SERPENTINE
VALENTINE

USA TODAY & WSJ **BESTSELLING AUTHOR**
giana darling

Serpentine Valentine
Copyright 2024 Giana Darling
Published by Giana Darling
Edited by Jenny at Editing4Indies and Erica Russikoff at Erica Edits
Proofed by Sarah Plocher
Cover Design by Cat at TRC Designs

"The serpent shows the way to hidden things..."—Carl G. Jung

This one is for me.
For bringing light to the darkness inside myself and hopefully, inspiring
other women to do the same.

TRIGGER WARNING

This is a Medusa retelling. Therefore, the book starts with the rape of Lex Gorgon. It occurs in Chapter Two and can be skipped if you are uncomfortable with reading about it on the page. The assault is only referred to after that. Although, if you are a trauma survivor, I want to warn you this book deals heavily with the aftermath and healing from sexual assault.

There are also instances of violence against men and women, bigotry, and exploration of sexual orientation.

PLAYLIST

"Medusa"—Kailee Morgue

"Autumn Leaves"—Eva Cassidy, London Symphony Orchestra

"Teacher's Pet"—Melanie Martinez

"No Time To Die"—Billie Eilish

"In The Woods Somewhere"—Hozier

"Achilles Come Down"—Gang of Youths

"Fire Burns Inside Me"—Andrea Vanzo

"Helios"—NNAVY, A.W.A

"mad woman"—Taylor Swift

"Vanilla Baby"—Billie Marten

"Maneater"—Nelly Furtado

"Boys Who Rape (Should All Be Destroyed)"—The Raveonettes

"Not All Men"—Morgan St. Jean

"Rêverie, L. 68: Rêverie"—Claude Debussy, Jean-Yves Thibaudet

"we fell in love in october"—girl in red

"Cherry Wine"—Hozier

"A Little Death"—The Neighbourhood

"Talk"—Hozier

"Lgbt"—CupcakKe

"Cold Water Swimming"—Quiet Houses

"Choke"—I DON'T KNOW HOW BUT THEY FOUND ME

"Woman"—Mumford & Sons

"Nothing New (Taylor's Version)"—Taylor Swift, Phoebe Bridgers

"Turning Page"—Sleeping At Last

"I Believe You"—FLETCHER

"Give It Up 2 Me"—Ojerime

"Sweater Weather"—The Neighbourhood

"La Lune"—Billie Marten
"School Nights"—Chappell Roan
"Woman"—Doja Cat
"The Secret History"—The Chamber Orchestra of London
"One of the Girls"—Otha
"I Wanna Be a Boy"—Addison Grace
"evermore"—Taylor Swift, Bon Iver
"Fix You"—Coldplay
"Love and War"—Fleurie
"Liability"—Lorde
"Aphrodite"—Honey Gentry
"Nina Cried Power"—Hozier, Mavis Staples
"The Yawning Grave"—Lord Huron
"Hallelujah I Love Her So"—Laura Zocca
"The Moon Song"—Brittin Lane, Mitchel Morse

CHAPTER ONE

"And fate? No one alive has ever escaped it, neither brave man nor coward,
I tell you—it's born with us the day we are born."
—Homer, The Iliad

Alexandra 'Lex' Gorgon

The wind whistled through the winding pathways of Acheron University's campus, whipping the discarded orange and brown leaves over the cobblestones and against old brick and stone buildings. My loafers skidded slightly on the wet ground, and I lost my balance, the heavy load of books in my hand slipping from my grip. They landed with a splat in a puddle, mud flying up to darken my white, sodden socks.

"Dammit," I groaned, squatting carefully in my short plaid skirt to retrieve them.

"Here, let me," a smooth baritone spoke from above me, and a moment later, Professor Morgan was beside me, reaching for my books.

I blinked the rain out of my eyes and offered him a small smile of thanks. In truth, I was in a rush and the man most students called Professor McDreamy had absolutely no effect on me. Rationally, I knew his wavy dark-hair and square jaw dusted in salt and pepper stubble were attractive. The hands that competently collected my texts were strong and tanned, even in October from the time he spent sailing his well-known boat *Poseidon*.

But I'd never fallen for his looks or his reputed charm. It seemed vaguely distasteful that he hosted his favorite students on board *Poseidon* at the end of every semester for a dinner party, and that his office hours were always filled with the prettiest girls from his classes.

He was harmless in the way narcissists were harmless. It was easy to see through the glamor if you knew him for what he was.

"I haven't seen you in my office hours yet this semester, Alexandra," he said with a click of his tongue to rebuke me. "After three weeks of class, I expected to see you there."

"I'm well versed in the classics," I promised him with a weak smile because I wanted to linger out in the rain like I wanted a hole in the head. "I've been getting As all semester. I won't slack off now."

"Mmm," he agreed, his eyes tracking over my face as he collected my last book and added it to his pile. When I reached for them, he held firm. "You know, I'd love to discuss your essay on Homer's homoerotic undertones in *The Iliad* over tea in my office sometime. I'm not sure if you're aware," he said in a way that meant he was certain I *did*, "but I'm the leading authority on Homer."

"In North America, definitely," I corrected and agreed simultaneously, noting the way his granite jaw flexed in irritation. "I enjoy Sir Scott Linley's work from England as well."

"Yes, well, a bit derivative," he harrumphed.

"When it comes to writers like Homer and Shakespeare, it's almost impossible not to be," I allowed, reaching for my stack of books again.

My fingers brushed his, and a spark shot up my arms. He seemed to feel it too, eyes widening then narrowing, darkening to a navy so black it was the sea beneath a night sky without stars.

He leaned just a bit closer, voice slightly hoarse as he whispered, "I admire you, Alexandra. A woman with your origins usually doesn't thrive so well here at Acheron."

Asshole, I thought even though I smiled humbly at him as I tugged my books out of his grasp and straightened. "'There is no substitute for hard work,'" I quoted Thomas Edison, ignoring Professor Morgan's gaze as it trailed up my tights-clad legs, lingering at the short hem of my plaid skirt. "For my whole life, I wanted to attend Acheron University."

It was one of the top universities in North America and one of the oldest. For a girl who grew up in rural Virginia to doomsday prepper parents who didn't believe in education, it represented both escape and enlightenment.

And I was here.

Starting my fourth year of my dual degree in philosophy and the classics.

Living my lifelong dream.

This time, when I smiled at Professor Morgan, it was genuine with gratitude. "I've never wanted anything else."

He grinned back at me, shared passion alight in his expression. It made him handsome enough for me to notice. "Come, have tea with me. My assistant is graduating after this year, and I need a replacement. Someone with your drive would be a perfect fit."

Excitement trilled through me. I was only minoring in the Classics, but an assistantship with one of the most renowned professors at Acheron could only help me in the future.

"I'd be honored to be considered," I told him.

A crack of thunder rumbled across the sky, followed quickly by a brilliant white flash. Seconds later, the light rainfall transitioned to knife-point bullets. Professor Morgan shot me a grin, then tugged my hand and started to run down the path to his office.

Bemused by his boyishness and hating the rain, I sprinted after him.

We were laughing by the time we reached Hippios Hall and pushed into the warm interior. Our shoes left large puddles on the red carpet lining the dark wood hall as we trudged down the corridor to his office.

I was too preoccupied by wringing out my heavy, drenched hair, still chuckling, to note the *snick* of the door locking behind us.

"Take a seat, please. I'll get the water on. You must be freezing."

I followed his gaze to my chest, nipples dagger points beneath the clinging wet fabric. It was a biological response to the cold, but his words sent a niggle of shame worming through me. As if I should be ashamed he noticed or had done it purposely to entice him.

I opened my mouth to retort, but he was already facing away, preoccupied with the electric kettle beside his desk. My mother had always called me combative and quick to offend. *Breathe*, she would tell me, pressing a hand to her own heart. *Breathe and be still.* I pressed a clammy hand to my sternum and breathed deep following the echo of her advice.

It wouldn't do to ruin my chances with Professor Morgan, not when I wanted to be a professor myself one day.

"So tell me what drew you to writing about the homoerotic relationship between Patroclus and Achilles?" he started benignly, a pleasant smile on his face as he took a seat behind his wooden desk and steepled his fingers. "Let me guess, you read *The Song of Achilles*?"

I startled over my own laughter. "I'm surprised you know about that book."

He shrugged. "Some girls have written about it, but none so intelligently as you. They refer to the novel more than the actual text of Homer's *Iliad*."

I settled the stack of books in my lap as I sat down across from him. My old, falling-apart copy of *The Iliad* was on top, its cover cracked, the pages peppered heavily with my blue-inked annotations.

"I read it for the first time when I was eleven," I explained, thumbing the thin, damp pages. "A local teacher took pity on me and gave me access to her library because my parents wouldn't let me get a library card. I was drawn to it as soon as I saw the secondary title 'The Wrath of Achilles.'" I shrugged, but a self-mocking smile twisted my lips. "Anger has always resonated with me best."

Professor Morgan laughed. "What does a young, beautiful girl have to be so angry about?"

Condescending men, least of all, I thought, but I kept the words locked up behind my breastbone.

Instead, I laughed lightly. "You'd be surprised. Anyway, I was first drawn to the topic because I'm gay."

The words tripped off my tongue lightly, skipping. I'd practiced saying them in the mirror since I was six and a neighbor told me that men loving men and women loving women was a sin. I didn't know it wasn't "normal" to want to kiss Penelope Hurst on the lips and hold her hand like my mother and father did until that moment.

Still, even with my ease of delivery, Professor Morgan seemed flummoxed. No, more than that, he seemed almost *offended*.

"Not really?"

"Quite," I confirmed with an arched brow.

His scrutiny sharpened, a pen tip tracing the edges of my face and the body beneath my wet clothes like a cartographer mapping new lands. And what he found, he didn't like.

"Well, girls go through these phases in university. It's perfectly normal," he allowed with a magnanimous smile.

"Thank you," I said, the sarcasm thick. "I feel much better about it now."

His grin widened as the kettle gave a sharp cry. He pushed out of the chair to prepare our tea, giving me a much-needed moment to collect myself. That all too familiar feeling pushed at my chest from the inside, a caged creature furious within its cage.

Tell him he's a homophobic, misogynistic prick, its growling voice demanded.

I ignored it as I had for years.

"It was clever to include Achilles' enchantment with Troilus in your argument," he continued casually as if the topic of my sexuality hadn't come up.

"Why would Aphrodite pick a male object of affection to trick Achilles with if he was hetero?" I agreed, excitement flaring inside me again as I started to sink my teeth into the topic at hand. "Homosexuality in ancient Greece wasn't shameful. In fact, it was often practiced by male warriors, who are often symbolized as the definition of masculinity. I honestly believe it's only in modern times that the idea of Achilles as a gay man rankled and was obscured."

"Interesting, as I said." Professor Morgan flashed me that thousand-watt smile as he turned to hand me a large, cracked mug of tea. Jasmine wafted from the curling steam, and the heat of his fingers wound around mine as he pressed it into my possession. It was an unnecessary move but one that spoke of intimacy.

Here, my darling, warm yourself with the tea I made for you.

Only, there was no intimacy between us.

I pulled my hands away quickly with a brief smile to ease the sting.

Professor Morgan didn't seem to notice. He leaned against the front of the desk, his calf pressed to mine before I moved it, so close I could smell the ocean brine of his cologne. The whole long, broad length of his body was on display in this pose, like a mannequin in a

18

window best positioned for admiration.

I ducked my head, hair sliding between us like a curtain as I blew on my tea.

"I would argue that the first texts mentioning Achilles and Patroclus say nothing of a sexual bond between them and that it was only later when pederasty was practiced, as you said, that they were given a homosexual bias."

And this was why I liked him, despite his peacocking. He had a sharp mind beneath his good looks, and I enjoyed listening to his thoughts unwind out of his eloquent mouth.

"Maybe you're right about the sexual undertones but not the romantic ones. There is a difference, and in this case, it's important. The almost berserker rage that overcomes Achilles at Patroclus's death, the way he mourns his dead body alone for hours, and keeps a lock of hair, a typical token of affection between loved ones? These are all acts of a man in love. Whether or not they ever consummated that love doesn't matter," I argued, passion saturating every word. My torso canted forward, my lips numb from moving so fast over the words.

"Ah," he said, soft, almost wonderous. "That's something I hadn't thought of. That's worth thinking about." Professor Morgan smiled at me then, and it was the first smile I liked all evening. A smile of kinship between the minds.

Looking back now, it was the moment that condemned me to what happened next.

CHAPTER TWO

"Pride goeth before destruction, and a haughty spirit before a fall."
—Proverbs 16:18

Lex

It was Halloween.

There was a party at a sorority house that Grace was trying to drag me to, but before that, I had a meeting with Professor Morgan at Hippios Hall. I could have ducked out. It was an evening to party, not one to spend curled up in the chair across from Morgan, sipping jasmine tea and talking incessantly about the Greek classics. In the weeks since I'd first dropped my books in the mud, the professor and I had developed a kind of friendship. He seemed to respect my lack of desire to flirt and fumble as men and women do, and instead, he focused on connecting with my mind. We met for tea in his office biweekly to discuss Homer, then Herodotus, Aristotle, and Plato. He wrote notes on scattered papers on his desk while we conversed, like my points had worth, and he wanted to cash them in later in reference to his own work. It was an honor to feel so valued for my mind when my parents had only ever condemned me for seeking to improve it. I was seduced, in a way, by the weight he placed on my opinion, and I found myself relating to the other girls tittering around him in class and in the halls. Not because I found him handsome the way they did but because I respected him and felt he respected me too. It was a heady thing. A dangerous thing.

When I looked at those girls, I snickered under my breath with scornful pride.

Look at them, I thought unfairly, *bees to honey.*

They don't know him the way I do.

And maybe they didn't, but what a silly thing pride was.

What a precursor to downfall.

I promised Grace I would meet her at the party later and tramped my way across the crunching autumn leaves to meet my favorite professor for tea. In keeping with tradition, I was wearing a costume, though Grace had turned up her nose at me when I'd stomped out of the bathroom wearing it.

"Really?" she'd asked.

My hair was done in thick barrel curls and braids, the ends closed off with golden coils shaped like snakes. My armor was only faux gray leather, a corset and pleated skirt like the ancient Greeks wore, and gladiator sandals that laced up my calves. I held a cheap shield and lance I'd bought online, and a fake owl was glued to my shoulder strap.

Athena, the Greek Goddess of War and Wisdom.

She had always resonated with me best, a female deity with typically masculine attributes. She was without consort, a virgin, and born fully formed from her father's head. I loved her sexlessness and valued her for it. She was all rational, all head, when most women were depicted as ruled by their hearts and guts.

"It's kind of more scary than sexy," my best friend and kind of foster sister had said, biting her lip.

"Good," I'd told her.

She rolled her eyes.

Regardless of feeling sexy or not, I felt strong and right as I passed the other costume-clad students in the commons. Amid a sea of sexy nurses, Targaryens, and *Star Wars* characters, I felt uniquely *me*.

"Alexandra."

I turned to see President Mina Pallas waving at me from a converging pathway so I waited for her to approach. When she did, she leaned close to give me a hug.

Most students wouldn't have hugged the President of Acheron U, but I was fairly uncommon. Mina was the reason I'd been accepted to the university at all, and I owed her everything.

"I love the costume," she said, beautiful face creased with laughter. She was middle-aged, but you'd hardly know to look at her. Soft blond hair fell to her shoulders, highlighting the cream-toned smoothness of her cheeks and the brightness of her blue eyes. She was classically elegant and refined, everything I'd always admired.

She was my hero.

The first female president of Acheron *ever* and one of the most acclaimed academics in the country.

"Thank you," I said, trying to ignore the heat in my cheeks. "I take it faculty members don't see fit to dress up."

Her laughter was so melodious, I swayed slightly toward her.

"Not exactly professional, no. Still, it's always fun to see the students enjoying so much. If I remember correctly, you were Cleopatra last year?"

"I can't believe you'd remember that."

Mina squeezed my bicep, a familiar move that made my chest light up like the Fourth of July. "Oh, I always keep an eye on our brightest students. Professor Morgan was telling me just the other day that he wants to offer you his assistantship."

Euphoria clapped through me like lightning. "Are you serious?"

Another amused chuckle. "I never joke about academics. I'm proud of you, Alexandra. When we first met, I thought I sensed a kindred spirit, but over the past three years, you've proven your worth again and again. My scholarship couldn't have gone to a more deserving woman."

Faced with her praise, I felt momentarily sick with joy. It overloaded my system until I was dizzy, nauseated by rolling waves of happiness moving through me.

"Thank you," I said breathlessly, feeling more like a fangirl than I ever had in my life. I'd never had anyone to make proud of me, not when my parents' idea of a good daughter would have stayed home in the mountains of Virginia tending to their homestead. "I'm honored you think so."

"Yes, well, keep up the good work." She moved her hand from my bicep to elbow and down to my hand, which she held for a moment before releasing. It sent sparkles of lust and idolized worship spiraling through my bloodstream. "Have a good evening."

"You too," I called out after a moment of dumb muteness when she had already continued on her path.

She shot a smile over her shoulder, the weak autumn light breaking through the cloud cover to shine over her blond head. I shivered a little, standing there looking after her. The surreal nature of having a dream come true never failed to daze me, and I took a moment to let it settle around me like a mantle, heavy and warm over my shoulders.

Her name was the first thing I spoke when I practically skipped into Professor Morgan's office, the words tumbling off my tongue as I explained how I bumped into the president. He laughed at my enthusiasm, walking around the desk to offer me a congratulatory hug.

I dropped my shield and lance to return the embrace, still chattering with enthusiasm, so happy I clung a moment longer than I would have.

"Can you believe it?" I demanded, releasing him even though he didn't release me fully, his hands falling to the indentation beneath my ribs above the curve of my hips. "Mina Pallas told me she didn't know anyone more deserving of her scholarship."

I pulled away from him to spin in a circle, skirt flaring, before falling into the chair I usually occupied. "I think I could float away on my happiness."

Morgan chuckled, watching me with a soft smile, eyes warm and bright. "It makes me happy to see you so happy. You're usually a rather subdued girl."

"True," I agreed easily. "'Though I am often in the depths of misery, there is still calmness, pure harmony, and music inside me.'" I quoted Van Gogh with a smile. "I feel joy. It just takes a lot to bring it out of me."

"What a fascinating girl you are," he praised, reaching forward to squeeze my knee. "I find myself a bit obsessed with what might come out of your lovely mouth next."

It was a vaguely sexualized comment, but I believed it was coming from a good place, so I beamed at him. "Well, your guess is probably as good as mine. I find I lack a filter most of the time."

"I've noticed," he said drolly, squeezing my knee once more before moving to his little station tucked between his rows and rows of books. "Tea?"

"Oh, yes, please."

"It's Halloween. What do you say we add a drop of whiskey for good luck and warmth?" he asked over his shoulder, his expression broken up with affection.

It felt so unaccountably *good* to have the praise of first Mina Pallas and then Dylan Morgan. It watered that fallow field in my soul where my mother and father's affection should have germinated as a child and sprouted into rich harvests.

"Why not?" I shrugged and reached across the desk for the notepad covered in his dark scrawl on his desk. He wasn't shy about sharing his work with me, and I loved to read the inner workings of his brain. "You've made progress on your book!"

"I have," he agreed. "Talking it out with you and some of my colleagues has broken that damned writer's block."

"I'm astonished I was any help." Then giddy and unfamiliar with this level of lightness in my soul, I leveled him with a sly grin. "Though President Pallas might have mentioned you were thinking about me for your assistantship next semester?"

His laughter was rich and straight from the belly. He was more relaxed around me now. There was no more posing and posturing, or at least, not as much. He laughed easily and didn't mind sharing his doubts and weaknesses. Seeing such a proud, powerful figure be totally human was oddly humbling and intoxicating.

When he handed me my customary mug of tea, cracked near the handle and chipped at the rim, I accepted it with a smile even though my cheeks hurt, unused to the expression.

"She shouldn't have said anything." His voice was mock sincere, but there were creases beside his eyes as he looked down at me. "I wanted to be the one to tell you that I made my decision."

"And?"

"And...I would like to formally offer the job to you, Lex."

My hand trembled with the effort to be professional and not fling myself into his arms. Instead, I lifted my shaking cup to cheers with his. "And I humbly accept."

We clinked glasses and drank the spiked tea in unison. It burned going down, an acrid taste buried beneath the alcohol.

"I think it's time for a new tin of jasmine," I told him, my nose scrunched with distaste.

He chuckled, watching me as he sipped from his own mug. "I brewed it too bitter. I'm sorry. But drink, you can't be warm in that getup after crossing campus."

"I can't stay long. I promised my friend I would meet her at a party."

He grinned. "You don't seem very enthused. You're what, twenty? Most kids are here to party, not study."

"I'm not."

"No," he agreed, looking me over again. "No, you're not. You'd rather curl up here with me, wouldn't you?"

"I'd rather be most places than at a party," I admitted with a grimace before taking another sip of tea and doing just as he said, curling my legs up in the chair. "But I do enjoy our chats. It's not often I get to speak with someone with so many of the same interests."

"Boys your age don't like Socrates?" he teased.

"Or most girls," I reminded him with a flat look.

Even though he knew I was a lesbian, he struggled not to refer to me in relation to men.

I bet you're popular with the boys in class.

I see the way men on campus look at you.

A girl like you probably has to keep them away with a bat.

Your father must own a shotgun.

It was irritating, and I never let him get away with it without reiterating my preference for female romantic company. But it wasn't enough to totally put me off, especially when a lot of people seemed to struggle with women liking women. Especially if we *only* liked women. Bisexual women were often unfairly sexualized and objectified by men, but at least they were "understandable" in the male mind.

Understandable and still fuckable if the mood struck them.

Pigs, the lot of them.

Morgan frowned at me, crossing his arms. "Really, Lex. You can't possibly be saying you aren't interested in men at all?"

I matched his expression, straightening in my chair. "I can, and I am. Men hold no interest for me romantically or sexually. Honestly, you are the only man I'm interested in, even platonically. I love women."

"Clearly, you have some daddy issues," he said in that smug way academics were all capable of, like mining texts for meaning had given them license to mine other's minds in the same fashion.

I bristled, anger sparking low in my gut, warming me better than the bitter tea. "Do I? I think I have parental issues. My father *and* my mother didn't believe in education, and I was born with this thirst for it I couldn't even begin to quench at our farm in the mountains. We owned four books, and two of those were different versions of the Bible. They didn't get me, so they didn't like me. After I ran away from home for the fourth time, they didn't bother looking for me.

"And do you know who took me in, Professor? A woman named Agatha Gorgon with three daughters of her own. They took me into their home and made me one of them. They taught me what nurture felt like and how easy it should be to be loved and accepted. Agatha gave me a mother's love for the first time in my life, and she gave me three incredible sisters. When she found out that attending Acheron was my life dream, she introduced me to Mina Pallas, her childhood best friend. And now, here I am."

I opened my arms wide, and Morgan looked me over, every inch, ending with his gaze locked on mine. I met it stubbornly, willfully. *Judge me*, I thought. *I don't care what you think.*

But the truth was, I did.

I loved Agatha, I loved Grace and Effie and Juno.

But I'd never had anyone to replace the love I should have had from my father.

Until Morgan.

So I cared, and when he bent forward to cup my cheek, I let him. I let him, and I leaned in to the affection.

"I wondered about the sadness on your face," he said softly. "It's hard to imagine why such a beautiful girl could be so sad, but I understand now. You've never had a man treat you right, have you, sweet Lex?"

I didn't answer. My heart was beating too fast, my breath coming too shallow. The heat of my anger beneath my skin felt too great, like a balloon overfilled and about to burst.

"It's hot in here," I told him, but my lips were numb.

"Really?" he asked, smiling gently, his face so close it was all I could see. He was handsome like the Roman statues they had on display in the Helene Art Hall, but I didn't like his callous hands on my face and the musk of his maleness in my nose.

"I think, I think I might need some air," I tried to say, but my tongue was thick and dry in my mouth. "I'm thirsty."

"Drink some tea," he encouraged, wrapping a big palm around mine on my mug to help me raise the drink to my lips. "Good girl."

Unease shivered through me, and my stomach cramped.

"I don't feel right," I mumbled, the mug falling from my suddenly ineffective hand to the Persian rug, where it broke along the seam of the crack with a gentle *pop*.

It was dark outside, the room only lit by the warm golden light of the task lamp on Morgan's desk and the standing shaded lamp in the corner. It made him seem bigger, looming over me like a monster.

"Morgan, please, I need to get outside," I reached up to try to pry his hand off my face, to push him away, but he only crowded me closer.

"Hush now, silly girl," he murmured, hauling me up out of the chair into his arms, my breasts pressed to his chest, one arm banded over my lower back to hold me to him. "Let me teach you what it's like to be loved by a man."

"No," I breathed, so shocked by his intent, I almost couldn't process it. "No!"

How could this be happening, I wondered, oddly disassociated from my body as he bent his head to kiss my neck? How could I have been so oblivious?

Later, I would be disgusted by my own naïvety, a sheep led so easily to the slaughter, but at the moment, I was stuck on Morgan's betrayal.

Because I'd trusted him.

The first man in my life to earn that since my father lost it when I was only a girl.

I thought about every conversation we'd had as I stood stuck in the cage of my mind, unable to move as Morgan laid me out on his desk and began to violate me with meticulous, almost gentle purpose. I thought about how he'd told me I was smart beyond my years, that he couldn't wait to see my name in academic journals. About how kind he'd been when I'd confessed I suffered from insomnia before exams, how he'd suggested meditation and melatonin. About how he'd smile at me, true smiles, smiles that seemed so much more than what he flashed like currency in his classrooms. About how he made me feel special.

About how he'd made me feel loved.

How bitterly, horrifically ironic that he was perverting that love now. Whispering words about how beautiful I was as he tore through me, about how perfect I was for him to use like this. About how he'd change my mind about loving women. I just needed to lie still and take it.

I cried.

Oh, I could feel the tears on my cheek, cold and painful on my skin before they fell off my cheek onto the papers he'd been grading on his desk.

He smelled like parchment and clove cigarettes, like sweat and man.

It made me gag, and at one point, I vomited on the desk.

He moved my rag doll form farther away from the stain and continued.

After the first time, he took a break, lighting a cigarette beside the open window behind his desk. I watched the smoke curl and fade into nothing as it blew through the crack, and I thought woodenly about how I was that smoke. Something used and discarded dissipating into nothingness.

He spoke to me, but I didn't hear him.

And when I didn't respond, something in him seemed to break. The zipper on his sheep's clothing fell clean away, and when he came for me the second time, it was the wolf who closed his teeth around my neck.

At one point, I passed out, and my last thought was that I hoped I never woke up.

CHAPTER THREE

"I do not exist. There is nothing left."
—Euripides from Hekabe

Lex

I woke up, and my first thought was this:

I wish I was dead.

The pain was so layered, I could not find its beginning or end. Like an ouroboros eating its own tail. There was the physical ache in every muscle from fighting, from the residue of drugs in my system, and the burn, oh God the burn, between my legs. It was so much that it seemed to echo even in my hair follicles, even in the roots of my teeth.

But no, it wasn't that ferocious, bone-chewing pain that prompted that first thought.

It was the spiritual chasm that had been carved out of my chest.

As if Professor Morgan had stolen not just my virginity, but the very essence of my soul. Punching his hand through my rib cage to wrench it free from my form.

I felt horrifyingly empty. Everything inside me was only an echo. Even months later, when people expected me to "move on" and "be whole again," I relied on those echoes to prompt me to act normally. To fit in, or at the very least, not be committed to the mental ward, where I might have honestly belonged.

It surprised people, later on, the few people I told, at least, that I didn't cry then.

But humans cry.

It was an emotional response and a physical prompt.

I wasn't human anymore, not after that, not in my own thoughts.

It didn't help that he'd left me in the woods like the bloody carcass of discarded prey.

The woods, the woods.

I'd loved them so much before.

Raised in the mountainous forests of Virginia, I remembered the scent of white pines and hardwoods as the fragrance of my youth, the soft spring of damp moss beneath bare feet as I chased my two brothers through the shadowed canopy. The woods had always brought solace to me in the same way the pious sought sanctuary in a church. It was where I could let down my shields, shed the armor of my anger, and open my senses to the world around me. It was where I found the courage to seek out peace.

And now, it was the setting of a tragedy.

For a moment, I thought about staying there, cold, bloody, and trembling. Letting death and the forest overtake and enfold me into the earth the way Oscar Wilde once spoke of.

Maybe I would have, but for the snake.

An ominous hollow rattle sounded somewhere to my left, drawing my gaze even though I had to turn my aching head, cheek pressed to the damp moss. I sucked in a sharp breath that ached in my ribs when I saw the Timber rattlesnake.

It was late for them to be active and rare to see them in

Massachusetts, where they were considered endangered. Yet there it lay, coiled and sunning itself on a rock in a shaft of sunlight piercing through the trees. It was a few feet long and dark, the zigzag design over its scales black, dark brown, and faintly green. I recognized it from growing up in Virginia, avoiding the faint rattle and roll when I played in the rocky forests they seemed to prefer.

Timber rattlesnakes were arguably the most venomous snakes in the United States.

And this one was three feet from me, its flat, triangular head hovering above the ground, tongue flickering.

Maybe I was still high from the drugs. Maybe my mind had broken along with everything else.

But something happened to me at that moment.

Locking eyes with a snake as if we could communicate and commune.

Here was a creature everyone feared, a being someone wouldn't think twice about fucking over. I read once that more people were killed by bees than snakes, yet we feared the latter so much we'd written them as villainous and ominous symbols in books for centuries. They were an object of power, smaller than us, easily avoided, yet so fearsome just the sight of them made people recoil.

I didn't recoil then.

I lay still and silent as that beautiful serpent unraveled across the space between us, undulating like a ribbon in the wind.

It will kill me, I thought, choking on terror and relief in the same breath.

But it didn't.

The snake slid over me as if I was as unthreatening and inconsequential as debris on the forest floor like a felled log or an overturned rock. Its tongue flickered softly against the bare skin of my belly as it slithered over my torso, body cool as textured silk, and down the other side of me. Without thought, my hand raised and lowered over the length of its tail, just a soft touch, my fingers tripping over the scales until it was gone and all I felt was my own skin.

My eyes burned, and my breath came hot and fast, pluming in the cold air. If I could have cried then, I would have.

Because somehow, the snake felt like a gift.

A promise.

That someday, someway, I'd be able to move on from this horror— shed my old skin and be reborn something stronger.

Something powerful and terrifying.

All the darkness I used to wear beneath my skin would become my shield and my armor while all the goodness—or what little remained— I'd hide deep within like the minotaur at the center of an endless maze.

As the rattle of the Timber faded, I sucked in a deep, agonizing breath.

And I stood.

I went to Professor Morgan's office in Hippios Hall.

It was too early for class, dawn just broken open over the grounds like a spill of yellow-orange yolk. There was no one to see me drag myself down the cobbled pathways, a blood-splattered trail of breadcrumbs in my wake. No one to see the way my knees knocked and my hands quivered. I was mostly naked, my skirt hanging askew over my hips by one button, my white blouse shredded by strong hands flapping like a white flag of surrender over my bruised breasts.

The door to the hall was unlocked, a low murmur of voices greeting me on a rush of centrally heated air as I struggled to pull open the door. Something was broken in my hand, and I could feel the pain and wrongness of a shattered collarbone in my left shoulder.

The corridor was empty, but doors were cracked open as faculty pored over morning lesson plans and sipped their start of day coffees and teas.

Professor Morgan's door was closed, but I didn't let that stop me.

It thudded open with a dull *thwack*.

I didn't have a plan. I didn't have much in my brain at all beside static hurt and fear and rage, rage that began to burn it all clear away, but I wasn't really expecting him to be there.

And he was.

Sitting in his great backed leather chair in a blazer with suede elbow patches drinking out of his favorite Hamlet mug. His hair was still damp from a morning shower, curling around the collar of his Oxford shirt, and he'd nicked himself shaving, a little cut on the edge of his clean jaw.

As if the sight of him wasn't enough, the insult of his cleanliness compounded how disgusting I felt, how rotten he'd made me feel straight down to the core.

And then there was her.

The girl sitting in my usual seat of pale lemon velvet with a mug of jasmine tea raised halfway to her red lips.

In a single instant, whatever remained of my humanity was lost to the voracious, all-consuming rage that possessed me like a hell demon.

I launched myself at him with a cry that tore up my already damaged throat. It left bile and the metallic tang of blood on the back of my tongue, but I didn't notice.

My focus was on Professor Morgan.

The monster that had turned me monstrous with pain and fury.

I landed partly over his desk, dislodging his computer and books, sliding across the surface with enough momentum that my fist hit the edge of that clean-shaven, nicked jaw like an anvil. His head *snapped* to the side, blood spraying over my chin from the way he bit into his tongue at the impact. His tea cup shattered on the floor, the scent of jasmine strong enough to make me gag.

I didn't stop there.

Nails ripped across his cheek, gouging long tracks, flesh lodged under my green-painted talons. He started to fight back, trying to find leverage where he was caught between his desk, my body, and the wall at his back, but nothing at that moment could have stopped me short of death.

The girl screamed and screamed behind me, but not as loudly as I'd screamed last night.

By the time someone dragged me off him, Professor McDreamy's famous pretty face was streaked with blood and swollen where I'd bruised him. He cursed me with a tongue too thick in his mouth, broken by his teeth and my fists.

I couldn't hear anything but the roar of blood in my ears urging me to take more. There was something frantically certain in me that if I lost my anger and gave way to sadness, I might very honestly die and never be reborn.

"Alexandra Gorgon."

The sound of my name spoken by such a familiar voice loosened the teeth of my fury enough that I could turn my head to see the doorway filled with bodies, in the forefront President Mina Pallas.

I almost didn't recognize her. Not because of the fog of my own colossal ire, but because of her own.

She was livid. Face contorted grotesquely with disgusted rage, her slim body suddenly huge and looming with aggression all aimed at...

At me.

I blinked, disorientated suddenly. Weak and woozy.

"What in the world do you think you're doing?" she demanded, storming forward to take me by the chin like a hook through the gullet of a fish. My head was wrenched back and up, pain exploding behind my eyes.

Something like a whimper leaked through my throat.

"Mina," someone murmured behind me, the person holding my arms behind my back to restrain me. "Wait, a moment. She's clearly been attacked."

She didn't listen.

"What do you think you're doing attacking a teacher? Attacking Professor *Morgan*?" She said it like I'd committed blasphemy. Like she was seconds away from excommunicating me from the only church I'd ever known.

"H-He attacked me," I found the strength to cough up the words that sat like rocks in my gut. "Last night, he drugged me a-and he raped me."

The word *rape* echoed in the silence that followed. I wondered if it would always be stuck in my head, a song on repeat I wanted desperately to ignore.

"I did no such thing," Morgan snapped, standing and shaking off the tending arm of a woman I recognized as a first-year anatomy professor. "I was with Monique Fournier all night, wasn't I, darling?"

The anatomy professor blinked behind her cat-eye glasses and then nodded slowly. "Yes, of course."

"Of course." The girl seated across from him when I entered broke free of the crowd and sneered at me. "You're pathetic for accusing him of something so horrible."

"Now wait," the woman holding me argued, loosening her hold on me to step to my side. I realized it was the Dean of Law, Professor

Diana Strong. "Whether or not it was Morgan, this girl has clearly been assaulted. Someone call the damn campus and local police. Get an ambulance here."

I swayed on my feet now that she wasn't holding me up, but she leaned into me, offering the support of her shoulder. She smelled of pine needles. When I turned my head to vomit violently, she held back my hair while ordering someone else to fetch her the garbage can.

"Really, Mina," Morgan was saying, holding out his hands, palms up as if in surrender. "You've known me for twenty years. Would I really do something so awful? Not to be crass, but I hardly need to force myself on some young girl."

I choked on bile, the only thing left in my stomach as I wretched again into the pail.

Someone at the door was ushering everyone out and closing it in their faces.

Suddenly, the idea of being in a closed room with Morgan was too much.

"I need to get out of here," I murmured, trying to pull away from Professor Strong.

"Not yet," she hissed, just for me. "Wait, I've got you."

I trembled so strongly in her hold that she had to hold me aloft, but I stayed still. I didn't have the autonomy then to disobey the orders of the only person who seemed to believe me.

"We'll need to take Professor Fournier's statement for the police, Dylan," President Pallas said, dragging a hand over her face in exhaustion before turning a glare my way. "Though, of course I believe you. What happened, Lex? Did he decide not to give you the assistantship, and you lashed out?"

A whimper got caught in my throat and turned into a harsh growl. "I would never."

I couldn't believe she would think that of me. The knife Morgan had stuck in my back twisted under her hand. How could the two mentors I'd loved so much, so purely, betray me like this?

The agony of it all crashed into me. Black spots danced in front of my eyes, but I held on to the anger tightly, my only buoy adrift in this sea of unending agony.

"He did this," I told President Pallas—Mina, the woman who had taken me under her wing, given me a scholarship and guidance—because I couldn't address Morgan, not directly, not when it reminded me of his eyes as he pressed into me. "He did this to me. I didn't ask for it. I'm not even..." I squeezed my eyes shut. "I'm not interested in men. He knew that, a-and he still did this. You have to believe me. You *know* me. You know I wouldn't fabricate such a horrible story. You know I couldn't..." I gestured to my body, war-torn and bloodied. "Do this to myself."

Mina stared at me, her eyes sharp as scalpels cutting through my body like a mortician through a corpse's chest. "I don't know that. I don't know that at all. Girls do foolish things for love all the time."

For love.

My knees gave out, but Diana Strong held me tight by my elbows. I sucked a breath past my teeth even though it scorched my scream-torn throat and hurt my ribs.

I'd loved Professor Morgan in my own way. It was true.

Like a father. Like a mentor. Like someone who would always give me a hand if I needed help to stand.

Only I was practically on my knees and neither Morgan nor Mina were helping me up. They seemed content, no, determined to see me crushed beneath the heel of what he'd done to me.

"Please," I whispered to Mina, and they felt like last words spoken to a priest. If she didn't believe me, I honestly thought at that moment I might really die. "Please, he did this to me. I need your help."

"Pathetic," Morgan scoffed, and I noticed he was sitting in his fucking chair again, dabbing the blood on his cheek with a handkerchief. "Really, Miss Gorgon, this is beneath even you."

"I will not take you at your word," the President of Acheron told me, looming over me like a dark cloud about to deliver a tempest. "There will be an investigation, and until you are cleared of suspicion, you are on academic suspension. You will leave campus immediately, and you will not return unless or until you are reinstated."

"What?" I gasped, but it was the final blow.

The loss of my bodily autonomy, the loss of my idols in Morgan and Mina, the loss of my pride and sense of security.

And now, the loss of my life dream.

The loss of Acheron U.

Before anyone could say another word, my eyes rolled up in my head, and I passed out.

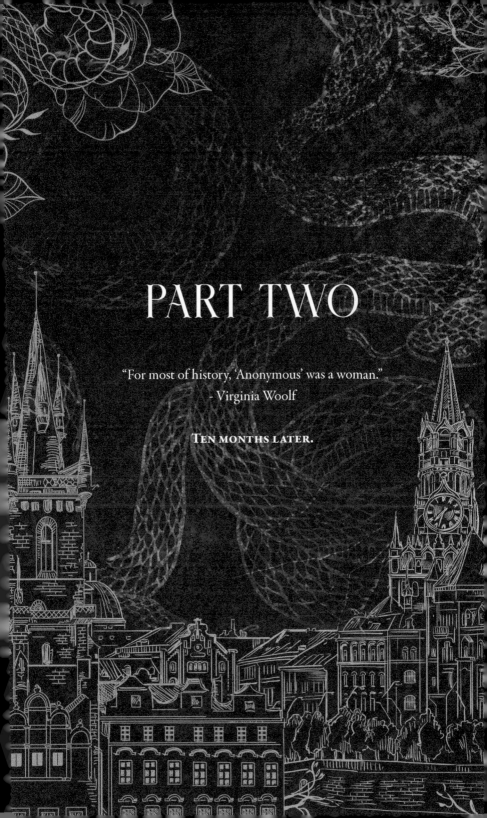

PART TWO

"For most of history, 'Anonymous' was a woman."
- Virginia Woolf

Ten months later.

CHAPTER FOUR

Luna

It was the third week of term, and everyone was still whispering about her.

Lex Gorgon.

The girl who was raped and tried to blame it on Professor Morgan last year.

Oh, most people didn't know the second part, but I did because my mother was the President of Acheron U.

I'd never forget her face when she came home that night, the almost blind fury contorting her features. She'd been in a rage, yelling into the phone as she stormed into the house straight to her office where she shut the door with a *bang*.

I shouldn't have been home.

I was supposed to be out with my friends from the field hockey team at some party one of the sorority houses was throwing, but I was bored by the end of the pre-drink at Courtney's house, so I'd decided to head home.

So Mom didn't know I was around to hear her, and having never heard her so angry before, I took advantage. The third stair to my basement suite creaked, so I skipped it, slinking up the case and the hallway to lurk behind her closed door.

"We need legal on this *now*," she ground out over the faint thud of her pacing footsteps. "This is a total shit show. Morgan is a Fulbright scholar, for fuck's sake. His book on Poseidon was a bloody *New York Times* bestseller. He brings more money to the Classics program than any other faculty *combined*. We cannot afford to lose him to scandal, let alone one like this."

There was a long pause, and then, "I don't know, Mary, I really don't. I never would have thought Alexandra Gorgon was the kind of girl to lie so flagrantly, but obviously, I was mistaken." A long, shaken sigh. "Yes, I saw her. She was...she was brutalized. But it was not by Morgan. Professor Monique Fournier told me she was with him all night, and you know those two have been on and off for a while now. No, whatever happened to Ms. Gorgon was done by someone else."

"Well, obviously he'd decided to pass her over for the assistantship," Mom argued. "The little, ungracious bitch decided to use the age-old play of crying rape."

I flinched, nearly falling on my ass in the corridor. I'd never heard my mother curse so much, never could have imagined the vitriol in her tone while she spoke about sexual assault against a woman.

Even if Lex Gorgon hadn't been attacked by Professor Morgan, she had still been a victim of a heinous crime. I learned later that her attacker left her in the forest behind campus, broken, bloodied, and torn at the roots of a gnarled tree like some ancient pagan sacrifice. So how could Mom lack sympathy for her? How, having seen her *brutalized*, could she not find forgiveness in her heart for a twenty-year-old girl who was taken against her will?

A crack opened inside my soul at hearing my mother speak like that, like somehow the student had deserved such treatment. A crack that split straight through the hero worship I'd harbored for my superstar mother all these years. The first sign of serious erosion in the total love and adulation I'd clung to even as I'd grown up and witnessed how flawed she could be. She was a single mother who'd made the decision to have a baby with a sperm donor. I'd only ever known her, relied on her, *trusted* her to set my world views for me.

I'd felt concussed by her words, mind ringing, world breaking into parts like a kaleidoscope.

It was ten months after the incident that rocked Acheron. Though, it was hushed up so poorly that threads of scandal still webbed the halls, catching students up in its snare.

"I heard she got what she deserved," someone said in the hall one day on my way to my Russian History seminar. "She was gagging for all her male professors. Everyone in her classes knew it."

My stomach clutched and wobbled like an open and closed fist.

"You can tell just by looking at her," a guy on the soccer team said on the sidelines of Godwin Field Complex when I jogged by on my way to practice. "She's sex on two legs. She's probably into that fucked-up shit."

It was impossible to escape the toxic whispers. Oh, I heard some people sympathize with her, but not many. Not enough.

I'd never really noticed Lex Gorgon before the rumors, but when she appeared on the first day of term following the incident, my eyes were drawn to her along with everyone else's.

I was sitting in the commons, propped between Haley's legs doing some reading for my History of Warfare class, when the energy in the quad went thick and still, like the atmosphere before a tropical storm broke. Flora stopped talking, Haley went stiff behind me, and Kenzie dropped the apple she was eating straight into her lap.

I knew she was there before I even looked up. Curiosity hooked me through the mouth, urging me to raise my head to see what everyone else saw. But a part of me hesitated. I felt a strange need to give her privacy, to avert my gaze when everyone else was making her an object of public consumption.

How vulnerable must she feel, I thought, the words of text beneath my gaze blurring as my eyes watered with sympathy. She had already been torn by the hands of some vile monster masquerading as a man, and now again in the court of popular opinion. If it had been me—I shuddered at the thought—I would have transferred schools. Maybe even changed my name.

Yet here she was, facing down the firing squad.

"Wow," Haley breathed, the word almost pulled from her involuntarily.

I lost my battle, and on a shaky inhale, I looked up at Lex Gorgon.

I'd only had a vague impression of her before the incident, and when I'd thought to look her up on social media, she wasn't there. So all I had in my memory was a pretty face, dark hair, and a full, sullen mouth.

That wasn't what I saw.

What I saw was a woman.

Not even a girl, not like the girls beside me in the field hockey kits because we had practice later that day, not the pimply-faced freshmen gaining fifteen pounds without the scrutiny of their mothers, not the fresh, eager smiles and giggles of newly independent boys and girls.

A woman.

It was hard to explain why I was suddenly breathless at the sight of her. Oh, she was lushly curved, deep hand holds between tapered ribs and flared hips, shapely legs bared beneath a short black skirt, and leather boots laced to mid-calf. Her breasts were obvious beneath her conservatively buttoned black blouse, but they would have been obvious in anything she wore, heavy, but high with youth. It was more than her coloring, which was striking, the pale eyes beneath dark, arched brows and thick lashes, the sun-warmed, almond dark complexion, and all that hair, a curly mass of black that writhed around her head like dark serpents in the wind. It wasn't even the snakes themselves, tattooed on her forearms peeking out from rolled cuffs, one on her throat, licking at her pulse point, another two curling down the length of one strong thigh like lovers.

All of that was good, better than good. It was *delicious*.

And even as I thought it, I wondered how I could think such a thing about someone, let alone a woman. That she was edible, worthy of drooling over, capable of satiating my sudden hunger.

But again, that wasn't why I felt breathless looking at her across the quad.

It was more this: She stood straight, evenly braced on both feet. It was an odd pose for a young woman, who usually cocked a hip or fluctuated from foot to foot. She was still and poised, her chin tilted up toward the sun. She was posing, flaunting the fact that she knew every eye was on her.

Look at me, she seemed to say. *Look at me. I have nothing to hide.*

And even more intoxicating, *I have nothing to say. You aren't worthy of my notice.*

Haley's "wow" was right.

"Isn't it kind of, I don't know, wrong or gross that she's just standing there like that?" Flora asked with a grimace.

"Jesus, Flo," Haley whisper-yelled, leaning over my shoulder to shoot her a glare. "Insensitive much?"

"I'm just saying it's weird. She has to know everyone's looking at her and talking about her. She's like...famous now."

"For what?" I asked softly, my eyes still locked on the victim who was not in any way acting like a victim across the quad. "For being raped?"

My words dropped like a nuclear bomb in the middle of our little group.

"Tucker told me she fucks anything with a dick," Flora argued, eyes flashing.

She was like that. Argumentative without caring much which side she landed on. In debate, it was amazing to watch, but in real life, it was callous and unfair more often than not.

"Tucker says that about any hot girl," I bit back. "He's a grade A misogynist. You said that yourself last semester when he asked you to suck his dick outside the Penny Farthing, remember?"

A sniff was her only answer.

Across the courtyard, Lex Gorgon finally tipped her head down and watched impassively as a group of three girls approached her. They didn't hesitate to fall in at her sides, touching her briefly in solidarity.

I didn't know her, but I felt profound relief seeing that she had friends.

For a moment, I'd seriously considered getting up and going over to her myself. Wondered how she would receive me if I got close enough to see just what color those pale eyes were. Imagined she might give me a smirk because she seemed like the kind of girl to smirk and then invite me for a beer at the Penny.

"Luna?" Kenzie said like she'd said it a few times already. "Did you finish that reading for Gibson's Shakespeare class?"

"Honestly, giving homework before classes even start should be criminal," Haley muttered, propping her chin on my shoulder.

I knocked her cheek with mine. "Don't think of it as homework. Learning shouldn't be confined to a classroom."

As a unit, my friends rolled their eyes and said, "Such a nerd."

I laughed, but even as I did, my gaze slid to the other end of the quad. Lex Gorgon was still standing there, holding court with her three friends, a similar image to the one I was part of. But there was no doubting, even from a distance, that she was different.

Scarred, rebellious...even dangerous.

So why was I so intrigued?

History of the Tragedies was my first class every Monday morning and followed for an hour each on Wednesdays and Fridays. I was doing an honors double major in English and History even though my mother told me it wasn't practical.

Maybe I even chose it because she told me that.

The truth was, I found it difficult to relate to people socially from an early age, and it was only through books that I began to understand them. The Harry Potter series taught me about courage and conviction, Jane Austen taught me about the longing every woman feels for something more outside of their norm, and the Gossip Girl books educated me on the currency of rumors and good looks in teenage girls. It was only by reading about the emotional landscape of others through the written word that I eventually felt like I could partake in real life without inevitably ending up an outcast.

So I felt a tender gratitude for literature for raising me in ways my mother never could.

I was excited about Tragedies, and not just because I was one of the dime-a-dozen college girls who fancied themselves obsessed with

Shakespeare. I'd always preferred sad stories, the kind that left an aching echo in my chest for weeks.

"You seem curiously excited for a class about tragedy."

The voice was low and rich, emerging from a throat like roughed-up velvet.

A shiver slid down my spine and every inch of my skin seemed to come alive.

I turned my head to the desk beside me even though I knew, somehow, she would be sitting there.

The girl who'd lived her own tragedy.

Lex Gorgon.

She was looking at me, features impassive, but those pale eyes—*gray! They were gray as wet stone*—were intent on my face. I don't know why I blushed, but I could feel the heat of it spill down my cheeks to my chest like red wine.

When I only blinked dumbly at her, her full mouth flattened into a line. She gestured to it with a black-tipped hand. "You were gazing into space smiling."

The class was still filling up around us, so I paused as a guy walked in front of us to take another front-row seat. It gave me a moment to suck in a sharp breath and scold myself not to be an idiot. She didn't deserve that after what she'd been through. Would probably think I was some judgmental prude ready to pin her with a scarlet letter.

"I like the tragedies best," I told her, my voice softer than usual because suddenly I was thrown back to my childhood when shyness crippled me, and I was unsure of every sound I made.

A thin black brow arched high on her forehead. "What do you know about tragedy?"

They weren't fighting words. There was no condescension in her tone or manner, more a gentle kind of curiosity, maybe even a playful dare.

Tell me the secret of your sorrow, she seemed to say.

And for some inexplicable reason, I wanted to share with her.

I shrugged a shoulder, fiddling with my ballpoint pen on the front of my notebook even though the ink was making ugly splotches on the page. "I think that's the point. Everyone can relate to a sad story. There are degrees of tragedy, obviously, but every person living knows some sort of unhappiness. It's love and laughter, success and happy endings that divide us. Pain brings us together."

Lex blinked at me then, a slow closing of those thick-lashed, stony eyes. When they reopened, a fresh intensity was there.

God, I thought, despite the way the words made me shaky, *she's so gorgeous*.

"That's an interesting thought," she said in that low, almost masculine voice that vibrated in my bones. "A clever one."

The blush that had receded to just my cheeks bloomed across my entire chest again. "Thank you. I'm Luna Pallas."

A thin smile that seemed more unhappy than not. "I think you know who I am."

I bit my lip, pressed my pen tip too hard to the paper, and rent the page. "I do."

She shifted a heavy sheet of wavy dark hair behind her shoulder, and I caught the flash of a scar like a starburst over her collarbone in the shadow of her collared shirt. Above it, a tattooed snake kissed the side of her neck with an undulating tongue.

It was erotic somehow, the snake and the scar. Tragedy stamped and inked on her body for everyone to see. It was bold and courageous. I liked that about her, and I didn't even know her.

"I know you, too," she startled me by saying, sliding her gaze to me out the corner of one eye. "So don't feel bad. Luna Pallas, captain of the field hockey team, popular and beautiful with too many friends to name and a boyfriend like jock Ken to her academic Barbie."

I laughed, embarrassed even though everything she said was true. "You make me sound like a stereotype."

"If the cleat fits."

The professor walked into the small auditorium then, stopping our conversation before I could defend myself. I was more than a stereotype. I had depth and angst galore. I just covered it up, hid it to make myself more palatable to the masses.

I opened my mouth to contradict Lex, but she was already facing forward with Shakespeare's *Hamlet* flipped open, the pages already riddled with blue-inked annotations. I leaned forward automatically, wanting to read what she'd seen in the famous bard's words. It earned me a glare and the angling of her body around the book, obscuring it from view.

I sat back, angry and embarrassed by her cold shoulder and my own blatant curiosity.

She was just a girl. A very pretty girl with thick dark hair down her back and features copied out of an art book. I'd known pretty girls before and pretty boys.

None had done to me what Lex Gorgon did with a single blink of those cold eyes.

That gray-toned gaze haunted me for the rest of the class. I couldn't stop sneaking glances at her even though she didn't once seem to return the favor.

Why was I intrigued by the way she held the butt of her pen against that plush lower lip that was as pink as the edges of a lotus flower?

Why did I want to read whatever notes she scribbled in sloping, cramped cursive over the pages of her notebook? Why did I love that she still took notes in longhand like me, eschewing the modern use of computers?

She was beautiful enough, almost flagrantly sensual with all those curves and that pouty, expressive pink mouth, to catch the eye of anyone. When I looked around the room, hoping to find someone else staring, three guys sitting behind her stared at the back of her head covetously.

But I wasn't like them. I didn't want to sleep with her.

I wasn't into women that way.

I just wanted...it was hard to say, but the closest I came to describing it while I sat beside her, nearly obsessing about her, was that I wanted to be in her orbit. Not close, if she wouldn't allow it, but in the vicinity of her energy.

Being near her made me feel itchy but alive.

I looked down at my notebook, trying to wrench my attention away from her and back to the lecture only to find a square folded piece of paper on my desk. My eyes shot to Lex, but she was bent over her own work, writing furiously.

Carefully, I unfolded the note under the table and read that cramped cursive.

Take a picture. It'll last longer.

Humiliation poured over my head like hot water. I wanted to look at her, to see if she was witnessing my shame, but I was too furious and afraid. She'd sensed my strange fascination and was belittling me for it.

It made it worse to know I wasn't the first one to find her captivating, that I was one in a long line of gazers to make her into an object of longing.

I wanted to crumple the paper, tear it to shreds, and swallow it. A juvenile way of erasing its existence.

Instead, I listened to Professor Gibson quote from *Hamlet*. "'My words fly up, my thoughts remain below: Word without thoughts never to heaven go.'"

Lex only had the power to make me feel small if I let her.

So I wouldn't.

I scrawled in my loose script:

Fine. Meet me in the library tonight on the second floor near the Ancient Greek section. I'll bring my camera.

I dropped the note into her lap without looking at her, then immediately turned back to my notetaking.

She hadn't returned it by the time class ended, and I was surprised by the bitter swell of disappointment that rose to the back of my throat. When I'd collected my things, Lex already gone in a swirl of black out the doors, I spotted the note left on her tabletop.

My fingers were damp with sweat as I unfolded it.

I'll be the girl in black.

CHAPTER FIVE

"The Gods have crazed you."
—*The Odyssey*, Homer

Lex

I couldn't remember the first time I saw Luna Pallas. She was everywhere on campus. Carving up the field hockey pitch behind Radcliffe House in a little blue pleated skirt, an orange ball glued to the end of her stick. Reading in the library amid stacks of books and discarded coffee cups like she had to match her study intake with caffeine intake. In my classes, because she was taking Classics as a minor and lit as a major and she was one of the try-hards who sat in the front row. Like me.

Only, she wasn't like me. Luna Pallas was the "It" girl on campus and not only because her mother was the beloved president. It was because of the way she looked, her skills on the varsity team, and the way her laughter bubbled over like the softly flowing water in the river bed that cut through campus. She had presence. Not bold, not brassy like gold, but soft and alluring like moonlight catching your eye in the dark night.

She was everywhere, but I always ignored her. She was a creature of the light and day, of sports matches and brunch dates with friends, of selfies and TikToks. And I was...not. It wasn't that I felt inferior—quite the opposite, it was that she held no interest for me.

Until that day in the Mathieson Library.

It was three weeks ago, at the very start of my first term back since the *incident*. I was on campus to speak with my academic advisor about my course schedule following my return and to meet with President Pallas. The first meeting went as well as could be expected. The courses I'd taken for half a semester before Halloween were incomplete, so I would have to retake them if I wanted the credits. I reenrolled for everything except for *that man's* Classics course.

The latter, well, it also went as to be expected.

Mina had a lawyer with her to cover her bony ass because I'd threatened to sue the university if they didn't reinstate my standing at Acheron this year. They had absolutely *zero* reason to suspend me, let alone kick me out, and she knew she didn't have a leg to stand on. But she hadn't been happy. Oh no, she'd been furious sitting across from me, white-knuckled, hard-hearted, hating me because I'd had the misfortune to tarnish her school's reputation.

It made me laugh in the hall afterward, a mean chuckle that hurt my throat. If she thought she was angry and hateful, it was nothing to the furious monster I'd become.

Oh, I'd gotten very good at concealing it. Hiding in sheep's clothing, though I was a very rabid wolf. But people could still scent it on me, the heat-baked, metallic smell of rage leaking from my pores like sulfur dioxide from a volcano. They cringed away from me in the halls and couldn't hold my gaze when I caught them staring.

They were afraid of me, of the violence that swelled against the barrier of my skin, dying to get out.

The only thing that kept me vaguely human and barely restrained was the crystal-clear idea of revenge.

Oh, it sounded sweet.

I spoke it like an incantation when I stared at myself in the mirror every morning and hated my reflection for the way it had betrayed me. I muttered it under my breath when I hit the gym every night, when I was so tired I could hardly breathe, but I still uttered it.

Revenge, revenge, revenge.

I'd have it, too.

I was smart enough to craft it and patient enough to see it through.

This would be my last year at Acheron U and the end of life as they knew it for Professor Morgan and President Mina Pallas.

They didn't know it yet, but that made it all the sweeter.

They thought they'd crushed me, obliterated the threat of me, and turned me into some weak girl subjugated by the shame they meant me to feel over inciting that animal into taking me against my will.

Well, I was not weak.

However, I harbored no small amount of shame, because no survivor I'd spoken to at my meetings ever spoke of moving beyond that hot coal of humiliation burning low in their gut. That idea society or history or our own female biology instilled in us that said we had to take the blame for others' actions, even if they acted against ourselves. I used that shame as fuel for my fury.

How dare they make me feel responsible?

How dare they take sleep from me, dreams from me, and leave me only with waking nightmares?

I thought about and plotted their downfall every single day for ten months. It got me through the healing of my body and started me on my way to healing around the chasm in my chest where he'd wrenched out my soul.

I was going to end them.

I had a plan for Professor Morgan, one I'd already set into motion. But what to do about Mina Pallas confounded me until the moment in Mathieson Library when I spotted Luna Pallas and truly saw her for the first time.

It was late, the windows made into mirrors by the blackness outside. It was the reflection of her in the glass that caught me. She had her eyes closed, leather headphones over her ears, her strawberry-blond hair tangled around the collar of her tennis sweater.

She was dancing, right there in her seat past midnight on a Monday deep in the abandoned edge of the library's quiet second story. Her body swayed, hands lifted, her blue ballpoint pen a conductor's baton arching through the air along with whichever melody played in her ears.

It was oddly lovely, catching that little moment. She was mussed from a long day, a coffee stain on the wrist of the cream sweater, an ink blot at the edge of her wide mouth from chewing on the end of a pen. It felt intimate, a window into a side of Miss Popular most people didn't get to see.

Fifteen minutes later, when I returned from retrieving the books I needed for my Epic Tradition Classics course, she was getting out of her chair. I pressed close to the books, hidden in the shadows, and watched as she toed off her patent leather loafers, wiggling her toes in frilly white socks. A moment later, she was moving, sliding across the polished wood floors, arms wiggling, hips shaking, hair flying like sunset gold streamers.

I wondered what she was listening to.

She looked so free, so without worries. It hurt my stomach because I knew I'd never be that way again. My memories were too heavy in my blood, weighing me down, taking me too close to the floor to leap or dance or be transformed by the simple magic of a song.

I hadn't felt it in so long, it took me a moment to realize what I felt was yearning. Not for Luna, exactly, but for that levity. I wanted to steal it from her or steal her for it, to watch it, be near it at least, even if I couldn't feel it myself. Joy by proximity, or something like it.

After a few long minutes of watching her, I was about to escape when she sagged suddenly, a marionette with her strings cut. One moment, she was dancing like a child, carefree and filled with light, and the next, she was slumped in her chair, forehead pressed to her folded arms on the table. Her shoulders trembled like a warning before they started to shake seismically, and I realized she was crying.

She sobbed, big rolling cries that wracked her whole body. When she lifted her head to drag the overlong sleeve of her sweater over one flushed cheek, I was struck by how pretty she was with tears on her face and sorrow crumpling her brow.

Suddenly, she was human. Fallible. Not quite so untouchable as her popularity and status as President Pallas's daughter made her seem.

And that was when I knew.

Men had been attracted to me since I'd grown breasts at eleven years old, but I'd never cared. Instead, I'd buried my head in the sand like an infant, content to believe that because I felt no attraction to them, the sentiment was returned.

I'd been born to love women, and they were all that intrigued me.

Yet I'd never tried to turn that charm that seemed to ensnare men in their direction. Before everything, I'd been too young, too blindly focused on my studies like any true academic. Now, now the idea had merit.

Not only because it might help the disgust I felt with my own body for unintentionally making itself an object of desire to men. But because I refused to allow what happened to rob me of the experiences I deserved. The smile of a future lover across the room filled with promise. The touch of a feminine hand cradling my breast, soft and coaxing. The taste of a woman's lips, how silken they might feel, how sweet the taste.

I would not live the rest of my life confined in the cage Morgan's actions had forced me into, bars between myself and freedom of sexuality, freedom of choice.

I'd take it back just as I'd take everything away from him and from Mina Pallas for disbelieving me and stripping away everything I loved.

And therein lay the true reason for my flash of brilliance watching a girl spin and sob in an empty midnight library.

Luna Pallas was the perfect tool to humiliate her mother.

All I had to do was seduce, corrupt, and destroy.

It was almost too easy.

The moment her startled green eyes locked on mine, I could sense it. Her interest. It burst like static electricity between us. When I moved my hand through the air, bringing my pen to my mouth, the currents tickled my skin and gave me goose bumps.

She couldn't stop watching me through class.

I wasn't even nice to her, but then, I understood women. We were disgusted by blatant cruelty, maybe, but gentle derision and a special kind of conceited pride intrigued us.

In five minutes of sitting in History of the Tragedies, I'd hooked Luna Pallas through the mouth like a fish. All I needed was to reel her in.

"She's pretty," Grace noted as she bent to polish her toenails black.

I leaned over to tug my copy of Edith Hamilton's *Mythology* out from under her foot before returning to my essay notes.

"Who?"

"Revenge plan B."

I rolled my eyes, but Juno was the one to say, "The whole point of code names is to be discreet, Gracie."

Grace looked around my large attic bedroom and scoffed. "It's just the four of us. I don't think anyone is listening through the walls."

"I don't know," Juno muttered, side-eyeing the portrait of Virginia Woolf I had hung up on the wall by the door. "She always looks like she's watching me."

"This is a revenge story, not a ghost story," Gracie said, tossing a box of tea at her sister. "You're so easily spooked."

Juno raised her brows as she paused in her task. She was wrapping barbed wire with gloved hands around the barrel of a wooden baseball bat.

"By ghosts," Grace corrected. "Not men."

"Damn straight."

"I'm terrified of men," Effie announced, even though we all knew this. She was the first of us to feel terror under the male gaze. She'd been abducted by her biological father when she was just a kid, before I even came into the picture. She didn't talk about the incident much, but there were scars on her thighs all of us pretended not to notice. "That's why it feels so good to hurt them."

A cruel smile bit into my cheeks. "I find anger and all its accompanying sins are the best kind of medicine."

"Is that right? Because you don't seem happy, Lex," Grace said.

I was saved from responding by Effie, who was dangling with her head off my bed beside where I leaned against it. Her soft Afro brushed my shoulders, tickling me. "It's only been ten months. We've barely started yet. You can't expect her to be happy."

The silence that followed her words was tacit agreement with what she'd said.

It was too soon.

I still couldn't sleep, plagued every night by black and white images of the incident playing out in the shadows of my room, in the reflection of lamp light on the windowpanes. If I managed to battle the shades of the past and actually fall asleep, I dreamt of the forest. The setting of my childhood, the only place that used to bring me solace in those lonely days, had been corrupted. Most mornings, I woke up with a scream lodged in my throat. Our neighbors complained until they realized who I was.

That girl.

It was one of the things that surprised me after the incident. If they knew what happened to me, women were frightened of me. As if being faced with a woman who had lived through their worst nightmares was a bad omen. I'd become a black cat, an umbrella opened indoors, the number thirteen.

Now, my neighbors didn't bother me even when I shrieked like a banshee.

"Still, Luna Pallas is pretty," Grace muttered petulantly. "That's something to be happy about."

"Why? I don't give a damn what she looks like," I countered mildly because if I protested too much, they'd read into it. "She's a means to an end."

"A pleasurable one, hopefully," she pointed out, waving the nailbrush in one hand so black speckles of varnish sprayed the stack of books beside her.

"Not the point," I gritted out between my teeth.

"So you haven't noticed?"

"Strawberry-blond, green eyes, dresses like the jock-focused collegiate girl she is."

"Perky breasts, round ass, and thighs like marble," Grace sing-songed.

"Not my type."

My three pseudo sisters gasped in tandem. Gracie pressed a hand to her heart, the drama-loving theater geek that she was. "You have a *type*? This is news to us. Please elaborate."

I leveled them with a glare and returned my gaze to the blinking cursor on my screen. Unwittingly, sometime in the past distraction-filled few minutes, I'd only typed two words.

Luna Pallas.

Fuck.

I slammed my laptop closed with too much force and shoved it off my lap as I rose to my feet. Cracking my knuckles, I checked my watch.

"You ladies ready to hunt?"

"Yippee," Grace crowed, jumping to her feet, dislodging the still-opened bottle of varnish so it spilled across the edge of my bargain-basement rug. "I thought you'd never ask."

Juno stood up to test the barbed wire-bound bat against her leather-gloved palm. "Ready."

Effie swung off the bed, grabbed the black suede roll of knives off my bedside table, and handed it to me. "I heard in the commons today that Jerrod and his lot would be by the lake for an evening row."

The anger that lay coiled around my soul, dormant during the day like any nocturnal creature, reared its head and gave a mighty, ominous rattle. The smile that claimed my face was the first true one I'd had in days. In the wake of the violence against me, the only thing that brought me any peace was seeking out violence myself.

So it was time to go hunting.

Acheron University was built in the 1700s by two men, Johnathon Wilcox Hammond and Demetrius Drakos. They were an unlikely pairing, one a scholar and youngest son of an earl from Britain and the other the fabulously wealthy son of a shipping magnate. They met, not unusually, through their wives, Hermione Wellington and Hyacinth Forbes. The two were best friends who, rumor has it, made a pact to stay that way forever. So when Hermione moved to America with her husband, Hyacinth convinced her husband to follow. The foursome was appalled by the lack of higher education in the New World and immediately set out to build something to rival the place where they met, Oxford University.

As a result, Acheron was born, a college to rival Harvard, one that focused particularly on the humanities because they were of specific interest to Hermione and Hyacinth. Many of the oldest buildings on campus were named in honor of Demetrius's heritage after places, people, or myths of ancient Greece, and the ones that weren't were called for Johnathon's and Hermione's favorite philosophers.

Hermione and Hyacinth even had statues in the small quad beside the lake. The duo was cast in bronze, two women sitting on a stone bench leaning together just a little too closely for propriety. One was reading a thick book, and the other balanced a set of scales on one petticoat-skirted knee.

One was truth and the other justice. Acheron's motto was *"Veritatis et acquitatis tenax."* Persevering in truth and justice.

There were other, bigger, and more impressive statues of Johnathon Wilcox Hammond and Demetrius Drakos around campus. Still, there was something impressive, almost compelling about those two bronze women down by the lake. Maybe because most women during that period were not permitted to leave a lasting impression in the sands of time, but somehow, they had succeeded in doing so. Maybe because something was beguiling about the way they were designed to sit together instead of with their respective husbands. Maybe because they sat just a little too close that any queer girl or boy seeing them would think for just a moment, "were they like me?"

I visited H&H a lot during my years at Acheron, and it seemed important, fateful even, that the first night of our rebellion took place under the view of their bronzed eyes.

Jerrod was there, as Effie said he would be. His friends had left, which was for the better, especially on our first outing, even though a part of me longed to get every single one of them. So it was just the single varsity rower, the son of some Silicon Valley tech start-up CEO, putting away the last of his equipment in the watershed beside the boat launch.

I watched him from the shadows, every predatory instinct alive inside me. It was late, the sunset behind the cloud-covered sky, and the wind was cool and scented with the sweet musk of decaying leaves. No one else lingered near the lake except this prey and his hunters.

He was tall as rowers are, with broad, quilted shoulders and a long reach. The girls on campus who cared about jocks thought he was a stud because he had swagger and attitude and a pretty face. Those same attributes on a woman would make her conceited, bitchy, and unlikeable, but on Jerrod Ericht, they were sexy.

He wouldn't be sexy when I was done with him.

The loud rasp of wood over wood echoed through the shed as Jerrod slotted his boat back into place alongside the others. It masked the sound of us moving in, a tight circle contracting around him until it was too late for him to escape.

When he turned around, wiping sweat off his damp brow, brown hair clinging to his forehead, he gave a croaked kind of yelp and took an instinctual step back.

I would have too.

It's not every dark autumn evening you're faced with a girl in a snake mask dressed all in black. His gaze flickered to Effie with her knives, Juno with her barbed bat, and Grace, as always, with a cattle prod. They were in black, too, straight down to the thick balaclavas obscuring their faces.

"What the fuck?" he asked, the slightest tremor of fear in his tone.

But then, then he looked at us again.

His eyes traced the shape of our bodies, the short length of Effie's skirt, and the swell of my hips and breasts beneath the leather leggings.

I knew the moment he understood he was surrounded by women because he relaxed slightly.

And then he *laughed*.

No woman surrounded by men holding weapons and wearing masks would ever have the luxury of laughing about it.

Anger and vindication surged through me.

"What the fuck is this? A practical joke?" He spoke through his laughter, rubbing a hand through his hair as he smirked at us. "Early birthday present, maybe? Man, Max told me he had something wicked planned, but fuck, you guys are hot. You going to take me to prison as your sex slave or something?"

I shifted on my feet as I unlocked the door on my rage, letting it spill through me like poison, bitter on the back of my tongue.

I liked it, though, that bitterness. I wasn't into sweet anymore.

I was into this.

"Or something," I told him in a voice like a snake's hiss.

And then, I moved.

He wasn't expecting it. They never do. Men are raised thinking they're better than women in most ways, but especially the physical. He'd never thought of defending himself against a woman, so by the time it occurred to him to try, it was too late.

Effie, Grace, and Juno stood back. I had it under control.

In fact, it was almost boring how easy it was.

By the time I had him strung up to the rafters by a spare coil of rope, his shoulders wrenched back nearly out of their sockets, his left eye swollen closed, his lip split and trickling blood down his chiseled chest, he was finally starting to panic.

"What the fuck is this?" he demanded as if he was still in charge. "What the fuck do you think you're doing?"

"Ah, ah, ah," I hushed him, pressing a gloved fingertip to his mouth. When he didn't heed my warning, Effie stepped forward and slapped a piece of duct tape across his mouth.

I leaned forward to paint a red mouth on the silver adhesive. "That's so much better," I said with a happy sigh.

And I was happy. That chasm inside my chest Morgan had left me with was filled with heat and crackling flames like the forges of Mordor. Fire licked through every inch of me, erasing my numbness and burning so brightly that I finally felt alive again.

"I'm sorry, you asked me a question, didn't you?" I asked pleasantly, running the talons at the ends of my gloves over his chest in two diagonal lines so that he was marked by a big red X. "You want to know what we're doing? 'If you prick us, do we not bleed? If you tickle us, do we not laugh? If you poison us, do we not die?'" I paused to lean in, wrapping my hand around his strong throat finger by finger, then holding tight until his face purpled. "'And if you wrong us, shall we not get revenge?'"

I released him when a blood vessel in his eye burst, flooding the white with a red stain. My laughter felt painful in my hot, tight chest. "You probably haven't read Shakespeare to know the quote, have you? It's from *The Merchant of Venice*. It's applicable to our situation because you wronged someone I know, Jerrod. Do you remember Rhea?"

His bloodshot eyes widened before he could curb his surprise.

"Oh yes, I know all about that night you spent with her," I continued conversationally as Juno handed me a large pad of poster paper and a pen. I uncapped the latter with my teeth and started writing. "Look at me, using euphemisms. I meant to say I know all about the night you hid in the girl's locker room after softball practice and waited until she was the last girl there. The night you hit her over the head with her own bat and sexually assaulted her."

Finished with my poster, I ripped the sheet free of the pad and slapped it against the middle of Jerrod's bloodied, overly muscled chest.

"You probably thought you were clever. No cameras in the girl's locker room. Late at night with no witnesses. I bet you thought she would be too embarrassed to tell anyone, especially after you made her feel like a slut for leading you on." I leaned close, my words sharp as the talons I dug into his pectoral, blood beading from the broken skin. "Was she just so pretty, you couldn't help yourself? Did she smile at you that one time right here by the lake after watching you row, and you thought that was her asking for it?"

His voice was a hoarse mumble behind his tape-closed lips, but I hushed him again as I held my free hand out to Juno, who handed me a staple gun.

"I don't care about your excuses, Jerrod. No explanation can erase what you did to Rhea, how you scarred her and scared her for life. Every time she goes into a locker room, every time she's faced with sexual desires, every time she is even alone with a man, what you did will haunt her. The fear you gave her will possess her like a demon. *You* did that to another person. *You* made a decision that took her ability to choose away from her. And me?"

I pushed the end of the staple gun to one corner of the poster I had slapped to the center of his chest and pressed the trigger, shooting the metal clamp deep into paper, skin, and muscle. He made a garbled cry, jerking in his bonds.

"I'm going to make you pay for it."

Click.

Another staple. Another muffled scream.

"I'm going to make sure everyone knows exactly what kind of animal you are."

Click.

Staple. Cry.

"I'm going to teach you what it's like to be hunted and haunted. You're going to walk away from tonight a changed man. Every time you come into this watershed for practice, every time you have your perverted sexual desires, every time you even see a woman, what I'm going to do to you will haunt you. Hopefully, it will make you think twice about ever touching another woman again."

Click.

Staple. Cry.

Tears slid down his cheeks, over the square of silver tape so his drawn-in red mouth leaked ink onto his chin, red ink mixing with red blood.

Satisfaction warmed my blood like arousal. My heart beat too fast. My mouth watered. My stomach felt achingly empty. I wanted to devour him. Break this predator apart piece by piece and eat him. Something about taking him into my body against his will felt like dark poetic justice. If he wanted to violate women so much, we would violate him.

It was such a small consequence of his actions.

The image of Rhea, sobbing and shaking, curled up like a fetus and just as vulnerable in my arms as I held her, flashed across my inner eye. She'd known what was done to me, but we were also friends. After what happened to her, she'd dragged herself to my apartment last week. Gracie and I took her to the emergency room, but Jerrod had worn a condom to forcibly take her mouth when she was passed out, so no genetic evidence was left behind. Only a bruised jaw, a swollen, split scalp oozing blood, and the start of bruises in the shape of fingertips on her throat.

But she knew who'd done that to her.

And then, I did.

And now, everyone would.

"It's over," I whispered to him through his muffled tears. "You can tell your friends, your bro/frat dude besties that the Man Eaters are patrolling campus now, and if any of you assault a female student in *any* way—verbally, physically, sexually—we will come for you. And this is the least we'll do."

I stepped back, and Gracie laughed manically beside me before explaining to Jerrod, "We're starting small."

And we were.

I had barely made this man bleed. Hardly enough for real retribution. Barely enough to curb that ferocious hunger in me for vindication.

But just enough, I thought, to prove a point.

To spread the fear.

There was a click of a shutter as Effie took a photo of our masterpiece. Jerrod Ericht strung up in the watershed like a bug suspended in a web, stapled with a poster that read "I rape women." In the bottom corner of the page, twin snakes curled together in a figure-eight ouroboros.

It was a symbol. A signature.

Xoxo, the Man Eater Crew

The only thing standing between women on campus and the men

who were systemically allowed to hurt us and get away with it.

CHAPTER SIX

"I'm not sure which is worse: intense feeling, or the absence of it."
—Margaret Atwood

Luna

Everyone was laughing, but I couldn't focus enough to find the joke funny. My mind was on Lex Gorgon. It irritated me that I was so fixated and that irritation led me to obsess over her even more. Why was I so intrigued?

She was defiant.

Maybe that was it.

I'd always been a good girl, a rule follower, and an overachiever. The kind of girl to sit at the front of class, to make friends with the quiet kid, to say yes to my elders and authority figures. I didn't do any of these things because I particularly wanted to.

I did them because I was told.

I did them because I was afraid of standing out, of being different and other.

So maybe something was compelling for me in Lex's defiance. In the way she didn't seem to care at all about anyone around her. It was this characteristic that set her apart from anyone I had ever met before.

Her exceptional beauty had nothing to do with it.

Not really, at least.

After all, I wasn't attracted to women that way.

But I was still human. Still moved by loveliness.

And she moved me, somehow.

"Luna," Pierce said, suddenly standing over me, leaning down to pick me up and take my seat so he could settle me on his lap. "What does a guy have to do to get you to pay attention to him, huh?"

He nuzzled into my neck, moving my hair to press a kiss to my throat.

I fought the urge to squirm. Public displays of affection—or really any physical affection at all—made me uncomfortable.

"You'd think being named captain this year would be enough," his best friend, Andrew, said from across the library table.

"Yeah, that definitely deserves a celebratory blow job, at the very least," Beckett joked, prompting the rest of our table to laugh.

Pierce didn't laugh, and I was grateful.

His hand tightened on my thigh as he shot his friend a glare. "This isn't the locker room, Beckett. Cut that shit out."

"Aw, is Princess Prude gonna cry?" Beckett sneered as he waggled his brows at me.

Humiliation and anger joined forces inside me. "Shut up, Beckett."

"What she said," Pierce snapped, tugging me even closer to his chest as if he could shield me from his teammate. "There's no winning with you, man. A girl is either a slut or a prude. Which would you rather?"

It was a good point, one that made me like my boyfriend even more, and I liked him plenty before.

But Beckett was the kind of man who'd been fed small doses of misogyny his whole life. Just little things like: girls are ruled by their emotions, not their intellect; girls aren't as good at sports; girls shouldn't show too much skin or flirt with too many boys, *but* if a girl isn't attractive to boys, she doesn't exist positively in the male mind.

So it wasn't surprising when he waggled his brows and said, "I'd rather a slut, of course."

"Oh yeah, you want some sloppy seconds or sixteenths like Lex Gorgon?" Potter asked, his lip curled into a sneer.

That surprised me. Potter was usually a quiet, nice guy. He struggled with acne, and his curly hair was beyond his control. I'd never seen him with a woman before, and the guys teased him about it.

Maybe that was why he said what he did. Because deep down, he hated Lex a little for not giving him the possibility of her affections when he thought she was otherwise so indiscriminate.

My stomach hurt, cramped around the unfairness of the conversation. I thought I might be sick.

"Dude, a guy could get herpes after just looking at her for too long," Beckett joked, and the rest of the table laughed.

Words sat on my tongue alongside the bile that rose from the back of my throat.

I should say something, I thought desperately, wanting to.

But I didn't.

And why didn't I?

Sure, I didn't know Lex, not really. What the guys said could have even been true, but still, shouldn't I defend her? Whether she was promiscuous or not, she didn't deserve to be talked about like that. Like an object on display. Like their criticism somehow determined her worth. Especially after she'd been assaulted and left like garbage tossed in the forest.

It was wrong. I felt that in my gut and knew it in my head, but I didn't say anything.

It made me realize that I wasn't drawn to Lex because she was defiant.

I was drawn to her because she was courageous.

Maybe I wanted to be in her orbit in the hopes some of that would rub off on my regular ole cowardly heart.

"You okay, babe?" Pierce asked, bumping my shoulder with his forehead to draw my attention to his tender smile. "It's like I'm holding a wood board in my arms instead of my girlfriend."

I smiled weakly and tipped my head against his. "I think I'm just tired. I'm going to head back to my apartment for an early night."

Lies.

"You want company?" he asked immediately, handsome brow creased. "I'll even watch *Pride & Prejudice* with you for the four thousandth time."

I almost choked on my startled laughter. "You're so good to me, you know that?"

"I do," he agreed with that easy charm Pierce Argent was known for throughout campus. Combined with his rich brown hair and long-lashed eyes, the flecks of cinnamon dusted across his cheeks, and the physique that made him captain and leading scorer for the Acheron U hockey team, he was the most popular guy on campus.

And he was, somehow, mine.

It still caught me off guard sometimes. Watching him across the cafeteria laughing with his jock buddies, seeing women swarm him like moths to a vibrant flame, hearing people cheer his name in the stands at games.

People said we were a perfect match. Mr. & Miss Popular Jock.

But there was an intangible quality to our relationship. Something missing. No, not something...*me*. Every time he touched me, I felt like a ghost, his fingers passing through me, his passions as easily ignored as mist moving over my skin.

Which killed me because Pierce was the best man I'd ever known. He was sweet and thoughtful without losing that edge that made him cool. He remembered everything about me, even things I often forgot, and he loved me. Our relationship wasn't fiery or overly physical, but hanging out with Pierce was one of the only times I felt like I wasn't going insane.

I'd always thought university was meant to be a time for finding yourself, but since I started at Acheron three years ago, I felt as if I'd lost myself even more. All those things I'd been doing all my life—field hockey, dating, going to parties with popular kids—felt wrong and left me empty. I wandered through my own existence like a shade, taking mute notice of changes but doing nothing to alter my course.

Until now, lying to my boyfriend about going to bed so I could sneak up to the secluded levels of the library to take pictures of Lex Gorgon, the most infamous girl on campus, and someone I had absolutely no business mingling with.

Someone who made my skin tingle for the first time in so long I couldn't remember the last instant I'd been so moved.

"Baby?" Pierce asked, his luminous eyes wide as he tried to look into mine, to read what I'd written in invisible ink on the surface of my soul. "Seriously, I don't mind ditching these guys."

"Well, we do!" Beckett protested. "We've got to celebrate your captaincy properly, dude. You can cuddle with Luna any fucking night."

"I can, and if I want to do that tonight instead of going out with you animals, I will," he declared.

God, I thought weakly, *any girl would kill to be with this man. He's almost too good to be true.*

"I'm fine," I assured him, kissing him softly, his stubble scratching my chin. "I'll see you tomorrow, okay? Have fun with the lads."

He squeezed my hip. "You're sure?"

Heart aching, I dredged a lie up from the churning mass in my stomach. "Yes, I'm just tired. Going to hit the hay."

"Love ya," he said before kissing me back, a little harder and deeper, like he needed a taste of me before parting.

I hummed my response.

We'd been dating since last year, but I wasn't convinced I loved him romantically or even that I could fall in love at all. Opening up to someone enough to fall for them seemed to take more bravery than I possessed.

The other guys called their goodbyes as I stood and collected my canvas shoulder bag, but I was forgotten as soon as I walked away. When I paused at the door to the stairs to look back, the group of them were laughing, Pierce gesturing with his hands like the leader he was, orchestrating their humor. They looked right together, a picture of young, carefree men in workout gear with two pretty girls in ripped jeans and little tops adorning them like bulbs on a Christmas tree.

My stomach cramped harder. I pressed a hand to it, looking down at my tweed skirt and the matching vest I had buttoned up over my chest. There was some cleavage, and my ass, round from years of field hockey practice, filled out my midi-skirt nicely, but I wasn't dressed to suit that tableau.

I didn't really want to be.

Relief slid over me like cool water as I ducked out of sight around the corner and started up the wide marble staircase instead of down, making my way to the dusty old stacks on the third floor.

It was dark on that level, old book spines limned in golden light from old-fashioned sconces and a few heavy chandeliers. The smell was strong here, the musk of aged paper, the slight sweetness of wood wax rubbed into the handcrafted railings and sturdy study tables. I dragged a deep breath in through my nose and held it, hugging my book bag to my chest.

Peace suffused me.

Here amid the books and the years of history housed in them and this very room, I finally felt settled in my skin.

It was late, after nine o'clock on a Thursday, which was *the* night to go out on campus, so I wasn't surprised by the quiet that permeated the space. Instead of marring the silence by calling out for her, I went in search of Lex.

All the large study tables out front were empty, but when I walked deeper through the stacks, I found my favorite small table decorated with a green plaid blazer and a leather backpack. I recognized the backpack, but even if I hadn't, the gold snake broach on the blazer would have identified the belongings as Lex's.

I wondered if I'd be bold enough to ask about her clear fascination with snakes, but I doubted it.

I dropped everything but my film camera on the table across from her seat and went off into the shadowed stacks to find her. My heart tripped, heavy and fast. I felt it drum in my throat, in my wrists, and that major artery near my groin. One big throbbing, thrumming beat.

I couldn't tell if it was from excitement or fear and decided it was both.

Alone in the library at night with a troubled girl hidden somewhere inside. It shouldn't have felt so poignant, but it did.

My search increased in intensity as I wandered, first slow, measured steps, then a quick patter of my loafers ringing out over the wood floors. From casual pursuer to something like a hunter.

I was hungry for the sight of her. The idea of stumbling upon her like an animal in the wild, watching her in a place that felt intrinsically like her natural habitat aroused something in me that was hot under my skin. There was an urgency, an almost panicked desire to find her and make sure she was actually real. Not some gorgeous creature I'd conjured into being with my imagination.

Finding her should have been anticlimactic.

A person can't get up to many particularly exciting things alone in an old library.

But it wasn't.

I lost my thready breath to the image she struck the moment I went sliding around the corner of the Antiquities section and found her in a row between D and E in the Ancient Greek texts section.

Before I could think, my camera was raised to my eye, sight trained through the lens, and I was clicking the shutter closed.

The sound didn't stir her, so, greedy, I took more.

She lay at the base of the wall at the end of the stacks with her torso flat to the floor and her feet perched high on the wall, an L-shaped woman with a plume of heavy black silk hair coiled around her head. Her small skirt had curled over itself like the drying petals of a flower to reveal long golden-hued legs, shapely and punctuated by those twin black snakes curling from the top of her left thigh to mid-calf where their tongues kissed. As I shifted on my feet, I caught a glimpse of the cotton at the apex of her thighs, black and scanty, her flesh paler and soft around its edges.

My throat went dry and tight. I found it impossible to swallow. To move, even, or think.

As I watched, she tipped the book she read higher above her head and used her free hand to slip, skip, and stumble over her bloused torso to that triangle of black fabric. Using her index finger, she slipped a nail under the cotton and adjusted it to lay flatter against her groin.

A noise like a groan rose unbidden from my throat and shivered into the air.

That, she noticed.

Languidly, she tipped her head farther back on the ground and stared at me upside down.

"Luna." My name in her mouth was a throaty song she stretched into three syllables. "I didn't take you for a peeping Tom."

I shook my strange fugue state off like water from my back and tried to respond as flippantly as I could. "You practically gave me permission when you told me to take a photo of you." I lifted my camera. "These will last longer."

Her smile was a reluctant curling of the left side of her mouth. "Tacit permission, maybe. But consent is important, don't you think?"

Why did a conversation about consent feel so...sultry? Like she was teasing me, flirting with me even.

"Yes," I agreed, shifting my weight because her scrutiny made me feel too hot, too raw and easily read.

"Well, then...?" She trailed off, one of her feet sliding farther down the wall so she was even more exposed. Her skin was so smooth, unmarred by hair or imperfections. It made me wonder if she waxed or shaved, how pale and soft the skin might be under that cotton triangle.

It took me three tries to find my voice. "Yeah?"

She cocked her head at a seemingly impossible angle and smirked at me the way I'd imagined in class. "Are you going to ask for my consent?"

"Um, yes." I paused, a furious blush scalding my cheeks. "Do I have your permission?"

"To do what, Lux?"

I couldn't believe the images that simple question triggered. My mouth around the index finger she'd slipped beneath her panties. My fingers tracing that same seam. My tongue against her tongue like the snakes kissing down her thigh.

I blinked, forcing the shameful thoughts away. "To take your picture."

Her smile flickered, brightening for a second as if she was laughing at me. As if she saw through me like tracing paper.

"Be my guest," she allowed and then, she turned back to her book.

I felt oddly bereft of her attention even though its intensity had made my skin itch. I rolled my shoulders, trying to ground myself, but my skin still buzzed, and my heart still pounded in that strange, erratic way.

Sucking in a deep breath, I set my mind to the task of photographing the girl with the snake tattoos. The girl who made herself impenetrable to the ridiculing masses.

She wasn't the same girl here tonight.

In the warm, dark belly of the library, cocooned by books on either side, she seemed softer. The gentle light turned her flesh to pale bronze, made her thin black blouse slightly sheer so the shape of her bra beneath it was a tantalizing shadow. Her face wasn't so hard, the strong features relaxed as her eyes traced the words on the pages of a translated work of Sappho's poems. As she sank further into the text, her red mouth began to form the words as she read them.

Oh God, but I was entranced.

It spooked me. As if I was a horse, I felt skittish and irrationally afraid. Something in me—this heated, writhing mess of *something*—sensed a storm coming.

A reckoning.

I both wanted to stay there in that narrow space between bookcases with a girl who scared me and awed me, and to run away, far away, never to return to Acheron U again.

"You're trembling."

That smooth-rough voice startled me so badly I dropped my camera. It plummeted straight down onto her face, but quick as a snake's strike, Lex caught it in her free hand.

"Careful," she murmured and I could have been going crazy, but I thought there was a flash in her eyes, a different kind of warning. "You could hurt someone with this thing."

"I'm surprised you let me take your photo," I said because I was muddled and off-kilter. As soon as the words were out, I regretted them.

"I don't believe a camera can steal my soul," she teased dryly.

"Still," I pressed even though part of me shouted to shut up. "It's vulnerable. I didn't think someone like you would enjoy the feeling."

"Someone like me?" She swung her legs down from the wall and turned to face me sitting on her bum with her legs crossed in one graceful motion.

"I-I..." I squeezed my eyes shut and took a deep breath to steady myself. I'd never been so ineloquent and clumsy in my life. "I'm sorry. I only meant you seem strong and invulnerable. And obviously, I know a camera can't steal your soul, but I'm a photographer, so I believe it can capture the essence of one." I huffed out a frustrated laugh and dragged a hand through my tangled orange-gold hair. "You just don't seem like the kind of person who wants to be known."

Least of all by someone like me, I thought but didn't have the nerve to say.

"Well, you don't know anything about me, so I'll forgive you the assumption." She said it in this way that was both superior and benevolent. Like I was a silly kid, and she was so much better than me.

I reacted bizarrely to that tone, but then, it seemed to be a reoccurring theme in Lex's presence. If a man had talked to me like that, I would have got my back up. Yet something about Lex's confidence and grace was charming, almost funny. If I'd known her better, I would have teased her.

But then I thought, why not? I'd been with her for ten minutes and already made a fool of myself. There was nothing else to lose.

"Thank you, oh benevolent queen," I said with a silly little bow.

When I raised my head again, my cheeks were flaming but I didn't try to bite back my smile.

And I was glad because even though her mouth was flat, her eyes sparkled back at me.

"It seems we're both more surprising than we seem."

Why did that feel like a compliment? To be found more than I seemed by someone as obviously complicated as her.

She stood so quickly, she startled me. I took a step back only to slam into the bookcase. A book beside my head trembled and fell forward.

Lex lunged forward and caught that before it fell, too.

"You have good reflexes," I breathed because she was close.

Close enough to smell—something dark and rich like tilled soil and crushed violets. Close enough to see the complete perfection of her complexion, not a pimple or stray hair in sight. Only a tiny scar like a silvery spider's web beside that full mouth.

And blood.

"Oh my God." I touched the base of her neck without thinking, rubbing a thumb over the splatter of dried blood there. "Are you hurt?"

Her hand snapped mine up in a punishing grip that made my bones grind.

"Ow."

She glared at me over our hands for a long moment before gentling her hold. Using our combined hands, she rubbed slowly at the blood until it dissolved under our touch.

Touching her felt sinful. My belly clenched hard and my thighs trembled.

I couldn't even begin to understand what was happening to me, and I didn't try, too caught up in Lex's swirling vortex.

"Gone?" she asked quietly, her eyes so intent on mine I couldn't blink.

I nodded.

She didn't release our hands. Instead, she opened my palm and traced the ridge of calluses across my upper palm with her thumb.

I trembled and told myself there was a draft.

"Strong hands," she noted, then scraped the edge of her nail across the thin skin at the center of my palm. "Calloused hands. I thought you'd be softer."

She'd thought about me?

My pulse throbbed so sharply I could barely focus on anything but its staccato beat and the feel of a girl holding my hand.

"Field hockey," I croaked out in explanation.

"Mmm," Lex hummed, dipping her head to look between our bodies, her hair swinging forward to brush my cheek like a silken kiss.

I almost choked on my sharp inhalation when she dipped slightly and one hand found the skin at the back of my knee under the hem of my skirt. She traced her nimble fingers up, up until she could curl them around the side of my thigh, flexing her grip to test my strength.

Without releasing me, her hand hiking up my skirt so I was exposed to mid-thigh, she looked up through her lashes at me with eyes like wet concrete, trapping me inside that gaze. "I should have known."

"Thunder thighs," I whispered because I couldn't gather enough breath for normal speech. "It can't be helped."

"Why should it be? Strength in women is underappreciated," she said, flexing those fingers again, then digging her nails into my muscle so I involuntarily clenched. "Strength in women is nothing but sexy as hell."

"You think?" I'd been insecure about my compact, athletic frame my entire life—ever since Sally Martinez told me I looked like a boy in second grade.

"I know," she confirmed, patting my thigh like I was a good girl, some prized bit of horse flesh.

Ugh, but why? Why was everything she did so sexy?

Why was I noticing it? Unable to walk away from it?

I felt like I was one lingering caress away from a mental breakdown.

"Why did you have blood on your neck?" I asked, straining to return the conversation to something less erotic.

She tilted her head in that way I was coming to notice was habit, an animal form of curiosity. "Why do you care?"

"Well..." I laughed, a little shaky because why was she still so close, only a thin wedge of pressurized air between us even though she'd let go of my thigh, my hand. "I guess that's a good question. Wouldn't anyone ask it?"

"Probably, but I wouldn't answer just anyone honestly."

"Will you answer me?" I asked, wincing at how eager I sounded. How eager I *was*.

Her eyes scraped over my face and neck, lingering at the upper ridges of my breasts pressed together by the button-up vest.

"Maybe, one day. I don't give up my secrets for just anyone."

I hadn't thought so, and the idea of being her confidante was like wine on the back of my tongue. Every breath I took was filled with her scent. I was getting dizzy. Forgetting myself the way I did whenever I'd had too much to drink.

I swayed closer to her. "What does a girl have to do to earn a secret?"

Was I flirting? I wondered dazedly.

"Why would little Miss Popular want one of my secrets?" she countered, and all I could think was *yes*, I was flirting, and *was she flirting back*?

"I don't know," I whispered honestly, a little wrecked. "I just know I can't stop thinking about you."

"Because you think I'm beautiful." It was a question, but not. She knew she was stunning. How could she not? But there was an edge to her voice, a threat.

There was a wrong answer here, and I had to be careful not to make it if I wanted to be this close to her (or closer) again.

"I do," I agreed because even a blind person would feel the warmth of her beauty. "But that's not it. I think I want to be you when I grow up."

"Hateful?" she almost snapped at me, white teeth glowing in the low light, a little too close to my throat.

Without thinking, I tilted my head, exposing myself even more to her sharp-toothed aggression.

"Strong," I countered. "Brave."

She hummed again, that rich vibration I could feel against my skin because she was ducking, bending her neck to breathe against my fluttering jugular. I shivered so violently that the bookcase rattled.

"You seem pretty brave to me," she praised a moment before she closed her teeth over my neck and bit me.

It was a hard bite with no mercy. The sharp pain punctured my haze of confusion and arrowed arousal straight through my carotid artery into my bloodstream. I'd never been bitten before, never thought to ask for it, but now, *God*, I wasn't sure anything had ever been so heady.

And then I felt a quick pass of wet warmth on my skin in the frame of the pain from the bite, and I realized something was sexier than Lex's teeth on me.

Her tongue.

A keening sound filled the air. It took me too long to realize it was coming from me. I forced myself to quiet, but I couldn't make myself move. My hands were pressed palm down on the books, my skin sweaty and sticking to the spines. I let my fingertips curl around the edges of the books as if they could ground me as they had so many times before.

Finally, Lex raised her head, her eyes so close they were all I could see.

"You taste good," she told me, almost conversationally as if she complimented other women on their flavor every day. The thought made my stomach hurt. "Have you ever kissed a girl before, Luna?"

"No," I breathed. "I'm straight."

Her smile was small and mean, purple-pink lips a hook that seemed to catch between my ribs. "Are you brave enough to test that theory?"

She was even closer, her breath a sweet mint draft across my lips, making them tingle.

I thought she'd kiss me then, but she only hovered.

"Brave girls use their words," she taunted me, so mean, so sexy that drool pooled in my mouth, and I had to swallow hard against the flood. Her hand lifted, found my throat, and her thumb rubbed at the bruise she'd made on the side of my neck. "Are you brave, Lux?"

"Why are you calling me that?" I whispered, desperate to evade the real question.

Which was, *why hadn't Pierce ever made me feel like this?*

"You're light." Her nose rubbed along the side of mine. "Bright and cheery. Friendly and sweet. A proverbial bonbon." She hummed and the noise traveled from her lips to my cheek as she brushed her mouth against me. "I wonder if you'll melt on my tongue."

My knees sagged a little before I caught myself.

"And what are you?"

"Dark," she said instantly, her pupils so blown that they looked entirely black. "Sinful and violent. Righteous and self-important enough to convict the wrongful when no one else will."

Her tongue slipped from between her lips, slick and pink, curling toward the edge of my mouth to trace the corner of it.

"Do you want to know what sinful tastes like, Luna?"

I didn't answer her. Not directly.

She'd said bravery meant words, but I'd always been more a woman of action.

So in response, I kissed *her*.

Her mouth was soft, so soft. Plump lips parted for warm breath, and for a moment, it was just that, just breathing into each other. And then she took control, sealing us together and gliding her tongue between my lips, past my teeth.

She tasted like Earl Grey tea and peppermint. Delicious.

But it was more than that.

It was the way she slid that hand on my throat around to the nape of my neck, sinking her fingers into my hair to tug me into the position she liked best to plunder my mouth.

It was the way her knee surged between both of mine, nudging against my groin with a firm pressure that made sparks explode behind my eyes.

It was the way she pressed my body between her body and the books like something precious to be preserved forever.

No man had ever kissed me like this.

It was like she'd been born to kiss me or that she'd been kissing me for years.

I never wanted her to stop.

So when she finally pulled back, eyes so black, lips and cheeks flushed darkly pink, I embarrassed myself with a whimper. My hand clutched at her waist, at the front of her black dress shirt, crumpled in my fist.

"Well?" Lex demanded, almost combatively.

Suddenly, the hold we had on each other didn't feel sexual or romantic. It felt like a fight, like one wrong step away from war.

I knew I shouldn't say it. They were fighting words, igniting words, and I had no idea what we were even fighting against or fighting for. Even if we were fighting together or against each other.

But I couldn't stop myself from whispering the honest truth.

"Like Earl Grey and peppermint."

Her smile was so small I would have missed it if I wasn't close enough to count her eyelashes. A soft curl of one side of her ripe plum-colored mouth.

"That bravery will earn you a secret." She swayed toward me again, and I held my breath, heart thumping so madly in my chest I thought I might die if she didn't kiss me. But she didn't. Instead, her lips brushed the shell of my ear as she whispered, "Now that I've tasted your skin and your mouth, I won't stop until I know what you taste like between those beautiful thunder thighs."

CHAPTER SEVEN

"We have to distrust each other. It is our only defense against betrayal."
—Tennessee Williams

Luna

Lex left me slumped against the bookcase after that dangerous whispered promise. It took me too long to find starch for my soft bones and peel myself off the spines. Even then, my head swam, and my pulse beat too hard between my thighs. I wondered idly if I'd ever be able to smell the scent of books again without getting wet.

Of course, that made me think of Pierce.

My *boyfriend*.

I braced myself on the table in the library and stared at my reflection in the mirrored windows. My hair was a glowing nimbus of pink-orange light around my head, its usual mess of overly thick, cowlicked chaos. But the rest of my face was not usual, not fixed in an expression I recognized. Flushed cheeks made my eyes bright, and my lips were swollen, the same dark pink as the teeth marks on the side of my neck.

Irrationally, I thought those rectangular indents would make for a pretty tattoo.

But I didn't have tattoos, and before seeing those snakes twisting up Lex's leg, I'd never even considered them sexy.

I collected my things in a daze and left the library, but the cold air of the dark September night doused me like ice water. My return to sanity wasn't smooth. I felt the turbulence in my lungs, and I had to lean against the black trunk of a tree cutting through the commons to lose my dinner in the bushes.

My skin was cold and clammy, but I felt feverish inside.

I felt like I was coming undone.

Who was that? That girl who kissed a girl.

The girl who kissed a girl and loved it.

Wanted it.

Begged for its return with a goddamn whimper.

Couldn't stop thinking about it even after spitting bile off the back of my tongue.

I was both disgusted and aroused, a duality that made me feel like I was coming out of my skin.

I was so lost in my own head, I almost didn't hear the argument.

Voices wafted out the open window beside me, honeyed light falling in a fat square at my feet.

"Don't be ridiculous, Mina."

A shiver bit sharply into the base of my spine and rattled up my back.

It was Professor Morgan's office in Hippios Hall.

And with him, my mother.

"I'm serious, Dylan. I can't afford to have any more fuckups. I'm interviewing at Cambridge University in the new year, and I have a real chance of being their new president."

"And a fine one you'll make," he agreed easily. "A word of advice, though. Maybe do not antagonize your best professors, hmm?"

"I'm not antagonizing you," Mom scoffed as I crept closer to the window, flattening my spine against the cold stone wall beside the opening. "Lex Gorgon has not gone gently into the night, Dylan. She's *here*. The girl came back, and she isn't doing it quietly. I'm worried she won't let this go."

"She'll have to."

He was so calm, so completely unrattled by Lex's accusations. It seemed wrong, deceitful. If someone innocent had been accused of rape, wouldn't they be horrified and panicked? Sorrowful, at least, that it had happened at all even though they weren't involved?

"How can you be so calm?" my mom demanded, echoing my thoughts.

"She's no one from nowhere. I'm calm because there is nothing to worry about. She has no power here at Acheron, Mina. I do. You do. And really, in the court of public opinion, Lex Gorgon has already been tried and found guilty. The girl has a terrible reputation."

She didn't before you, I thought as anger surged through me, bright and cutting as the edge of a knife through soft tissue.

It brought with it a certainty, a knowledge that Professor Morgan had raped Lex and left her for the carrion birds in the forest.

He seemed like the kind of man capable of taking what he thought he was owed.

And Lex...

Lex, with her breathtaking beauty and her aloof, ephemeral charms, was exactly the kind of prize a hunter would want to take.

Lex, the girl who had kissed me, was exactly the kind of girl who wouldn't fall for Acheron U's dreamiest professor.

And Lex...

She just didn't seem like the type of girl to lie about her tragedy. It was seared so deeply in her soul it radiated sorrow from those wet stone eyes and emanated off her like dry ice. To be near her was to feel her anger and her malcontent.

I didn't know her beyond a bite and kiss in Mathieson Library, but I felt more certain about her integrity than anything I ever had before.

My intuition cried out for her salvation.

"You're right," Mom killed me by saying slowly, convincing herself of his words because it was beneficial for her, not because she believed him. "She had a lawyer threaten to sue if I didn't let her enroll for the semester, but I hope that's the end of it."

"Even if it isn't," Professor Morgan said flippantly, "no one will believe her now. She's the campus pariah, and she's too proud to speak out against the rumors about her. Trust me."

Trust him?

I couldn't believe my mother would. She was the one who'd set an example for so many women in academics. She was the first female president in the history of Acheron U, and before that, she'd been the Provost at Stanford. She'd raised me with only a little help from my grandparents. Started the Pallas Scholarship to reward high-achieving female scholars without the money to attend Ivy League schools. Written a book on female empowerment in the 21st century that was on *The New York Times* Best Seller list for forty-two weeks.

She wouldn't trust this man.

How could she when every alarm she'd taught me to install in my body against the chauvinism and misogyny of men was ringing madly in my head?

"Okay," she said finally, words soft but binding as a promise. "I'll trust you."

Those alarm bells clanged louder, not just for Morgan but also for Mom.

I felt betrayed by her easy confidence in a man who seemed so much like a predator. The woman I knew would have championed Lex, conducted a thorough investigation, and suspended Morgan, not Lex, pending the results.

But then, work was the most important thing in Mom's life. I was a close second, but growing up, I'd always known her entire identity was wrapped up in her academic crusade. She had never been the type of mother to play with me. Instead, she was the kind to assign me homework on top of my classwork, and take me to museums and art galleries. I was an extension of her, and as such, I had a responsibility to be just as accomplished as she was.

So maybe it made sense, in a sickening way, that she would give in to her need to smooth troubled waters and believe Professor Morgan. It made sense for her, but I knew in her heart she knew it was wrong because I did too.

I'd read once that one of life's biggest upsets was when children discovered their parents weren't the faultless heroes they'd grown up venerating, but human beings just as infallible as themselves. Until that moment, I hadn't thought such a blow was possible for Mom and me, and it broke my heart more than anything else ever had before.

After a night of chaotic revelations, my knees gave out beneath me, and I fell bottom first to the cold, damp grass. I closed my eyes as the world tilted wildly around me, restructuring itself around Lex, around Mom, around the new knowledge I had after tonight that burned holes through the tapestry of life as I knew it. Nausea rose and receded, but I fought the urge to vomit. Instead, I sat there within the dark cold for a long time. Long enough for my skin to go numb, my hands frozen into claws dug into the earth as if they could anchor me in the chaos.

Long enough for the nausea to slowly ebb away, for the world to clumsily right itself in new colors and patterns my eyes didn't seem ready to recognize.

There were only two things clear in the wreckage.

I'd kissed Lex Gorgon, and I liked...no, loved it.

And if my mom wasn't going to do what was right and stop Professor Morgan from preying on female students, someone had to.

And I thought madly, that person should be me.

CHAPTER EIGHT

"There is no greater agony than bearing an untold story inside you."
—Maya Angelou

Luna

The next morning arrived, too bright and throbbing. I felt hungover from the emotional whiplash and exhausted after only a few hours of tossing, turning slumber. I showed up to early morning practice like a zombie, but thankfully, years of conditioning meant I could play center mid-field in my sleep, and no one commented on my grogginess.

Besides, they were distracted.

"They found him in the boat shed," Courtney said as we all crowded into the locker room, taking off our shin pads and cleats, stretching, changing, and chatting before heading out for classes. "He was tied to the rafters, and someone *stapled* a sign to his chest."

"What did it say?" Cornelia asked, leaning forward with the rest of the girls, pulled in by the gravity of the story.

"'I rape women,'" she whispered. "Can you believe it?"

"Yes," Taya murmured beside me, head bent as she peeled off sweat-damp socks.

No one else heard her.

"No!" Flora cried dramatically, curls flying in her face, sticking to wet skin as she let her hair down. "Jerrod is *Jerrod*. He's, like, one of the most popular guys on campus. Why would he have to rape someone?"

"Rape isn't just for insecure men, Flo," I said, quiet but firm. There was a new weight in my stomach, not a hindrance but a ballast. A rightness and conviction that hadn't existed before last night. It came from knowing a bit of Lex Gorgon, now, and what type of human she seemed to be. Angry, yes, sad, definitely, but also, honest to the point of brutality. No one believed her story, and that seemed like a crime for which she unfairly bore the punishment. "It could be because someone rejected him, and a guy like him isn't used to rejection. Or he grew up in a violent home. Or maybe he was just drunk, and things got out of control."

She scoffed. "If he was drunk, the girl was probably drunk. That's not rape."

"Do you hear yourself when you speak?" I demanded, suddenly rearing up on my knees, looming over my friend with a glare I could feel like a funeral mask on my face. "How can you say something like that?"

"Where have you been the last decade, Flo?" Haley asked, backing me up the way she always had and always would. "Consent is everything."

But Flora did what she always did, which was to dig in her heels even though she probably knew she was in the wrong. "If you're drunk and making out with a guy, you have to accept that he's going to think you want to fuck him."

"But you don't owe him that," I rebutted, thinking of Lex, thinking of whoever the girl was that Jerrod had attacked.

"If you're going to be a tease…" She shrugged.

"I mean, it's a good explanation. Maybe the girl just regretted sleeping with him afterward," Cornelia suggested.

My stomach cramped so hard, I hissed. "This is why girls don't come forward when they're assaulted. Listen to the way we're talking about the victim, and we're *women*."

"Oh, get off your high horse, Luna. You're always so fucking righteous." Courtney rolled her eyes. "We don't even know who the victim *was*. It's not like she went to the police or anything. Some random, weirdo vigilante strung Jerrod up in the boatshed and assaulted him! Why don't you have some sympathy for him, huh? The rowing team is going to be *shit* without him while he recovers."

"He hurt me."

The words were soft, but they landed with a bang that vibrated through the entire girls' locker room. Everyone stopped midmovement, and the side chatter ceased.

At first, no one knew who had spoken, but then Taya lifted her head, blond hair parting like curtains to reveal a tearstained face.

"He hurt me last year at the party after they won sectionals," she continued in this dead voice like a recording over the speakers. "I was there with Andrew, but I drank too much and told him I was going home. He called me a cab and waited with me until it arrived. But on my way down the path, I got sick. I threw up in the bushes, and when I was done, the cab had left. Jerrod was outside. He offered to drive me."

A tremulous pause, only the sound of her laboring breath echoing against the lockers. Fat, crystalline tears beaded in the trough of her lower lids and slid down her cheeks, fast and then faster, and she started to speak again.

"H-He was friends with mutual friends. I didn't think about it. I just said yes. He had a water bottle in the car, and he gave it to me and said it would help with the hangover. I guess I fell asleep in the car...

when I woke up, I was in the back seat, and he was on top of me."

I slid closer on the bench, not touching her because it didn't feel right, but just letting her know I was there. I was there, and I believed her. Behind me, Haley moved from her open locker to stand behind us.

"Why didn't you say anything?" Kenzie asked, her mouth hanging open in shock.

It felt so much more real to the girls, I realized, now that one of our own had spoken out. It was so much harder to disassociate from someone you spent six days a week with, sweating beside, cheering with over wins and consoling over losses. We all liked Taya. She was a solid defender, quiet, but also there if one of the team needed her. It was almost appalling how simple the difference was. The team knew Taya. They didn't know Lex or the victim who'd come out first about Jerrod. If agony had a familiar face, it was easier to sympathize.

It killed something in me to know we hadn't been there for Taya when she needed us. The knowledge that Lex had been essentially alone with her truth for so long was like salt in the wound.

I gave in to my selfish temptation and placed a hand in the center of Taya's back.

Relief coursed through me when she leaned back into it.

"I did," Taya whispered, swiping at her runny nose with the sleeve of her training jacket. "I went to the school counselor the next day. But Jerrod's teammates vouched for him, said he was with them the whole time." She shrugged. "He didn't...I mean, he wasn't inside me, but he humped me and then came on my face. That's when I woke up."

"That's still sexual assault," Haley said softly, placing her own hand on Taya's shoulder.

"Yeah?" she asked, desperation in her tone, eyes so filled with tears they seemed magnified, bulbous. "I thought so."

"You thought right," I agreed quietly. "Can I hug you?"

She hesitated for a moment, chewing her lip, and tears sprang to my eyes. She reminded me of a wounded animal, too scared even to accept help.

When she nodded, I carefully and slowly wrapped her up in my arms and stroked her hair.

"I'm sorry, Taya," I murmured.

Her sob broke like a wave against the crest of my shoulder, and then she was crying wildly, moaning tears that filled the small room like a mournful symphony.

Haley was there then, hugging her too. And then Kenzie and Cornelia and Margie and Devon and the rest of the girls, surging forward to envelop our friend in the comfort and safety of our love. Even Flora and Courtney stepped forward, the last two, looking horrified and ashamed.

"It's okay," Taya said, voice thick with snot and tears and wild relief. "I almost didn't believe it myself."

A tear rolled down Flora's cheek. "I'm so sorry, YaYa."

"Thanks," she breathed, smiling tremulously. "I-I can't even believe I said anything."

"I'm glad you did," Courtney muttered, not looking at any of us, scuffing her bare foot on the floor. "I was being a dick."

No one argued with her.

"I think you should go to the director of student life," I said, curling my hand around one of hers. "She should know what Jerrod did. Even if you can't press charges, they'll start a file on him. It'll be harder for him to get away with that bullshit."

"Yeah," she said, but her lower lip trembled.

"We'll go with you if you want?" I offered, looking around at the pale faces of my teammates. "Right?"

As one, they nodded.

"Really?" Taya asked, startled, eyes wide. "I don't want you guys to have to get involved."

"We're already involved," I said because it was true. "Whatever you need, whatever you want, we'll be here, okay?"

"I thought you might think I was a s-slut like L-Lex Gorgon," she admitted on a hiccough.

My stomach fisted, and I was mute with sadness and rage.

"Never," Courtney assured with a tender smile.

I tried to feel happy about the way the team had come together. About Courtney and Flora realizing how wrong they'd been not to consider the validity of a rape accusation just because they knew the guy and thought he was cool and hot and popular. I was happy when we all finished dressing and walked as an ensemble through campus to the admin building so Taya could speak her truth.

But mostly, I felt like there was a pit of snakes in my belly, coiling tighter and tighter, hissing out one name.

Lex.

And I couldn't help but feel a sense of devastation knowing she'd never feel the same sense of community comfort after her tragedy.

As I sat outside the office waiting for Taya, I wished I had Lex's number to text her, but what would I have said?

I'm sorry no one believes you.

I'm sorry you've become an example of what not to be. I'm sorry your beauty made you dangerous.

How could I be the only one to empathize with her?

It occurred to me only when I looked at the girls waiting beside me, at their struck expression and horrified eyes. At the very real stink of their fear in the air.

They were imagining what happened to Taya happening to them, or maybe even reliving their own traumas.

What had happened to Lex was horrible not just because of her sexual assault but also because of the *punishment* she'd been doled out because of it. Suspended from Acheron for months, condemned by her peers as a slut. It was every girl's worst nightmare.

Maybe that was why they ridiculed her and kept her at a distance.

They feared what had happened to her so badly they almost didn't want to get close enough to catch whatever fate had done to her.

I thought it was a good theory, but it didn't explain why I reacted so contradictorily.

When I saw Lex, all I saw was awe-inspiring strength. I wanted to be closer to her so I might catch whatever made her so fearless even after she'd been through a woman's worst nightmare.

I was an overthinker by nature, but this drove me mad.

So I decided right there, as Taya emerged from the office with a tremulous smile, and the entire team surged around her in a show of gorgeous unity, that for once, I'd stop thinking, and I'd follow my gut.

CHAPTER NINE

"Never interrupt your enemy when he is making a mistake."
—Napoleon Bonaparte

Lex

Iknew they'd call me into the Acheron University Police Department before I'd gone after Jerrod, and it was almost disappointing when they did an hour after the first photo of him in the boatshed was posted to social media.

They were so predictable.

I wasn't surprised when they brought in Jerrod to try to identify my voice and frame, either.

He looked beaten but not too badly. He was lucky I'd kept a stern grip on the violence churning inside me. He was lucky I was theatrical enough to enjoy the song and dance of its aftermath.

"Is this one of the girls who attacked you?" the officer prompted him when he only stared at me.

"I already told you, Officer Ponce," I said silkily in my normal pitch. Last night, I'd spoken to Jerrod in a high, lilting voice like a girl. I liked the contrast between its softness and my violence, and it made for a good disguise. "I have an alibi for the time of the assault. I was eating dinner with my sisters at the Maenad, and then I went to Mathieson Library to study."

Jerrod's frown deepened. "They were wearing head coverings. But she doesn't sound like the bitch who attacked me. Besides, that girl was bigger, taller."

"She'd have had to be to get a shot at you," the officer said, blowing smoke up Jerrod's ass because some fancy lawyer was no doubt waiting outside.

Jerrod didn't smile, at least.

I stared at him impassively, but I was delighted he'd exaggerated his attacker's stature. I'd guessed he would. What six-foot-four varsity rower wanted to admit a five-foot-eight girl who weighed one hundred and forty pounds had put him out on his ass?

Pride was so predictable.

I should know. It'd led to my downfall too.

They ushered Jerrod out and left me alone in the observation room to sweat it out.

I didn't sweat, but I did enjoy the quiet and the solitude.

Finally, the door beeped and swung open to reveal Mina Pallas.

I had to fight back the triumphant smile that threatened to overtake my expression.

"Hello, Alexandra," she said coldly as the door closed behind her, and she took a seat across from me.

"Hello, Mina," I responded easily. "I wasn't aware you'd taken up police work."

Her smile was thin and ugly. I liked it on her.

"Tell me you had nothing to do with this," she demanded. "Because you know if you step even an inch out of line, I'll have you expelled from Acheron without blinking an eye."

"Oh, what a surprise!" I pressed my hand to my breastbone in exaggerated shock. "I never would have guessed you'd take any excuse to kick me out. Not when you gave every sign of support and understanding after Professor Morgan raped me on Halloween."

She flinched at my words, fingers curling into her palms on the top of the metal table before she hid them in her lap.

I didn't let the toxicity in my blood, that thick black sludge of hatred, alter my expression at all. I'd become adept at hiding all the pain, all the wonderful rage that boiled and churned in me as if my body was a cauldron mixing the poison of death.

"Do not spread that toxic lie, Lex. I'm warning you."

I held my hands up in supplication. "Consider me warned. I know you won't let anything risk your precious career. How are talks going with Cambridge?"

For one precious moment, shock and fear seized her features before she smoothed them clear. "I don't know what you think you know, but I assure you I am very happy at Acheron."

"I wish I could say the same."

"Then why did you insist on coming back?" she hissed, leaning forward to bare a feral kind of grin at me.

Only a handful of old friends still spoke to me, and only a few of those were brave enough to ask me the very same question. They all seemed horrified that I should want to return to the place of my death. Obviously, they didn't understand why ghosts haunted the scene of the crime. They were tied inexplicably to the injustice of the acts done against them, hovering in wait for someone to bring them peace through vengeance.

The only difference between me and a ghost was that I intended to do my own dirty work.

"This was my dream," I said. "I already lost more than I can say to what happened. I won't lose this. Which is exactly the reason I did *not* assault that guy."

"What were you doing last night?"

This time it was me who claimed a mean smile, mine curling like the edges of a villain's mustache. I sat back in my chair and cleaned beneath my already clean nails.

"Didn't they tell you? I have an alibi."

"They did not. You will tell me now."

I shrugged one shoulder, flicking my gaze up to lock on hers so I could watch her reaction. "I went to dinner with my sisters at the Maenad, and then I went to Mathieson Library to study."

"Can anyone corroborate you were there?"

"Apart from the access pass system and the security cameras in the lobby, I believe one person can for sure, yes."

Mina's jaw ticked like a bomb counting down to detonation. I wondered if her nails had cut crescent wounds into her palms.

"Who?"

"Oh," I drawled, bringing up my Virginia roots. "I thought you'd know. It was your daughter, Luna."

Shock again, this time blowing her pupils wide. "She saw you."

I laughed, but the sound was more of a purr. "Yes, she saw me. She was with me for almost an hour."

Pleasure unfurled in my belly, warm and heavy.

They say you should rise above, be the bigger (wo)man, take the higher road.

Well, no offense to those people, but fuck *that*.

I subscribed to an entirely more elemental system of ethics.

An eye for a motherfucking eye.

And I was coming for both of Mina's.

"Why would my daughter have anything to do with you?" she

ground out, cheeks flushed with fury.

Luna's had been flushed like that last night too, but from something much softer than fury. Her arousal had stained her lips, cheeks, and neck like wine. I'd wanted to lick up every inch of that stain and see if it tasted just as heady as it appeared.

And I had, in a sense. Biting her had been spontaneous, calculated to intimidate her as much as seduce her.

Unfortunately, it seemed to affect me much the same.

"I know you have selective memory, but you used to enjoy spending time with me too, on occasion," I reminded her dryly. "In fact, that first time, when Agatha introduced us in Richmond, and we had lunch at that little place that smelled like garlic, you spent three hours talking to me. Maybe it's a case of like mother like daughter?"

"Shut your mouth," she whispered, trying to control her rare show of fury.

I smirked. "You were the one who asked."

"Stay away from my daughter."

"Okay," I agreed. "But I can't promise she'll stay away from me. I seem to have some kind of charm. Even when I don't want attention, I get it."

The rage snuck into my voice again, threatening to overtake me. I let myself imagine slamming Mina's elegant head into the table, the crunch of her nose breaking and the wail she'd let out before she cupped her ruined face.

It made me feel better.

"I can make life very difficult for you here at Acheron," she warned, trying to compose herself by tucking a loose strand of hair behind her ear and fiddling with her pearl earrings. "You don't want that."

It hurt, her words and the laughter they produced in my throat. I'd admired her so much for so long. Loved her even.

And now this.

I was glad we had this meeting, though. It only proved I was on the right path.

I stood slowly and braced my palms on the table to lean over her and spoke slowly, so she would feel every word.

"Every single day is more difficult than you can imagine. I wake up screaming. I don't sleep right. It's a hardship to leave my room knowing I'm going onto campus with men everywhere. With *him* as close as the other room sometimes. I hate my body. I hate my peers for calling me a slut. I'm alone and broken, Mina. And *you* contributed to that. So go for it. Try to make my life worse than it is. I doubt I'll feel a difference.

"What I do know is that I get out of bed every day for three very important reasons. One, I refuse to let my education at Acheron U be taken from me when it's all I've ever wanted. Two, I fully intend to showcase exactly what kind of monster Professor Morgan is. And three, Mina, is you."

I pushed off the table and knocked on the door.

When the cop opened it, I said, "Unless I'm under arrest, I believe I'm free to go?"

After he reluctantly looked at Mina, then nodded, I turned back to the woman who had helped make my life a living hell.

My smile was genuine, warm, and bright. It seemed to take her aback because she blinked.

"Tell Luna I said hello," I tossed at her before I turned on my heel, hair swinging behind me like a cape, and left.

CHAPTER TEN

"I was about half in love with her by the time we sat down. That's the thing about girls. Every time they do something pretty... you fall half in love with them, and then you never know where the hell you are."
—J. D. Salinger

Lex

It turned out that my words to the president were unnecessary because when I walked up the path to the heritage home I shared with my sisters that evening, a familiar rose gold head gleamed from the swing on my front porch.

I didn't greet her as I approached, and I was surprised she didn't say anything either. Most people were too anxious to let silence unfold around them, but I often found it more eloquent than words.

And Luna's quietness said something.

There was no fear in it, which surprised me after last night. I figured even if she didn't fear me for all the reasons most other women seemed to, she would fear what we had done.

The kiss.

That fucking kiss.

It made me feel like that Timber rattlesnake had that morning I lay broken and bleeding in the woods so close to spiritual death.

It made me feel like I'd been given a gift.

When you're given something precious after years of being handed only hexes, it feels like it's been rigged to explode the moment you open the box. Whatever goodness inside can only be a ruse. The question is whether to throw it away immediately or enjoy it while it lasts even if it blows up in your face.

My platform loafers thudded against the old wood stairs leading up to the porch, the crunch of leaves beneath my heels little bursts of joy. I loved the sound of fall, the smell and the aura of everything celebrating before the long sleep of winter set in. Morgan had mostly ruined it for me, but as I leaned against the post and stared at Luna curled up in the porch swing, I found some pleasure in it again.

She didn't look up at me, her gaze fixed on a folded newspaper I knew instantly was *The New York Times*, her black pen scratching out answers in the tidy boxes of the famous crossword puzzle. That she did it in pen, so assured in her responses, was oddly arousing.

She shouldn't have made such a pretty picture tucked against the wood slates in an oversized green sweater with the symbol for Slytherin house on the breast, the sleeves pulled down over her knuckles to keep off the chill. But the way her silky red-gold hair fluttered in the spiced autumn breeze, tickling her cold-flushed cheek, and the way she tapped the end of her slightly bitten-off pen against her plump lower lip was outrageously compelling. She had Debussy playing from the speaker on her phone perched on the railing, and her shoes made a tidy pair set beside the swing, strangely lonely like they were waiting for another pair to join them.

It almost hurt to look at her, something in my chest panging like a discordant note. It was just that she looked so *fresh* and so *young*, so untouched by the cruelty of the world. We were the same age, but I felt ancient standing there bearing the burden of my nightmarish memories.

"Slytherin doesn't suit you."

She smiled a little at the crossword. "No, I'm decidedly Ravenclaw, but I've always had a huge crush on Draco Malfoy."

Of course, she did. The woman didn't know what was good for her, but could I blame her when she'd been raised by the heartless Mina Pallas?

"Why are you here?" I asked, all the weariness I felt suffused in my words.

"I had a difficult day," she said finally after a pregnant pause, pen poised over the newsprint. "You seem to be able to make me forget myself. Everything, really. So I thought..." She shrugged eloquently.

I wondered if it had anything to do with Jerrod. His name was on everyone's lips today, whispers and echoes of other transgressions that had been hushed up and buried over the years by his wealthy parents. Juno had texted earlier to tell me two more girls had gone into the director of student life's office to talk about their pasts with the varsity rower.

It made me feel giddy and reckless to know I'd done that.

Forced that monster out from under the bed into the harsh light of day. I hoped he was suspended and arrested, but I was realistic enough to know that probably wouldn't happen.

Still, he'd bear the mark I'd put on him for the rest of his life, those whispers of rape haunting him like the memory of him haunted his victims.

"How did you know where to find me?" I asked.

"My mother is the president, so it wasn't hard. Everyone on campus knows the mansion on Charity Lane is haunted. It makes sense that you'd live here."

"I didn't move in for the poetry of it," I drawled. "Rent was cheap. Typically, students don't like to room with ghosts. Lucky for me, I'm used to them."

Luna hummed, mouth pursed as if she wanted to question me about my ghost stories but didn't have the courage.

Silence settled between us like dust on unused furniture. Still, she didn't look at me, but it felt welcoming instead of dismissive. Almost as if she wanted me to study her.

So I did.

I traced the lines of her features until I thought I could memorize them in my sleep. It irritated me to do so. I was supposed to be a spider casting a web for her to fly witlessly into, yet I felt bizarrely like the one ensnared in her unintentional grip.

"Word repeated four times in the last line of Shakespeare's 'all the world's a stage' speech," she asked me the crossword clue without raising her gaze, sucking at the tip of her pen.

It led me to wonder what her lips might feel like sealed over something else. My fingertip, the shape of my nipple, the swollen glands of my clit.

"Lex?" she asked, looking at me then, her eyes so green against the green of her sweater they looked unreal.

I cleared my throat and crossed my arms and ankles, affecting an aloof pose because I felt anything but. "'Sans teeth, sans eyes, sans taste, sans everything.'"

Her eyes lit with admiration, and she smiled. "Which play?"

"*As You Like It.*"

"Jacques," she agreed, naming the character whose monologue it was. "It's not my favorite, but you have to admit, it's got merit."

"I don't have to admit anything, but yes, I like the play."

She was playful today, so totally unlike the shy or furious woman I thought I would be met with at our next encounter. It was disarming, which, for me, was dangerous.

She's pretty. Grace's voice echoed through my head.

I snorted. She was pretty like Botticelli's Venus was pretty. The word didn't do either justice. She was...she was like something from a dream.

Only I'd stopped dreaming so long ago, I almost couldn't believe she was real.

"Let me guess, you prefer *Hamlet* or *King Lear*, something dark and singularly unromantic."

I could have laughed at that. Would have last year before the incident.

Now, the humor only flared and faded in my chest.

"Not quite." I pushed off the post and sauntered toward her, lifting her socked feet so I could sit beside her, then replacing them on my lap. She wore frilly socks and had delicate ankle bones I wanted to trace with my tongue. "I like *The Merchant of Venice.* 'I hold the world, but as the world, Gratiano, A stage where every man must play a part, And mine a sad one.'"

She clucked her tongue, waving her pen as she spoke. "It's still sad."

"I like sad things. I wouldn't be in our Tragedies class if I didn't."

"Because you understand them?" she ventured, finally looking something other than bright and warm. Finally looking a little something like me.

I didn't like it.

"Yes," I agreed, but I didn't want to linger on me and the things I was known for, so I reached out to wrap a lock of her pretty hair around my finger. It gleamed yellow, orange, and red like the leaves falling from the massive oak in the front yard. "I like *A Midsummer's Night Dream,* too."

"'Though she be little, she is fierce'?" Luna guessed at my favorite line with an impish grin.

"No," I said slowly, pulling the word apart like taffy as I leaned close enough to count the faint freckles on her milky cheeks. "'So we grew together, Like to a double cherry, seeming parted, But yet an union in partition, Two lovely berries moulded on one stem.'"

Luna's full mouth parted, a small pink tongue peeking through her teeth. "I'm surprised you have that one memorized. It isn't particularly famous."

"No," I agreed, wrapping my finger up her strand of hair and down again, watching the play of the setting sunlight against it. "But I always like the imagery of it. Two beings on one stem, separate but together."

"Why, Lex, that seems romantic," she gasped, then laughed when I pulled hard on her hair. "I'm sorry, it's just surprising to hear you speak like that."

"Because I was raped or because I'm gay?"

The words dropped between us, ugly and rude. I winced at my own self-cruelty. What Morgan had done and how he had done it had tainted even my view of my own sexuality.

Let me teach you what it's like to be loved by a man.

The twin snakes of anger and fear that lived in my belly seethed and writhed.

"You're gay?" Luna asked like it was a big reveal.

I slanted her an unimpressed look. "Don't quote Shakespeare to me, then insult your own intelligence by acting surprised."

"But I *am* surprised," she insisted earnestly, leaning forward like an eager child. "I didn't know you were a lesbian."

"Forgive me, but you do remember our kiss in the library last night?"

Her blush was instant, white to pink from one second to the next. I watched her gaze slide away from mine, unable to look me in the eye as she remembered our embrace.

"Of course, I remember," she murmured, tucking a wayward piece of hair behind her ear.

God, even the shell of that ear was sexy.

I gave in to an impulse and reached for her slightly pointed chin, pinching and lifting until her green eyes locked on mine. Only then did I reach up and smooth a thumb over her pink cheek, testing its warmth.

"You seem unsure," I said, soft and husky, already moving toward her. No, not moving, but pulled to her by some gravitational force. "Shall I remind you?"

"'O, how ripe in show, Thy lips, those kissing cherries, tempting grow!'" she whispered against my lips, and I couldn't help the moan that slipped from me.

A beautiful, ethereal girl who quoted Shakespeare back to me?

Why did Mina Pallas's daughter have to be like this?

So pure.

So fucking perfect in ways I hadn't expected.

I thought I knew Luna, the pretty, popular jock, but she kept proving me wrong.

And it made the game I was playing feel even more dangerous than the others I played with the Man Eater Crew.

I couldn't afford to lose the anger now. Not even for a second.

Not even a second spent kissing a very pretty girl's very pretty mouth.

"I can't, though," Luna muttered, echoing my own thoughts for her own reasons.

I didn't pull away or make it easy because I didn't want to.

"I have a boyfriend, Lex," she explained patiently.

I noticed she had her hand curled over my hip, fingertips flexing as if she liked the feel of me and didn't want to let go.

"And?" I asked flippantly.

I knew all about Pierce Argent, the golden hockey player already garnering NHL buzz. He seemed to treat women well, but I hated his type. There were too many entitled jocks on campus who thought their star power would dim the glaring light of their misconduct against women.

Her brows tangled. "And I don't believe in cheating. He's a good man, and he doesn't deserve that. And, honestly, I'm straight."

My laughter felt like a cough in my lungs, painful and brittle. "Ah, that old classic."

I pulled away to sit on my side of the swing, ignoring her pugnacious frown.

"Well," she insisted, clutching the crossword to her chest as if it were a shield, "I am."

"You were," I amended, then thought again and corrected myself. "You thought you were."

"Um, I'm pretty sure I know my own sexuality better than you," she argued, bristling so beautifully the meanness in me wanted to push her even harder to see how glorious she'd be with even an iota of my rage.

"Do you?" I taunted, baring my teeth at her. "Because I see things you don't. The way your skin flushes when I'm close. The way your eyes dilate and your nipples pucker. Your body isn't lying to me, Lux. You're just lying to yourself."

"Fuck you," she said, but it lacked heat, and the profanity sounded wrong in her mouth like she didn't often curse.

"You want to," I agreed, egging her on.

Slouching in the swing, I spread my legs, my small pleated black skirt riding higher up my thighs. I could feel her gaze like a warm wind on the inside of my thighs as I smoothed my palms from my knees to my groin. A low, seismic moan quaked through me as I touched myself over my panties lightly, fluttering over my clit.

Luna didn't move. She didn't even seem to breathe.

"I want you, too," I admitted. Even though I spoke the words like an insult because I *was* insulted that my body could so easily betray me. "I want your pretty face between my thighs. I want to be the one to give you your first taste of a woman. Do you know the flavor? Have you ever played with yourself, then sucked your fingers clean of the cream?"

A little gasp. Maybe she wanted to protest, or maybe she couldn't believe I was capable of speaking such filth.

I didn't care either way.

"I think you'd like it," I practically purred, the words rolling off my tongue. "The way I taste. Like salted pasta water. I think you'd become addicted to that slick sweetness. To the feel of it on your tongue. I think I'd have to pry you out from between my thighs, greedy little thing that you'd become. It makes me wet just thinking about it."

"Lex," she breathed, and it was there, both the protest and the longing for more. "Don't."

"Don't what? Don't stop? I won't," I promised darkly, tossing the hem of my short skirt up and over my belly to reveal my underwear-clad groin to her hungry gaze.

It was a quiet residential street, and we were partially hidden by the half wall of the porch railing. The sun was dropping quickly now, smearing the sky in tangerines and pinks deepening to indigos and blues. We had privacy beyond the intimacy of the bubble we'd created around us.

"Are you imagining what I must look like under here?" I continued baiting her, running a nail under the hem of my panties. "If I'm smooth and wet and plump like a rose almost smothered in dew?"

"I-I saw in the library." She cleared her throat but didn't take her eyes off my fingers playing over my panty-covered sex. "I mean, it looked like you shaved."

"Waxed. You should feel me," I taunted, pulling the edge of the fabric down low so the top of my mound was visible, a paler gold than the rest of my skin and as smooth as silk. "I'm so sensitive like this. One touch of your hand, one suck from your mouth, and I'd shatter for you."

"I can't," she said, but the words were more air than sound.

She wanted to. Oh, but she wanted to.

The worst part was how much I wanted her.

I'd honestly wondered if I'd ever feel desire again, yet here I was, exposed on my front porch beside a straight girl, the daughter of my sworn enemy, and I was so close to orgasm. All I needed was a vicious roll of a thumb over my clit, and I'd burst open like ripe fruit.

"It's okay," I soothed but not kindly. My teeth were bared, my gaze hard as I stared her down, as I forced her with the weight of my gaze to look at me as I spoke. "I'll make myself come for you, Lux, but next time, I expect you to get on your knees for me and ask nicely to do it yourself."

A hard swallow and blown pupils were the only response I got, but it was all I needed.

I didn't take off my underwear, not only because it was practical, but because I couldn't bear to be so vulnerable before her or anyone, not now and maybe not again.

Instead, I framed my swollen clit between two fingers and rubbed like that, back and forth as if I was swaying through the binds that tied me down from pleasure.

God, I hadn't come in months.

I hadn't wanted to.

But the way Luna watched me, eyes so bright they glowed, demonized with pleasure, made my heart skip and trip. My pulse beat heavy in my belly, throbbing so hard in my pussy I had to fight to match the tempo. Harder, faster, the higher I flew.

Yet I couldn't do it.

I strained and burned and almost whimpered from the pained frustration.

I was seconds away from giving up, furious and embarrassed that my power trip had somehow failed and made me defenseless when a soft, sweet voice said, "Here."

Here like she was handing me an apple.

Here like she was answering roll call.

But Luna's *here* was so much more than that.

She swiveled on the bench, from leaning away from me to leaning toward me, laying down her head against my shoulder and placing her other hand on the inside of my thigh. She squeezed hard, the pain morphing into flames inside me.

"Come for me, Lex," she urged, breath hot on my neck a second before she placed a neat kiss there. "I want to watch. I want to know what you look like when you do."

A moan rattled through my hollow chest, but it was enough.

The feel of her soft body pressed along the side of mine. The way her hand opened and closed around my inner thigh, just inches from my leaking folds. The sharp pant of her breath over my neck and collarbone, the way her lips brushed just a little against my throat.

This.

This was it.

What it should have been like for me my first time.

So sweet and simple and sure.

I broke apart for her then, but it wasn't a gentle shattering, frost shaken from winter leaves, but a colossal cracking, breaking, demolishing inside me. I lost something of myself to the pleasure, something vital and important like breath. Like I was falling beneath the icy crust of my shields and drowning in that cold dark chasm left where my heart used to be.

For long moments, I couldn't breathe, coming and fighting to keep everything I was close to me in the chaos that reigned in its aftermath.

When I came too, I was gasping for breath, and my face was wet.

"Am I bleeding?" I asked because it made sense.

It hurt so much. The pleasure had ripped me apart from the inside out.

"No," Luna said, her fingertips on my cheeks. She pulled away to show me the clear wetness. "You're crying."

I stood so quickly, I almost fell over and had to catch myself on the railing. My hair fell forward like a welcomed curtain, shielding me from Luna's gaze, enfolding me in gloom. I stood there trying to hunt down my breath, trying to close the gaping crater that single orgasm had left inside me. Everything wanted to spill out of that gap—my rage, my pain, my awful, bone-chewing loneliness.

"Lex, I think you're having a panic attack." Luna's voice reached me from leagues under the sea.

I spun around to tell her to fuck off, but halfway there I lost consciousness and everything went black.

Honestly, it was a relief.

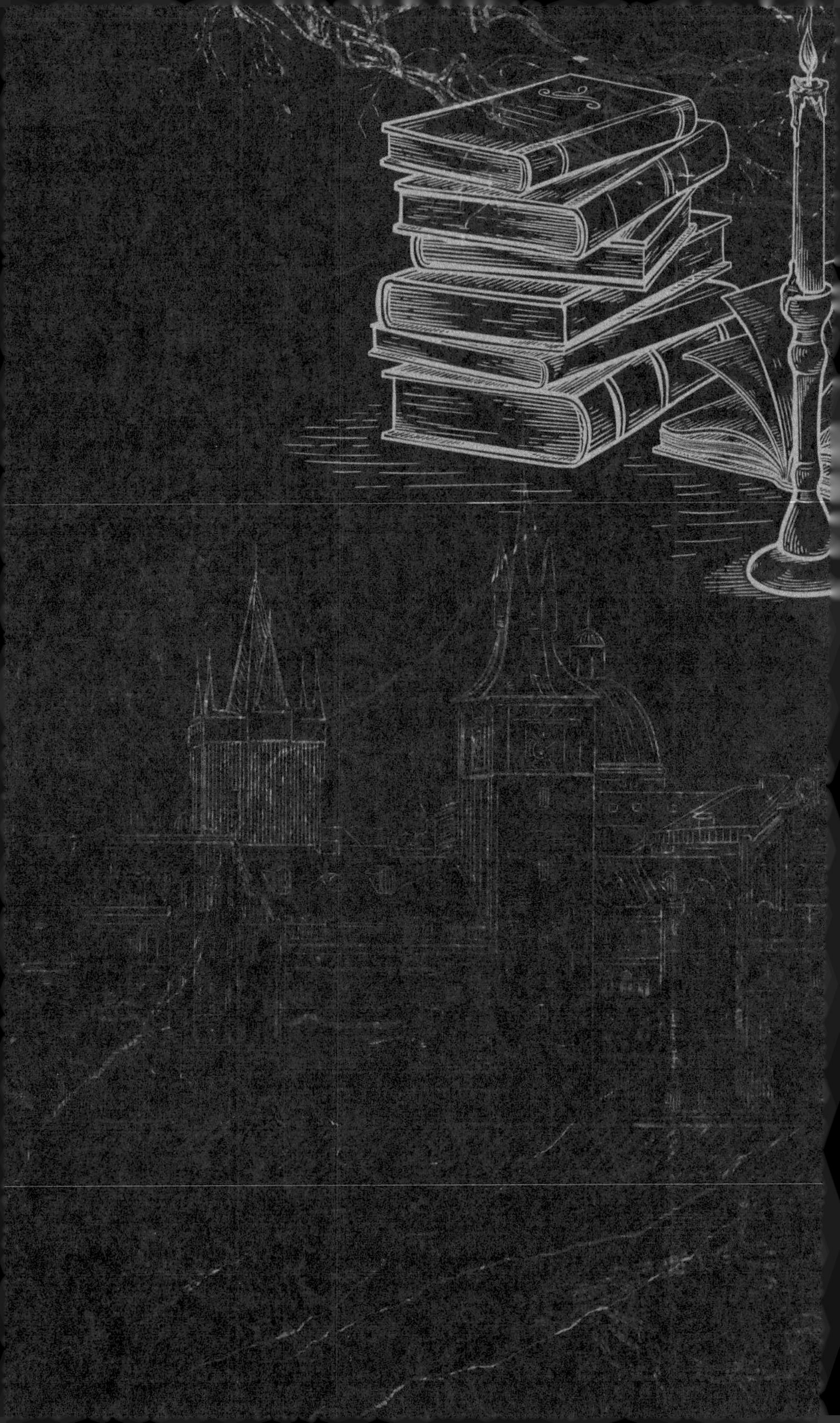

CHAPTER ELEVEN

"Life isn't about finding yourself. Life is about creating yourself."
—George Bernard Shaw

Luna

I tried to catch her, but she was too far away. Helplessly, I watched as Lex fell gracefully to the ground like a fallen silk scarf, almost dissolving into herself. Aroused, frightened, and panicked, my first response was to try to pick her up to take her inside, but she was too heavy for me to lift from the ground without breaking my back. I considered calling an ambulance, but I had the feeling Lex would be furious with me for doing that.

So I stared at the oversized front door of the Victorian home and sucked in a deep, bracing breath before I knocked on it, then pushed through without waiting for an answer.

"Hello?" I called out, walking into the narrow front hall.

"Yeah?"

I followed the sound of that feminine voice to the right into a kind of front parlor with a round table set before large bay windows. Three girls sat around it playing cards and sipping rosé wine from vintage water glasses. One was dark-skinned with a sun-kissed halo of fine, curly hair, while the other two were almost as pale as me, one blonde and the other brunette with twin ski-jump noses and enormous brown eyes.

All three of them stared at me as if suspended in animation.

The brunette, the one with a cigarette hanging by the edge of her lower lip, was the one to recover first. "You're Luna Pallas."

"I am," I agreed. "I'm sorry to barge in here, but, well, Lex fainted on the porch, and I don't know what to do."

"Fuck," the Black girl grumbled, pushing out of her chair to stalk into the kitchen at the back of the long room.

The brunette rolled her eyes. "She's so dramatic."

"No, I mean, I think it was serious," I tried to explain, wringing my hands at the thought of Lex just lying in the deepening dark and cold lie without supervision. "She had a panic attack."

The blond frowned at me. "What was she doing?"

Touching herself for me, I thought but didn't say.

I think the blush that set fire to my skin was answer enough though because the brunette snickered as she got up to go out on the porch.

When I moved to follow her, the blond reached out to catch the sleeve of my sweater. "Ignore Grace, we mostly do the same. I'm Juno."

"We're not having the girl over for tea, June-bug," the girl came back from the kitchen and glared at me as she passed through the hall to the front door. "Get out here and help me."

"That's Effie," Juno explained as she stood, then started to lead me back out to the porch. "We're Lex's sisters."

I wasn't sure how four multicultural girls of around the same age came to be sisters, but now wasn't the time to ask. There were too many other questions on my mind, the predominant one being my concern for Lex.

"Has this happened before?" I asked as we stepped outside, and I saw Grace and Effie kneeling beside Lex.

"Unfortunately. Since the incident..." She trailed off, suddenly letting me go to kneel beside her sisters.

Effie was holding a small vial and twisting the lid off. When she caught my gaze, she lifted it to me in cheers. "Smelling salts work like a charm."

"May I?"

The three of them blinked at me in comic unison, but I didn't feel well enough to laugh.

"Why?" Grace demanded.

"Because I was with her when she fainted."

It was a weak explanation, but I couldn't find words to explain that I wanted to be the one to wake her. It seemed foolishly romantic, as if I fancied myself some kind of Prince Charming waking the princess with a kiss. In truth, I knew it would take more than a single kiss to wake Lex up from the nightmare her life had become since last Halloween.

"Stop being such a bossy boots," Juno reprimanded Grace, wrenched the vial out of Effie's hand, and passed it to me. "Have at it."

I caught it easily, then walked around to Lex's head. I was incredibly aware of the Gorgon sisters' gazes as I carefully lifted Lex's head and kneeled down on the ground to cushion her skull on my thighs. Only then did I gently brush the thick curls from her face and wave the smelling salts beneath her nose.

She came to with a tremendous, soul-quaking scream.

The hair on my arms and the back of my neck stood on end, and my ears throbbed from the noise. That scream baptized me in a miniscule amount of the enormous pain wedged inside her small, feminine form and made me feel sick. How much was there inside her just waiting to get out? And when it did release, what form would it take?

"Hush," I told her when she settled, taut as a board in my lap. I bent over her face to view her upside down and pressed my cool palm to her hot cheek. "You're safe."

Her eyes were wide, wreathed in mink lashes, and textured like wet concrete. Such lovely eyes so filled with knee-weakening fear. I watched up close as she came to her senses, and that soft gray hardened into stone.

She pushed up and off me so quickly that she was lying down one moment and standing over me the next. Her beautiful mouth was twisted like hot metal into an ugly snarl.

"I told you, next time you are on your knees for me, it better be because you're willing to beg for more." She spat the words at me like venom and then stalked into the house, the door slamming so hard behind her the wreath of pine cones fell off the door and broke apart on the ground.

One of them rolled into my thigh and pricked my thumb when I picked it up.

"You should stay away from her," Effie said, but she'd lost her edge. Instead, she looked sad and burdened, shoulders sagging, mouth a downward droop. "She's been through enough without some straight girl teasing her."

"I'm not teasing her," I said automatically, but the truth of her words resonated deep inside me and made my stomach ache.

Wasn't I?

Only minutes ago, I'd professed my heterosexuality to Lex. Argued for it, even. When so much evidence was pointing to the contrary, or at the very least to the possibility of bisexuality.

Hadn't I been one stiff breeze away from orgasming myself watching Lex touch her long, agile fingers against the swell of her groin? Hadn't I breathed deeply just to catch a hint of her sweet musk beneath the cool spice of the autumn breeze?

"I'm not teasing her," I repeated slower. "I want to be her friend."

That was the truth, as much as I could give anyway.

"Yeah? Benevolent Miss Popular wants to take on the charity case of the girl who was raped?" Gracie asked with snapping teeth. "I heard you like taking in strays. Be careful with Lex. She bites."

My mind instantly conjured the memory of her strong teeth clamping over my throat, but I shook my head to clear it.

"That's not the epithet I would give Lex," I argued. "To me, she's gray-eyed and lionhearted. I know she's been wronged, not just by whoever attacked her, but the rest of them, of *us*, on campus. But to me, she's not a victim. She's the strongest girl I've ever met, and I want to know her. I wish I was more like her. I *want* to be strong like her."

And for her, I thought but didn't say.

My words seemed to mute the sisters. They sat there staring at me with cold, shrewd, reptilian eyes. There was violence in them, like there was in Lex, but it was better restrained. Still, I wasn't sure if they would hug me or tear me to pieces like crazed maenads.

"It takes courage to love someone who thinks they are broken, and you reek of fear. It's easy enough to say that to us," Juno said softly, standing up in eerie tandem with her sisters so they loomed over me, pretty yet somehow monstrous beneath their skins. "Come back when you're ready to tell the world."

I was so exhausted from the day, so tangled in my own tormented thoughts that I completely forgot about my standing Friday night date with Pierce until I pushed through the door of my basement apartment and found him cooking in my kitchen.

Happily, he was playing music loudly, totally in the zone because of course, he was the perfect man, and he loved to cook and did it well. Otherwise, he might have seen the crestfallen look on my face, and the whole minute it took me to drag the remnants of my tattered identity around me like a funeral shroud.

The me I played at being hadn't felt right for a very long time, but now I felt almost sick assuming the role.

Pierce made it a little easier just by being him, so I took that minute to watch him exist in my space. He was comfortable there, swaying his slim hips in low-hung gray sweatpants that molded beautifully to his hockey player's bubble butt and thick thighs. He sang freely to Hozier's "Talk," his voice low and smooth. Meatballs were sautéing on the stovetop along with a bubbling pot of water for pasta he'd rolled out by hand. His confidence and competency reminded me slightly of Lex.

What a weird thought, one that cramped my stomach again like something worse than period aches.

I forced myself across the small living room into the kitchen and wrapped my arms around his waist, pressing my cheek to his back. He smelled like pleasant male sweat and the Old Spice of his deodorant.

Unexpectedly, tears sprang to my eyes and leaked into the material of his white tee.

"Hey," he said, hugging my arms to his washboard stomach. "Hey, pretty girl, what's wrong?"

I wasn't ready to tell him, not really. Not when my emotions and thoughts were clear as sludge circling the drain, threatening to take me under.

But I also didn't have the capacity to lie to him.

I'd never been a liar, even when it would have behooved me to be so. I was a crappy poker player as a result, but I secretly loved my integrity. It was one of the few character strengths Mom had ever complimented me on too.

"I think we need to break up," I whispered brokenly.

His hands spasmed over my arms. Slowly, he maneuvered us around until we were facing each other and then gently, like I might run away, he cupped my face in his huge hands. His gorgeous eyes tracked my tearstained face, searching for answers. Honestly, I hoped he found them. It would make everything a lot easier.

"Come sit with me, okay?" When I nodded, he turned down the burners and moved us to my vintage love seat.

Usually, he'd complain about how uncomfortable the Queen Anne couch was, but he sat lengthwise and mutely encouraged me to sit in the bracket of his open thighs.

"I think I need space to do this," I admitted.

His fingers clenched on my hips as he settled me closer, facing him, enclosed by him. "No, if it's all right, I think you should stay right here. Whatever you have to say to me, Lune, I want you to know that I'm always here for you. No matter what."

A sob burst into my mouth, but I trapped it behind my lips.

"Breathe," he coaxed, rubbing my arms.

"I don't know what to say, really." I pressed one hand to my churning stomach and attacked my other thumbnail with my teeth. "Everything is jumbled. I feel like the last few days have changed me somehow."

"What happened?" No judgment, just an open expression and support.

God, I wanted to love him. How much easier it would have been to love this perfect boy. Instead, I was drawn inexorably to a complicated girl who redefined what it was to be emo.

"I met someone," I said so softly, I barely formed the words in my throat.

Pierce's face tightened, then slowly relaxed. "Okay... And you want to be with them?"

"I-I honestly don't know. I just don't want to be in a relationship with you when I have this...this thing burning inside me."

"You're in love with him?" he asked, the first signs of anger burning the edges of his words.

"Not love." I laughed hollowly at the thought. I'd never thought I was capable of such passion or bravery.

It occurred to me that I'd been floating along on the easy current of who I thought I was supposed to be based on other people's judgments for all the twenty-one years of my life. How sad was that?

I sucked in a deep breath, trying to channel some of Lex's unflappable strength. "Not love, but I've never felt like this before. I'm so sorry, Pierce."

He sucked in a huge breath, held it for a moment, and then let it all out in a rush between his teeth. "Okay, yeah, I'm not gonna lie and say that doesn't kill me a little. I was half in love with you before you even gave me the time of day."

I barked out a surprised laugh, then covered my mouth with my hand. "You were not."

"Oh totally," he said with a wry grin. "I wouldn't shut up about you to the guys. They thought I was pussy-whipped." He rolled his eyes. "They're idiots, but they're my idiots, and they were right in a way. I was like enchanted with you or something."

"Pierce," I groaned. "God, you're making this even harder. Don't you think I know how stupid I am to break up with you? If I was normal, I'd thank God or whoever every day for being your girlfriend. You're as perfect as they come."

"Nah, you know I'm a slob, and I have a wicked fucking temper when it's triggered." He winced as if remembering some past event. "And obviously, I'm not perfect for you if you can have feelings for someone else."

"It's not you," I said, then winced again when he laughed bitterly. "No, honestly. It's *not*. I think..."

Did I owe him this honesty? I wasn't sure, but I decided it wasn't a matter of owing him anything. I actually wanted to tell him. To test the words stirring inside my chest. How would I ever know if they were true if I didn't let them see the light of day?

He waited patiently, still rubbing his thumbs over the balls of my shoulders, bringing me comfort even though I was causing him pain.

I focused on enunciating every single word, framing it in my mouth before releasing it so I wouldn't throw up.

"I think I might like girls."

I squeezed my eyes shut like a child that I might block out his reaction. Not because I was scared, exactly, but because it occurred to me that I'd just come out.

Coming out.

What a strange concept for a girl who'd always believed she was straight.

But it felt right, the doing of it and the phrase.

Because I was coming out, out of that easy river into the rapids, into a life that was filled with peaks and troughs, risks and rewards.

It was a cold plunge into those icy waters, but it wasn't like drowning. No, it was like breaking free of the frigid waves after being chained to the murky depths for years. The light was brighter, sound clear and crisp. I was still gasping for breath, floundering, but I was doing it knowing the shore was in sight, and one day, I'd get there.

Maybe Lex would even be there, toes in the sand, snakes bright on her skin, waiting.

"Okay."

It took me a second to register Pierce was even there. That I was sitting on the same antique couch I sat on every night in the same apartment I'd had since second year. That nothing was unchanged but me.

I peeked through one eye at my boyfriend—*ex*-boyfriend.

"Huh?".

He smiled, a genuine one though it was small. "Okay, Luna. That's cool."

That's cool.

It startled a laugh out of me. "You think?"

"I mean, yeah. It's 2023. What do you expect me to say? Sexuality is a spectrum, and I gotta believe most people fall somewhere in the middle of either extreme."

I blinked. "Even you?"

He shrugged, then dragged a hand through his hair so it stood in golden brown spikes all over his head. "I dunno, maybe. There was a guy growing up in Vancouver..." He trailed off, following a memory I couldn't see. "Yeah, he was a good guy, and I thought maybe he was cute or whatever, but I didn't do anything about it."

He took my cold hands in his and squeezed. "Obviously, you're braver than I am."

My laughter shot out of me like machine fire. "You've got to be kidding. I'm such a sheep. It's kind of embarrassing."

He frowned and leaned closer. "Hey, don't say that. The girl I know, the girl I've loved, is brave. She always sticks up for people and champions what she believes in. She's kind to everyone, even people society judges. She's honest." His mouth twisted into that wry grin again. "Even when it would be easier to lie. All of that takes courage, Lune, and you have that in spades. You think it didn't take some serious balls to come out to me just now?"

"No, that one took everything I had in me," I confessed, squeezing his hands back. "The thing is, even though I don't think we should date anymore, you're still my best friend."

"You're mine, too. It might take me a minute to get over the urge to fuck you." He grinned when I laughed. "But I'll get there. You won't lose me, yeah? Not if you don't want to."

"I don't want to."

"Good. And I won't tell anyone about your epiphany, yeah? It's yours to share when you're ready."

"Same goes to you."

"Hey, I didn't come out. I just said I thought my teammate was hot back in the day," he protested through his smile.

"Po-tate-o, po-tah-to," I joked and then laughed when he pushed me.

We grinned at each other, and I felt lighter than I had maybe ever.

"You wanna have the kick-ass pasta and meatballs I made, then help me with my stupid philosophy paper?" he asked.

"Yeah," I said, feeling so giddy, so invincible I almost wanted to go to the top of the Mathieson Library and scream from the rooftop. "Just give me a second."

Pierce kissed me on the forehead, then went into the kitchen, and I got up to grab my phone from my backpack I'd dropped by the front door.

Before I lost the high from my first act of bravery, I committed another and sent Lex a text that I thought her scary sisters would approve of.

CHAPTER TWELVE

"Each of us must suffer his own demanding ghost."
—Virgil, The Aeneid

Lex

Luna: "I will not choose what many men desire, Because I will not jump with common spirits, And rank me with the barbarous multitudes." I'm not afraid of you, Lex. Far from it. I'm moved to be a better person, a braver person because you inspire me. Even if you don't want me, please let me be your friend.

The screen of my phone was the only light in the dark, turning my face blueish-white. I should turn it off and put it away. Now wasn't the time for distractions. Only, it didn't seem to matter what time it was, Luna Pallas wouldn't stop haunting my every hour.

How was I supposed to remain cold and immovable against a girl who quoted *The Merchant of Venice* to me, knowing it was my favorite of Shakespeare's plays? Who used it to persuade me to take a chance on her?

She was supposed to be a goddamn pawn, not a prize worth risking everything I'd rebuilt inside me to win.

I hadn't seen her since my panic attack eight days ago nor had I responded to her text since then. It was cruel to leave her hanging like that, but I found I grew crueler by the day, my heart shriveling away like a flower hung to dry from my rib cage.

Anyway, I had more important things to focus on.

Like the fact that even though two students had gone in to tell their truths about being assaulted by Jerrod Ericht, the bastard was still walking free and clear on campus. I'd even caught him last Monday, days after we'd attacked him, walking with his chums and laughing like he didn't have a care in the world.

It enraged me.

I'd known that Mina Pallas was quelling any signs of sexual misconduct for a while, but not to this degree, not when a photo of the rapist in question had made the rounds of the entire university. She was getting bold.

She had reason to, in a way.

I'd attacked Professor Morgan after what he'd done to me, and she'd quashed news of that like a bug beneath her sensible heel. Now, Jerrod, no doubt with the help of his family's money, had been purged of his crimes.

Bullying, Mina said in an article that was published in the school paper, *The Delphi*, wouldn't be tolerated at Acheron.

Bullying.

As if what we had done to Jerrod wasn't warranted.

Well, we planned to expand her lexicon tonight.

What we had planned wasn't bullying.

It was vigilante justice.

I tucked my phone into the back pocket of my tight black jeans and pushed out of the accessible washroom into the bright, noisy bar.

The Penny Farthing was the most popular bar on campus, which meant that normally I'd stay the hell away from it.

Even before, I hadn't been a party girl, even a particularly social girl.

Now, large crowds gave me hives.

But it was important that everyone saw me here.

After all, I needed an alibi.

"Sorry about that," I said as I slid into the booth across from Bryn. "I always need to wash my hands before eating."

Bullshit, but the pretty girl across from me bought it with a warm smile.

"No worries," she said. "Like I said, I'm just happy you asked me out."

Of course, she was. Bryn Harper was in my Ancient Philosophers class, and she'd been flirting with me for weeks. She was cute, too, in a kind of boyish way with cropped hair and a propensity to wear clothes from the men's side of the store. She pulled it off with confidence that came from being out for a long time.

I didn't really have a type, and normally, she would have intrigued me. I liked her self-possessed nature and the way she took my hand the moment I sat down, touching me in public without shame. It was a good example to set, one I was happy to follow.

But I wasn't interested in the slightest.

How could I be when a pretty, fae-looking strawberry-blond wouldn't leave my thoughts?

She had even made an appearance like a lightning flash against the darkness of my nightmares. I never remembered what the brief dreams were about, but I woke up with her face lingering in my mind's eye.

It was rude of me to use Bryn's interest as an alibi, but my agenda was more important than her hurt feelings. And anyway, I did want to be her friend. As Juno liked to remind me, it was healthy and healing to have friends in the LGBTQIA+ world who could make me feel safe and seen.

"I have to be honest," Bryn continued, eyeing me warily. "I had another reason for coming tonight."

Unease slithered under my skin. "Oh?"

"Yeah." She laughed awkwardly and rubbed a hand over her chin as her eyes darted over my shoulder. "I'm not sure if you know this, but my mom is Quinn Harper."

Of course, I knew who Quinn Harper was. An editor at *The New York Times* and author of three books about modern-day feminism and sexuality. Bryn was something of a celebrity in the queer community at Acheron as a result.

"Yes, I'm aware."

"Well..." Bryn collected the perspiration on her beer glass with the tips of her fingers to avoid looking at me. "She wanted me to ask you about doing an interview with her for an exposé she wants to write."

Deep beneath the numb layers of my body and spirit, something like hope stirred.

"And why would she want to interview a nobody scholarship student at Acheron?" I asked mildly even though, of course, I knew.

She wanted me to talk about Halloween.

Bryn finally looked up at me. "About what happened to you last Halloween. About how unfairly President Pallas and the university treated you. I know the consensus around campus seems to be...biased against you, but there are people who believe your story."

"It's not a story," I corrected before I could remind myself to act unaffected. "It always bothers me when people say that. There are many sides of a story. What happened that night isn't a matter of perspective. It's my truth."

"Okay," she agreed easily, lifting her hands palm up in surrender. "I apologize. I only meant to say that Acheron seems to have a tendency to hush up these things without correcting any of the wrongs. My mom wants to shine some much-needed light on what's going on here."

"Why now?" It was a valid question. It had been nearly a year exactly since Professor Morgan had attacked me.

Still, it was another question I knew the answer to.

Bryn leaned closer, eyes sweeping our surroundings to make sure no one was listening. "Have you heard about the Man Eaters?"

I raised a brow but didn't confirm or deny it.

She went on in hushed, excited tones. "They're this vigilante group on campus. It was the Man Eaters who outed Jerrod Ericht."

"A lot of good that did," I muttered darkly.

Bryn winced in agreement. "Yeah, he should have been expelled or prosecuted. That's one of the reasons Mom wants to write this article. It's important. After I told her about you last year, she's been keeping an eye on things here. What the Man Eaters did...it still had an effect. People are talking on campus, watching out for predators, banging on locked closets looking for skeletons. They've shaken things up. And yeah, Jerrod is walking free, but he won't get rid of the massive stain on his reputation. My roommate told me he's been banned from parties on Greek Row."

A spark of satisfaction flickered in my dark heart and died.

It wasn't enough.

Bryn read the malcontent in my expression and nodded. "I know, it's not enough. That's why I agreed to talk to you for Mom. What's going on here...what's being hushed up? It's not right, Lex. You, more than most people, know that. I'm just asking you to help do something about it."

I stared at her, my tongue playing over the ridge of scar tissue through my bottom lip.

She didn't know what I was already doing to help. What I had planned for that very night. How Shakespearean that I'd asked a girl on a date as an alibi only to have her want revenge against the very same people I was hunting.

But an exposé wasn't enough.

A local reporter or two had approached me after I'd been suspended following Halloween last year, but they were ineffectual, small-fry fish in an ocean that would drown whatever they tried to say. It hadn't been tempting then, not in the tsunami crest of helpless rage I'd felt. It still wasn't enough to satisfy the dark hunger in me to see predatory men suffer and bleed for their crimes against us.

But it was intriguing.

A small voice that sounded a little like Luna's whispered in my ear that it was the *right* choice, at least morally speaking.

I didn't give a fuck about morals. Not everything could be so easily slotted in black or white boxes.

The written word couldn't exorcise the predator demon that haunted me since that night in Morgan's office and never would.

But maybe that wasn't the point.

I could punish these men all I wanted with my fists and my ire but I was just one (very angry) woman. Quinn Harper could reach the masses so that no one would ever go blindly into Professor Morgan's clutches ever again. So that the way President Mina Pallas had sold her soul for academic and financial gain would be highlighted for all to see.

As far as revenge plots went, it was a good angle.

On the other hand, it also compromised what I was doing with my sisters. I'd be the obvious suspect for the hate crimes the Man Eaters committed. Professor Morgan would be more careful, even more insidious than before, and Mina would bury her bad deeds six feet beneath the earth.

And I couldn't afford to give up my crusade, not when I was just starting. It wasn't just about appeasing the monster I'd become. My hunger for male pain and humiliation as an antidote for my own. It was about dragging them out from under the beds of innocent women on campus who had, could, and did fall victim to them in the shadows. I knew I was nothing but darkness, the last of my light snuffed out as I'd lain in the forest on November 1st, but at least I could hunt other creatures in the gloom. At least I could shed light on those dark corners so other girls wouldn't stumble into them as unknowingly as I had.

"I don't think so," I said slowly. "No one believed me before, so I have no reason that would change, even if your mother was the one telling my truth."

Bryn sighed and reached across the table to touch the back of my hand. When I pulled it away automatically and hid it beneath the table, her gaze softened with sympathy that made my empty chest burn.

"Just think about it, okay? I know I'm biased, but my mom has done a lot of good with circumstances like these, and I think she could make a real difference here. When she and my mama were young, they faced a lot of discrimination and hate crimes. She wouldn't pressure or paint you like a victim, if that's what you're worried about. Acheron is one of the oldest and most prestigious universities in the country, but what does that matter if female students don't feel safe here?"

A-fucking-men, I thought, liking Bryn even more than I thought I would.

Maybe, if I hadn't set out to seduce Luna Pallas, hadn't seen the play of autumnal light in her sunset gold hair and seen the tenderness of her good heart at play, I would have asked Bryn out for real. As it was, I was so tied up in knots about Luna, I couldn't even begin to imagine dating someone else.

I'd lost the plot around Luna the moment she showed up at my house, valiant in the face of her curiosity, eager to know about a girl most people were eager to fear and hate.

My phone buzzed in my pocket, and I knew without looking it would be a text from Juno.

My cue to leave.

It was perfect timing, really. I took a moment to look down at my hands on the table, willing tears to pool in the troughs of my lower lids. They weren't genuine. I hadn't really cried at all since before the incident, and nothing Bryn had said was particularly triggering. Not like orgasming eight days ago in front of Luna was, anyway.

But tears also worked for a get-out-of-jail-free card.

"I'll think about it," I said weakly as I looked up at Bryn with those forced tears shining from my eyes. "I-It's still hard to speak about it, I guess."

She made a noise of sympathy in the back of her throat and made to reach for me again before catching herself. "I'm sorry I upset you."

"You didn't. I mean, it's hardly your fault," I assured on a flimsy laugh, dashing at my cheek as a tear rolled loose.

Her grin was self-deprecating. "I really fucked up this date, didn't I?"

Another laugh, this one more genuine. "Honestly, I'm not in the best place to date anyway."

"Yeah, that's fair. I'd still love to be friends with you," she suggested. "You've always intrigued me. A beautiful girl who skulks around campus with her nose buried in Homer or Socrates is a rare enough sight to draw the eye. I have a feeling your looks are the least of your charms."

Oh.

But that one hurt. An arrow to one of the last soft spots behind my breastbone.

I hadn't made a new friend in...too long. People had stopped even pretending to see me as more than a victim or a slut.

It was good to be seen for me. Wanted platonically.

It was something I'd yearned for in the secret recess of my soul my whole life.

"Yeah," I agreed, and this time, real emotion clogged my throat. "Yeah, that would be nice. If you'll excuse me for a second, I just need to clean up." I gestured to my wet face and no doubt running mascara.

"Take your time," Bryn said graciously. "Why don't you get some fresh air, and I'll order us some food? When you get back, I promise we'll talk about pleasanter stuff."

I smiled at her in thanks and slipped from the booth. Her eyes were hot on my back as I walked to the back and around the corner to the restroom. It was empty, so I didn't hesitate to take the last stall. I opened the sanitary disposal container screwed to the wall and took out an airlocked plastic bag.

Inside, a black full-face snake mask, talon-tipped leather gloves, and my Hogue X-5 matte black tactical knife awaited me.

When I emerged from the bathroom and stalked out the emergency door into the back parking lot, Professor Morgan's victim was nowhere in sight.

In her place walked a vengeful harpy on a crusade.

CHAPTER THIRTEEN

"A burnt child loves the fire."
—*The Picture of Dorian Grey,* Oscar Wilde

Lex

The Delta Alpha Fraternity was housed in a colonial mansion at the far end of Greek Row at the western edge of campus. It wasn't a prestigious frat for anything in particular, athletics or academics or hot guys.

But I hadn't singled it out for its accomplishments.

When I'd decided to start this vigilante shit, I'd wondered how I would find predators on campus without some sort of system. I had Juno, who was an IT whiz and who frequently searched the dark web forums for conversations about brutality on campus, and Effie, who was so popular and warm, friends often flocked to confide in her. But it wasn't exactly enough.

Then one day a few months after Halloween when the spring was thawing winter and making everything weep, I'd escaped the rain to duck into a little coffee shop in Richmond. Sipping a cup of Earl Grey, I'd noticed a few local young folks peruse the bulletin board at the front of the café. It seemed like an archaic way to spread news about things in the age of computers, but the corkboard was still littered with flyers for babysitters, music lessons, and tutors. I watched as someone ripped a tab off a poster for karate lessons, and I knew exactly how I'd get the insider information at Acheron when I returned.

I'd just ask.

The tips about Delta Alpha had come into my burner phone in a flurry. One, two, three...ten.

It seemed they had a reputation for drugging girls and sharing them in the basement of the frat house.

Two of the messages we'd received had even spoken about their assaults being filmed. They didn't have proof, but they distinctly remembered a camera in their faces at different points in the horrific evening.

Upon further investigation, their claims seemed to have merit. Juno found a thread buried on Reddit that talked about Delta Alpha being a fraternity for "primal" men who were ready to take what they wanted. They spoke in ambiguous terms, but it was easy to discern that they used mythological terms as stand-ins for their true meanings.

Going "Greek" on someone was a fairly thin-veiled allusion to raping women. The Greek gods were known for raping mortals and goddesses alike. Poseidon with Demeter and Medusa, Zeus with Leda, Callisto, Europa, Antiope... The list went on.

So tonight, I'd done as the ancient Greek gods and these Delta Alpha predators did, and I'd assumed a different form to fuck with them.

Earlier that night, before I met up with Bryn, I'd showed up at the party in a short blond wig and blue contact lenses. My unique snake tattoos were covered up by leather pants and a mock turtleneck crop top that still left my belly exposed from the lower swell of my breasts to well below my belly button. The boys had been such easy prey. The moment I showed up, they flocked to me like moths to a flame. I wondered if any of them sensed the violence barely contained beneath my skin, flickering at the edges of my forced smile. If a part of them wasn't drawn to the danger.

Either way, it was easy enough to find the ring leader, Mitchell Paxton, and lure him to his room. Easier still to wrap my fingers around his throat when he bent to kiss me and press just firmly, just long enough for the guy to pass out on his own bed.

The idiot kept the drugs inside the only book on his bedside table, the pages cut out to house three vials of Rohypnol. That it was a copy of F. Scott Fitzgerald's *The Beautiful and Damned* was wonderfully ironic.

I left after that, knowing Mitchell would wake up thinking he'd drunk too much and head back to the party. That whatever use the frat had for those drugs would go unfulfilled even if they slipped it into girls' drinks because I'd taken the vials myself and switched them out for powdered sugar.

On my way out, I'd handed them off to Gracie in the kitchen who was wearing a pink wig that oddly suited her. She stayed inside with Juno as backup to drug the guys when the party wore down so I could go on my date with Bryn.

And now, I was back.

The house was empty when I pushed through the front door. It was only eleven thirty at night, way too early for a university party to be over, but the girls had done good work. I followed the hallway past the archway to the living room and kitchen, both filled with party detritus. Music still played throughout the house, growing louder as I made my way deeper. The door to the basement staircase was cracked open, and my heeled shoes thumped on the wooden treads as I made my way into the bowels of the house.

I wasn't surprised by what awaited me. My sisters knew what they were doing. Even before we'd become the Man Eaters, we had fought together. My foster mother's second husband had been abusive, so Grace, Effie, and Juno had already been enrolled in self-defense and Muay Thai classes when I started to live with them. As preteens, we had coordinated fights like most kids choreographed dances to top forty music.

So no, I wasn't surprised when I saw the twelve live-in fraternity brothers tied together elbow to elbow in a circle with their bodies facing outward, duct tape over their mouths, ankles crossed and zip-tied.

"Good work, girls," I said in my high, flighty voice.

Effie jerked her chin up in acknowledgment, sharpening one of her knives where she sat on the edge of a sofa. Juno stalked around the grouping of men, tapping her barbed wire baseball bat against her hand. Blood stained one end, correlating with the side of a blond guy's skull. Obviously, he'd put up a bit of a fight.

I recognized him instantly as Mitchell.

"Did you find it?" I asked.

Grace stepped forward, her short skirt swinging over skull-patterned fishnets.

Even tied up, the eyes of two men tracked her progress across the room.

Anger burst inside me like a rotten tomato thrown against the wall of my chest.

"Eyes up here," I snapped at them, stepping forward to slap one of them across the cheek.

His face snapped to the other side, blood flying from the gashes my talon-tipped gloves cut into his cheek in a wide arch to paint the man beside him like a Jackson Pollock painting. It was lovely.

Sure, we dressed provocatively when we went hunting. There was something poetic in being beautiful in our wrath. Vengeful women throughout history and literature were too often portrayed as ugly, the narrators of their stories inevitably male.

The harpies, the Morrigan, the furies.

Well, the Gorgon sisters were not ugly, and our anger didn't taint us, it empowered us.

"Here," Gracie said, handing me a computer. "It was on the floor of his room."

"Want me to crack it?" Juno asked, affecting the same high, floating tone as the rest of us.

"No, I think Mitchell will open it for us." I stalked over to the president of Delta Alpha and crouched before him. His eyes widened, ripe with fright, as I traced the edge of his jaw with the end of a talon. "Won't you, Mitchell?"

He mumbled something behind his taped lips, and I didn't have to be a mind reader to know it wasn't very kind.

I clucked my tongue at him. "Have you ever heard of the saying 'it takes a monster to destroy a monster'? No? Well, let me explain."

As I spoke, I pressed harder with the metal talon at the tips of my gloves, cutting a precise hole into the top of Mitchell's smooth cheek and then slowly, carefully drawing a diagonal line down to his mouth. The skin opened up cleanly like drawing a line on paper in red ink that pooled slowly along the crease then wept down the slope of his face.

One. Two. Three.

Cut. Cut. Cut.

"You and your lot are monsters, Mitchell. Maybe you think you're owed something, maybe you think it's harmless, that the desire you feel for the women you drug and take without their consent is payment for services you make them render. Honestly, I cannot comprehend the evil path your mind takes you down to convince you what you did to these girls was okay. Honestly, I don't know the first thing about how you live with yourself."

I paused to stand up and take a step closer, planting my black boot on the soft swell of his groin before I leaned forward into his face. The pressure made him whimper like a stuck pig.

It felt good and right.

He was a monstrous animal. I was only peeling back the layers of disguise. If I let myself lose the taut hold I had on my anger, this wouldn't be enough. Nothing would be, short of real torture, flaying and quartering and staking him. Until he was a mess of bloody, pulpy flesh. Until he was no longer human because he didn't have a right to the term.

I sucked in a deep breath that tasted of stale beer and acrid male sweat.

Then I ground my foot harder into his soft flesh. How strange, I thought, that something so soft and repulsive could be such a formidable, horrible weapon.

"All I know," I told Mitchell as I sneered into his face. He couldn't see my expression through the mask, but disgust layered my saccharine tone. "Is that in order to take your kind down, I have to be willing to do things some people might call barbaric or evil. But you know what? That's okay with me. Someone did something to me like you've done to women in this basement, and it changed me. It turned my heart to stone. I don't care anymore if I'm evil or monstrous, Mitchell. I'll be both those things if it means taking men like you to your fucking *knees*."

I reared back, cocking my arm, and then landed a brutal blow with the metal knuckles built into my gloves against the side of Mitchell's objectively attractive face.

And then I did it again.

And again.

Again.

Again.

Again.

Until Mitchell's face wasn't even close to pretty anymore, objectively or not.

"Now," I said sweetly as I kneeled before him and opened his computer. His blood dripped off the cover and onto the beer-stained floor, poppies blooming in memory of the virtues lost here. "Tell me your password, or your frat brothers get the same treatment."

It only took four men to get Mitchell to capitulate, but I let Juno, Effie, and Grace have fun with the rest.

After all, we were a team.

And in the end, those bastards got a little taste of what they deserved.

I didn't stay for the setup.

Once the computer was unlocked, it was easy enough to find the hidden folders containing the forced pornos they'd made of five different girls over the past three years. Juno brought each video up on a different computer from the men tied up in the room, wrapped them with red ribbons, and attached a note for the Acheron PD to find when they arrived after Effie called them just as they readied to leave.

We'll continue to do your job for you if you insist on keeping your heads buried in the sand. Do better for the women on this campus.

Xoxo,

The Man Eater Crew

I was the one under suspicion, and I'd already been gone twenty minutes. It was stretching my breath of fresh air a bit long, but I'd texted Bryn to let her know, and thankfully, the Penny was close to Greek Row. I entered through the back entrance again and went to the last bathroom stall. I'd already ditched my blood-stained hoodie and gloves in Effie's Bronco, but I still had to change back into my date night clothes and wash my upper chest in case there was blood residue as there had been after I'd beaten Jerrod.

There was no Luna there tonight to clean it off for me.

Something moved in my chest, a stretching or a yawning like I was coming awake at the thought of her.

I ignored it.

Instead, I stared at my reflection in the small mirror, yellow light spilling down my face. All my life, people had told me I was beautiful, but looking at myself, I could only see all the pain I refused to let myself feel. It settled in the tight line of my pursed mouth, in the strain beside my eyes, the color once bright as a new nickel now dull, stained concrete on the floor of a dirty bar. I felt used up and old, but I was only twenty-one.

A small part of me wondered if the anger wasn't making it worse. I knew the incident had started the erosion, but the rage that hammered against me every day like waves crashing the rocky shore had to be taking effect.

I looked as battered as I felt.

Ironically, Bryn smiled hugely when I rejoined her with an apology and said, "You look better. Always beautiful, but lighter, now."

My sharp-edged grin was genuine. "I feel it."

"Sometimes it's good to get things out."

"Oh, definitely."

"So how come I haven't seen you around the LGBTQIA+ Society socials?" she asked just as a server brought a huge plate of nachos and curly fries to the table. "Honestly, I didn't even know for sure you were gay until you asked me out."

I shrugged, popping a fry between my teeth and chewing as I thought. "Being gay isn't something I externalize."

Bryn frowned. "I haven't heard it referred to like that before. What do you mean?"

"I mean that loving women is special to me the way the things I love best and my passions are. I suppose I don't like to talk aloud about those things because they seem...precious. Sacred. They give meaning to my life and who I am, but, like anything sacred, I don't like to share them very much."

"That makes a bizarre Dali-esque kind of sense," Bryn said after a moment. "As long as you're sure it isn't fear."

I cocked my head in question.

She stared at me with an intensity I didn't often find in other people. "You've been through a lot. I can't pretend to know your whole history, but it occurs to me that a girl whose entire community knows more about her than they should would want to keep some secrets. And that, maybe, she wouldn't trust anyone lightly. It shouldn't be the case, but being out can make you vulnerable. People are assholes even in the 21st century."

"It's a good theory," I allowed, but when I tried to smile, it cut like a knife wound into my face. "But no. Maybe when I was young...I grew up in rural Virginia. Being a lesbian wasn't an option. Now, no. What do I have to fear when the worst has already happened?"

Bryn froze with a nacho halfway to her mouth. Hot cheese dripped slowly off the end, but she didn't stop it from falling with an oily splat to the table.

"That's horribly sad, Lex."

"I'm a horribly sad girl," I quipped, but the joke of it fell flat under the weight of the truth.

My phone buzzed in my pocket. I had no idea who would be calling me unless something went wrong at Delta Alpha.

"Sorry, this is so rude, but do you mind if I take this? It could be important."

Bryn gestured for me to take it with a wave of her hand.

"Hello?" I asked into the cell.

"Lex?" Luna's scared voice sheared through the radio waves and hit me like a whip across the face.

"Luna, where are you?"

I turned my shoulder to Bryn, using the thick ropes of my dark curls to curtain me from her gaze. After that, her presence, even the entire bar—raucous laughter, the clang of dishes and cutlery, Taylor Swift playing over the speakers—faded away completely. All of my focus was on Luna and why there might be that keen edge of fear in her voice.

"I-I'm at Flora's house—"

"Are you safe?" I demanded.

"I don't feel so good," she admitted tremulously. "Could you maybe come get me?"

The sudden warmth in my chest nearly took me to my knees. That Miss Popular would call *me* to get her when she was scared—not her idiot boyfriend, Pierce, or her field hockey friends or her mother—seemed monumental.

It hit me all at once that it was because she *trusted* me.

And suddenly, I wanted to tell her my truth. That awful truth with snapping teeth and three heads chained to the pit of my belly that I wouldn't let anyone, even myself most days, get close to.

"I can call someone else," Luna offered after I hadn't spoken for too long a moment.

"No." The word was harsh enough to sound almost vicious. "No one else. Stay there. Get somewhere safe and lock the door. I'm coming."

CHAPTER FOURTEEN

"It's quite an undertaking to start loving somebody. You have to have energy, generosity, blindness. There is even a moment right at the start where you have to jump across an abyss: if you think about it you don't do it."
— Jean-Paul Sartre, *Nausea*

Luna

Flora lived in a big house a few blocks away from campus with a few other girls from the field hockey team and two from the university soccer team. All this meant their Saturday night party to celebrate our team's sixth undefeated game of the season was an absolute blowout.

The truth was, I didn't really like parties. I much preferred to curl up at home with a good book, a mug of decaf coffee, and one of my sad girl playlists. But I was the captain of the field hockey team, and certain social obligations went along with that. Attending team parties was one of them.

My usual trick was to show up, stay for the early hours when people were too preoccupied with getting drunk themselves to question the clear liquid in my red Solo cup (water usually, or soda water with lime if I was feeling fancy), and then slip out the back when everyone was too busy reveling to notice my absence.

But tonight was different.

It'd been officially over a week since I'd last spoken to Lex.

It shouldn't have mattered, really.

Breaking up with Pierce should have meant more, maybe the undefeated streak the team was on and the pressure I felt to keep that going, or the fact that my mom had called to grill me about my dating life before tonight's game.

"How are things going with Pierce?" she'd asked in that cloyingly sweet voice that meant there was a wrong answer to her question.

"We broke up," I'd said calmly, even knowing it was the wrong answer.

It was the truth, though. Pierce and I would always be friends, but even if nothing more happened with Lex, I felt better, more myself than I had in ages now that I wasn't his girlfriend.

The pause that followed was so long I almost hung up just to avoid the drama.

But that was the funny thing about being a daughter. Even when you read all the signs correctly and know you're in for a telling-off, you stick around to take it. Some kind of biological and emotional manipulation we're all helpless to resist.

After she finished laying into me about how I could have let such a wonderful catch slip through my fingers, she asked the one question that had actually chilled me.

"Luna," she said, soft and slow. "Do you have any classes with a girl named Alexandra Gorgon? Maybe you know her as Lex."

"Yes," I'd said, trying not to panic. "I think she's in my Tragedies class."

"Avoid her, please," Mom said, a simple order she expected me to obey. "She's a bad apple."

A bad apple.

It was such a stupid expression, almost archaic and juvenile.

The only way that Lex Gorgon resembled a bad fucking apple was that she was as tempting and taboo as forbidden fruit. My mother expected me, as God had done with Eve, to follow logic and avoid the obvious temptation.

She didn't know how much I yearned to claim her sweet flesh for myself against all rationale. And how could she? I'd never in my life disobeyed her will, and I was twenty-one years old.

After I hung up, I moved through the motions of making my dinner before my game on autopilot. It was a state of mental numbness like meditation while I let my emotions germinate and grow in my gut.

So it wasn't until I sat down at my lonely little table in the basement apartment I rented in my mom's house eating butter chicken curry that it really hit me. I was eating butter chicken curry because it was what my mom made me every Saturday night growing up. In truth, I didn't even really *like* it, at least not as much as I enjoyed Vindaloo or Thai Panang.

I only made it because it was my routine and it was only my routine because it had been my mother's.

I shoved the curry away so viciously, the bowl tipped over my placemat and spilled out onto some of the photographs I'd developed of Lex from the library. After I lost the curry in my stomach in the trash beneath the sink, I'd carefully cleaned up and sat heavily in my chair. My eyes fixed on one of the photos of Lex, her legs against the wall, skirt folded over like the peel of a banana to reveal the gold flesh of her legs, the snakes slithering the length of her left thigh.

I played field hockey because my mother had growing up. I went to Acheron because, of course, I would attend the school my mother was president of even if I'd always dreamt of going to Cambridge instead. I still lived in her damn basement because she'd convinced me it would be easiest, best. She could pop by whenever she had a moment, which wasn't often because she was always working, but still.

She presided over my life like the gods on Mt. Olympus, ruling and interfering as she saw fit without any qualms about how it might affect me.

Get back together with Pierce if you know what's good for you.
Avoid Lex.

God, I couldn't have been more her puppet unless she had her hand up my ass. Even as I thought that, I winced because I'd been crude, and Pallas women were not crude or crass or in any way undignified.

Well, fuck that.

I was done with it.

What was the point of being alive and healthy if I didn't live for myself?

I worked with enough disadvantaged youths as a tutor at the local at-risk high schools, so I knew most people were not as lucky as I was. So why was I wasting it by acting on someone else's wishes?

Especially when I was now faced with something I wanted more than anything else I could remember.

Not something, someone.

And then, not even a man as I'd always assumed I would want, but a woman.

And then not just any woman, but Lex.

Gray-eyed, bravehearted Lex with thick dark curls like coiled serpents and eyes like twin wounds.

It was a powerful revelation to have alone in a dark apartment that reeked of curry, but it lingered with me all through the game against Cornell, which we won handily in part because I was, as Haley said, in "beast mode." Even after, when I dashed home to get showered and ready, I thought of Lex as I dressed in an oversized white men's button-up shirt and belted it at my waist to make it into my version of a sexy dress. Heeled loafers, my signature frilly socks, an oversized blazer, and my strawberry-blond hair down around my shoulders in its usual unkempt mess, and I thought maybe Lex would have approved.

Not verbally, but with one of those heavy-lidded looks that made heat pool like melted wax in my belly.

Of course, I knew I wouldn't see her at Flo's party. She would never be invited, and even if she was, I couldn't see cool, aloof but guarded Lex letting loose with friends.

But it still made me feel aroused and confident to dress for her.

If I was being honest, it was also the reason I drank more than I usually did, and completely lost my window to leave the party early and sober. By the time I realized I was too drunk, everything was playing out with a significant lag time. It was nearly midnight, and I was swaying on my feet. Pierce had left early with some girl, a wry grin on his lips when we'd caught eyes over her shoulder as he guided her out. I'd winked at him in blessing.

"You okay, girl?" Haley asked, appearing as if I'd conjured her. "You look toasted."

"I am." A burp burst from my lips, startling both of us. Haley laughed, but I covered my mouth in embarrassment. "Ugh, I am so gross right now."

"You want some water?"

"Please. I'm going to hit one of the empty bedrooms and lie down for a second. The room is spinning."

Haley squeezed my shoulder, then tugged on the ends of my hair. "Okay, Lunatic, I'll come find you in a minute." When I burped again, she laughed and added, "And maybe I'll bring a bowl."

I staggered through the house past a couple making out on the stairs up to the second floor, where things were dark and quiet. Flo's bedroom was at the back of the house, and I shut the door behind me. Before I could rethink the impulse, I flopped on the bed and pulled out my phone from my little tweed purse.

"Hello?"

I closed my eyes to relish that husky voice and also because the room was spinning so madly, I thought I might puke.

"Lex?" I knew it was her not just from the sound of her distinct voice but also by the way it made me feel. Like I was both anchored and floating away, a balloon at the end of a strong string tethered to her hand.

"Luna, where are you?" Her voice was sharp with panic.

Panic for me.

Even though my world was twirling and I felt more ill by the second, something inside me that had been planted that evening in the library grew roots and sprouted.

"I-I'm at Flora's house—"

"Are you safe?" she cut in.

"I don't feel so good," I admitted. Chewing on my bottom lip, I let myself take a risk. "Could you maybe come get me?"

There was a long enough pause that my stomach started to churn and rumble ominously with more than just sickness. This was the second time I'd put myself out there for Lex, and if she left me hanging again, I didn't think I could give it a third chance.

"I can call someone else," I muttered.

"No," she snapped, and I wondered if she was angry with me. "No one else. Stay there. Get somewhere safe and lock the door. I'm coming."

I stared at the phone screen after she hung up, but before I could digest what I'd done, bile rose to the back of my tongue.

I lurched up and stumbled over Flora's purple shag carpet to the en suite bathroom with my hand over my mouth as if that would help.

My knees hit the tile with a bang, and the pain ricocheted through my bones all the way up to my teeth. But I was desperate. The toxic combination of bile, booze, and remnants of butter chicken was already clogging my throat.

My sweaty fingers clutched at the toilet seat desperately as my entire body contracted around the mess in my stomach. I moaned between expulsions, too hot and too cold and aching all over as if I'd been steamrolled.

When I was done, I dropped my head right there on the toilet seat and passed out.

At some point, warm hands smoothed over my hair and gently gathered me into strong arms. The chest against my cheek was hard, and for a moment, I nuzzled closer, thinking it was Pierce.

But no, Pierce had left, and the cologne was all wrong, musky when it should have been salt-sweet like ocean brine.

I murmured a protest, but my tongue was thick and dry in my mouth, heavy and ineffectual. When I was placed back on Flo's bed, I relaxed automatically and black edged in to the sides of my vision. Vaguely, I was aware of the bed compressing on the other side of me, someone rolling snug against my body and smoothing a hand down my stomach.

I was ten leagues under the sea, my own intoxication threatening to drown me in numbness, but beneath it all, there was a kernel of fear struggling to make itself known.

I must have passed out again because I was awakened by an almost feral, growling kind of scream.

When I opened my eyes, it was to see Lex in the doorframe, red lips peeled back over white teeth in a vicious snarl, hands fisted at her sides. There was a girl I didn't recognize in the doorway behind her, and Haley, holding a glass of water sideways, liquid spilling out unnoticed.

They were all looking at me in horror.

No, not me.

Someone shifted beside me, sending a cool rush of air over my exposed torso. My oversized dress shirt was unbuttoned, the chunky belt undone.

Before I could register what that might mean, Lex was arrowing across the room on another ear-splitting howl. She hauled the person—a man—on the bed beside me off the mattress and *threw* him with more strength than she should have possessed into the wall beside the window. He landed so hard that a painting hanging next to him swung and fell to the floor, glass shattering over the hardwood.

And then, she brutalized him.

The flurry of her fists froze him in place, pinning him to the wall with each blow. Face, torso, knee to the groin so he doubled over, and Lex used that same leg to knee him again in the nose. Blood sprayed over the ground, over the man's white shirt, and when he reared back against the wall in pain, over Lex's snarling face.

No one stepped in to stop her.

Maybe they were too afraid, and I didn't blame them. She looked... monstrous in her rage. Capable of murder or worse, if there was such a thing.

I had no doubt she would have killed him then, but thankfully, I found my voice just as she cocked her arm, elbow bent sharply, and crashed it down over his temple.

He went sliding down the wall to the floor, passed out.

And I said, "Alexandra."

I'd always believed there was power in a name. Maybe it was fanciful, but in fae mythology, the ancient faeries didn't give out their true names because they had the power to control them.

It seemed to work on Lex exactly like that. The sound of her name in my mouth lassoed her around the torso and physically jerked her away from the man a moment before she would have landed another punishing blow.

She whirled then, facing me for the first time since she'd started her attack.

It sobered me.

Blood peppered her face, staining her teeth still bared in an animal snarl, a growl working in her throat behind those sharp canines. Her hair was an untamed mass of black curls, the ends tangled over her heaving chest where a few buttons on her cream silk blouse had popped open from the strain of her fight.

She looked dangerous and entirely untameable, a wild thing trapped indoors crazed by claustrophobia.

And I'd been the one to stop her.

Me.

Something like peace crowded beneath my breastbone where fear and confusion already did battle.

"Can you take me home now?" I whispered, unable to look away from the beauty of her savagery.

She sucked in a few deep breaths through her teeth, eyes scraping over every inch of me. Then instead of answering, she stalked around the bed to my side and gently, hands shaking with the strain of that gentleness after a flurry of violence, she started to button up my dress. Her bloodstained fingers left red residue over the fabric, but I didn't mind.

"Tell me you're okay," she ordered under her breath. The words quivered with supressed fury.

"I'm okay. Now." I placed a hand over her wrist and squeezed until she looked up at me again. It was humbling and incredible to see fear for me shining in those cold stone eyes.

"Lunatic?" Haley asked softly, creeping closer. "Are you okay?"

Lex snarled at her without turning to face her.

"Hush," I told her, then looked at my best friend. "I think I purged the worst of it. I just feel...weak and out of it."

"I'm sorry I didn't get up here sooner," she whispered brokenly. "I got caught up in the kitchen and..."

"It's okay."

"It absolutely is *not*," Lex corrected, finally turning her head to pin Haley with a vicious glare. "If you knew Luna was like this, you should have looked out for her. Where is your sense of sisterhood? You can't just leave another woman alone in a house with strangers when she's had too much to drink."

Haley blanched at her words, and tears filled her big brown eyes.

"Lex—" I tried to admonish.

But her gaze snapped to mine, and she growled, "Not now, Lux. You do not want me to get started in front of your so-called friends. Can you walk? We're going now."

Before I could answer, she slipped a hand under me and basically pulled me to my feet. Her scent, something dark and warm and entirely *Lex*, filled my nose and made me sway on my feet for a completely different reason than I was before.

"Do you need me to carry you?" she asked, her nose brushing my cheek.

I shivered. "I think I'm okay."

She stared at me with hard eyes for a moment before nodding. Haley and the other girl, a pretty butch girl with bright-blond hair, moved out of the way as soon as we got close, but they followed us through the house as we left.

Everyone watched us with burning curiosity, conversations fading to nothing, bodies freezing midmovement.

What the hell, they wondered, *was Luna Pallas doing in the arms of the most notorious girl in school?*

Even though she was clearly helping me, my unlikely lady knight in silk armor, I still heard the odd snicker and murmur of "slut" and "whore." At one point, I tried to dig in my heels to snap back at them, but Lex just propelled me forward.

The cold air of mid-October felt like a blessing on my overheated, clammy skin. I tipped my head back and closed my eyes to enjoy it, trusting Lex to guide me forward. She'd pulled up in front of the house in an old cream-colored VW Bug convertible that seemed at odds with what I knew of her.

"Do you need help?" the strange girl asked Lex as she opened the passenger door and helped me into the seat.

Lex clipped my seat belt before turning to face her, blocking me from her sight in a move that was endearingly protective, though entirely unnecessary.

"No, I've got it. I'm sorry about tonight..."

"Don't be." There was a smile in her voice. "Seeing this, I get it."

"It's not..." Lex trailed off, then huffed with frustration.

"Some things don't need a label. Take care, okay? You have my number if you need anything. I hope I'll see you again soon."

I watched with a pit the size of Tartarus opening up in the base of my stomach as the girl stepped forward to brush a kiss over Lex's smooth cheek. She met my gaze over her shoulder and grinned.

Possessive anger coiled around my chest like a boa constrictor.

"Night, Bryn," Lex said, stepping forward to shut my door before making her way to the other side of the car.

I looked out the window to see Haley standing at the end of the walkway to Flo's house, her hands tangled together, the orange light of the antique streetlamps casting her wet face with a ghoulish sheen. She lifted one hand in farewell as Lex started the car and pulled away.

People gathered in the doorway behind her, watching as I left with Lex, and I knew that gossip about tonight would be all over campus by morning.

Were Luna and Lex...unlikely friends?

Or even unlikelier lovers.

Given that most people knew Pierce and I broke up, I knew there would be some whispers about the latter.

Panic chewed at the edges of my lingering intoxication, sobering me further. But beneath the acidic feeling was something else.

Something like relief.

Because the truth was, Lex and I weren't lovers.

But I wanted to be with a desperation that usurped any previous level of desire I'd felt in my entire life.

Wanting her was one thing, but having her was another. It would change the entire scope of my life. My reputation as Acheron's golden girl, my relationship with the only parent I'd ever had, and my own feelings about myself.

But as I sat in the car, feeling safe and cared for, feeling *seen* for the first time in so long, I thought Lex was worth the risk.

CHAPTER FIFTEEN

"Yes yes yes I do like you. I am afraid to write the stronger word."
—Virginia Woolf

Luna

We didn't speak in the car. Only the gentle swell of music I recognized as the Vitamin String Quartet played through the space between us. I was too tired, too discombobulated to make sense of the emotions churning inside my empty, clutching belly, and I had the sense Lex was too incensed and preoccupied with trying to calm down.

She didn't take me home, and I wondered if she avoided it because she knew I lived in my mother's house.

Instead, we pulled up to her haunted home on Charity Lane, the enormous Victorian looming purple-black in the shadows. Lex stopped the car and got out so quickly, I was still staring after her when she opened the door for me and reached in to help me out.

I wanted to say something, but she didn't let go of me when I gained my feet. Her fingers loosened to slide down my forearms over my hand, tangling our fingers together.

The feel of her hand in mine took my breath away. The rightness of it made my eyes burn with tears.

I loved it. Holding hands with a woman. This woman, particularly.

As it always did around Lex, my sense of self shifted a little closer to its true form.

She led me across the leaf-strewn path to the door, keeping hold of me even when she fiddled with the key to open the door. The light was on in the parlor, and I caught sight of the Gorgon sisters sitting around the round table playing Scrabble and drinking ginger tea that spiced the air with fragrance. They stared at us as we passed by, but Lex didn't stop to acknowledge them.

I thought Effie might have shot me a sly wink, but it seemed too unlikely to be true.

We went up the dark stairwell, the steps creaking under our weight, to the attic. Large skylights cut into the roof had moonlight falling in silver fragments across the huge, steepled ceiling room.

Lex's domain.

She left me then, moving around to light lamps and do something in what I assumed was the bathroom to the left of me.

I took the opportunity to snoop.

The warm light of vintage lamps, some draped with gauzy scarves, filled the room with golden warmth and gilded the heavy antique furniture. A wrought-iron bed was pushed against the far wall, made with black and gray linen sheets and piled with soft, wrinkled pillows. Beneath it a faded Persian rug, one of many layered over the big space. There were remnants of a carpet picnic by the other wall, which was lined with stacks upon stacks of yellowed, well-loved books. In the corner amid the stacks sat an overstuffed leather chair layered with cozy blankets, a standing reading lamp curling over the arm. The windowsill next to it was burdened with a bronze platter of melted, stacked candles and an old brass looking glass.

It smelled of old books and incense, that burning, honeyed smell of Lex herself.

I loved it.

Even the large glass enclosure built into one corner that housed an enormous black and brown snake.

I moved closer even though a cold trickle of fear dripped down my spine.

The serpent was coiled loosely on an angled flat rock, sunning itself in the warm red light cast by the heat lamp within. It lifted its head on my approach, fixing me with shrewd black eyes.

"His name is Chrysaor," Lex said, startling me with her silent approach. "He's a Timber rattlesnake."

"I didn't know you could keep rattlesnakes as pets."

"It's not recommended for the faint of heart," she agreed, touching her fingers lightly to the glass.

Her snake moved toward her instantly, his long body undulating smoothly, scales shining gold and black.

"He's beautiful," I admitted, a little surprised to find him so.

"I'm glad you think so. Most people are afraid of snakes."

"Most people are afraid of you."

We both seemed startled by my words, our gazes catching on each other.

She seemed softer somehow, up here in the safety and seclusion of her own den. Less dangerous and more understandable, much like seeing her snake in his own habitat.

"But not you," she confirmed, cocking her head in that reptilian way she had.

"Not me," I agreed, more breath than words as I found the courage to step closer. "You make me feel a lot of things I've never felt before, but not fear."

She raised an arched black brow. "I wouldn't blame you. You just watched me beat a man half to death. That wasn't a random act for me, Lux. If you're the light, I'm the darkness. Violence becomes me like kindness does you."

"Maybe I need a little violence in my life. Maybe I like a little chaos," I taunted, boldly stepping even closer so that our breasts brushed and our breaths comingled. "Maybe I long for your brand of darkness."

"Don't play with wild animals unless you're ready to get bit," she warned.

I canted my head to the side, baring my throat where she'd once sunk her teeth. "I want your teeth on my throat more than I've ever wanted someone else's mouth against my lips."

A little shiver moved through her, and her eyes burned like banked coals under the shadow of her brows.

For one suspended second, I thought she would kiss me, and when she hesitated, I thought my heart might burst with longing.

But she didn't.

She took one large step away from me and turned to walk toward the stairs. "I drew you a bath. It should help to sober you up and make you feel better. There is a spare toothbrush on the sink basin, too. I'll make you some ginger tea to settle your stomach while you get in."

Before I could protest, she disappeared into the dark mouth of the stairwell.

A sigh unwound from me like a spool of thread.

The bathroom attached to her room was cramped, but Lex had made it suit the aesthetic all the same. A full-size clawfoot tub took up the entire back wall, and a skylight spilled silver light directly on top of the gleaming bubbles frothing across the surface. She lit beeswax candles on the rim of the sink and in a wide circle around the tub. Music played from a speaker she'd placed on the closed toilet lid, Hozier's smoky voice filling the room like steam.

I shed my clothes without hesitation, grateful to be rid of the stink of vomit and sweat. It was impossible not to catch my reflection in the large gilt mirror over the little sink. Pale skin smattered with freckles across my shoulders, breasts, and the tops of my strong thighs. My body was taut with strength, but my waist was small and lean, my ass dense and round with muscle from years of field hockey. My breasts were small, perky, and topped like sundaes with bright cherry nipples. I wondered as I stared at my body with new eyes, with *her* eyes, if Lex might like it.

After I brushed my teeth, I used a black velvet ribbon on the sink ledge to tie my hair off my back before moving to dip a toe in the tub. The water was almost too hot, but I settled beneath the surface with only a long hiss and instantly relaxed in the heat. Lex was right—the last of my drunkenness seemed to leech out into the fragrant water, leaving me sober and sleepy.

I must have drifted off a little because when I opened my eyes, Lex was leaning against the sink holding a huge mug of steaming tea. The steam from my bath curled around her, dampening her skin so her silk blouse stuck to her breasts and pebbled her nipples beneath it. Little curls popped up around her hairline, black commas and question marks I wanted to trace with my fingertips.

"You're so beautiful," I told her, because I couldn't stop myself and I was too tired to try. "Everything about you seems to call to me."

"Alarm bells?" she snarked, all her shields firmly in place after her act of rage and honest feeling at Flora's house.

"No, like a siren's song," I corrected, and maybe the lingering alcohol in my system made me brave or maybe it was just my proximity to her, the most courageous girl I knew that prompted me to say, "Will you join me?"

She seemed startled by my question, tensing like an animal about to flee a predator.

"Please?" I asked, holding out my sudsy hand to her.

She stared at it with the same fear and mild curiosity I'd felt looking at the rattlesnake. But she didn't shy away from me. She procured a pitcher from beneath the sink and placed it along with my tea in my reach then stepped back again. I watched as she straightened her shoulders and slowly toed off one leather boot and then the other. Her hair slithered over her shoulders, obscuring her face as she bent to peel off her socks and then her black trousers. I watched, throat dry, breath suspended in my lungs, as she slowly unbuttoned her silk blouse and let it fall from her shoulders to float gently to the floor.

Finally, she stood before me in a black mesh bra that strained to contain her beautiful breasts and matching high-cut panties that accentuated the long, strong line of her legs. There was still blood on her face and hands, in the v exposed by the blouse she'd worn to beat up the man who'd tried to take advantage of me, but it only heightened her beauty in my eyes.

Here was a woman and a warrior.

Here was a woman who had trusted me enough to shed her armor and bare herself to me after everything she'd been through, even after a panic attack that had taken her to her knees the last time we'd been intimate together.

"So brave," I murmured. "So achingly beautiful."

My words seemed to spur her into action. She walked lightly on her toes across the cold tiles and stepped into the tub between my spread legs, sinking beneath the bubbles still wearing her underwear.

I understood why she kept them on. It was a vulnerable thing to be naked like this with her. Not sexual, but intimate in a deeper way.

"Come here," she ordered, reaching for the clay pitcher and dipping it beneath the water.

I didn't hesitate, twisting to face away from her and moving until my bottom hit the apex of her thighs. A shiver worked through me, but Lex ignored it as she teased the ribbon from my hair, letting it fall across my shoulders, ends dangling in the suds. She pressed gently against my forehead to get me to tip my hair back and then used her other hand to pour the warm water over my hair.

I hummed with pleasure and a little awe.

She was washing my hair for me.

It felt achingly wonderful to be so taken care of. The shampoo she plucked from the windowsill smelled like cinnamon as she worked it into a lather between her hands. When her fingers sank into my hair, massaging my skull, I melted into her touch, moaning without shame at the sensation. Her legs cradled my body, her hands my head, and when I leaned farther back, the tips of her breasts in her sheer bra abraded my back.

Arousal built in me like water filling a well, a soft surge of languid heat building inside me until I felt full to the brim.

"Lex," I panted, softly as she rinsed my hair with clean water from the bronze tap.

She didn't respond with words. Instead she squeezed conditioner into her palms and lathered the ends of my hair, coiling the strands together until they formed a rope. She used it to cant my head farther back and to one side until my panting mouth was accessible to her own.

"I'm going to kiss you," she told me, but there was a question there.

Her need for consent saddened me for a moment. Of course, it was important. The last sexual encounter she seemed to have had lacked any consent at all.

I vowed to try my hardest to ease the pain of that memory with this new one.

"Please," I asked her, flicking my tongue along the swell of her lower lip.

Her moan vibrated from her mouth to mine as she sealed them closed and slid her sweet tongue against my own. I ate the sound out of her mouth and gave her my own groan as I swallowed it down.

The taste of her affected me more than the liquor I'd consumed that night. It made my skin too tight, too hot over my racing blood and aching bones. I wanted her to take me apart piece by piece with her teeth and knit me back together with that talented tongue. My body arched farther into her as she tugged hard at my hair. Our breasts rubbed together, my naked flesh sensitive against the buff of sheer fabric over her chest. I rolled over farther so her leg was nestled between my thighs.

"That's it, my sweet girl," she murmured against my mouth before nipping at my damp bottom lip. "Rub your pussy against me. Use me to get off."

A groan quaked through me as I pressed harder to her thigh, undulating into her so my clit was stimulated again and again.

Lex ate the sounds off my tongue between murmuring praise for me.

Gorgeous girl riding me like that.

I can't wait to see you come for me.

If I dipped my hand beneath the water, how wet would I find you? Would you soak my palm? I would lick your sweet nectar from my fingers, and that alone might make me come too. Would you like that?

I rode her harder and harder, water sloshing over the tub to splash against the floor, candles hissing as they were snuffed out.

But it wasn't enough.

I needed her to really touch me. I wanted her fingers inside me, her tongue on other places than just my swollen, aching mouth.

"Please," I begged her, unable to articulate exactly what I needed, only that I needed her. "Lex."

"Hush, Lux, I've got you."

My hair was coiled around one of her fists but she dipped the other beneath the water to wrap around my hip and palm my ass, urging me to thrust harder. The sensation of her nails digging into my flesh sent electric currents of pleasure straight to my pussy.

"Oh my God," I panted, tipping my head back as Lex pressed kisses from my mouth down my jaw to my neck.

Her teeth scraped my throat, sending sparkles through my blood. "I'm dying to touch your sweet pussy, Luna. To feel your wet heat around my fingers and press into you knuckle deep."

"Yes," I hissed, drawing the exclamation into four long syllables.

"But you have to earn that," she teased wickedly, nipping at my earlobe. "You have one minute to come apart on my thigh or I'll put you on your knees and use you to get off myself."

"Holy shit," I croaked a second before her teeth closed over my neck and clamped down hard.

I broke apart like waves against the shore, dissolving into particles of bright energy that surged and bucked against immovable Lex. She pinned me to her with those strong teeth, the hand wrapped tight in my hair and the one squeezing my bottom so tightly I knew I would bruise. I wanted to stay there forever, panting against the damp shoreline of her hair, pressing open kisses to the cliff drop of her jaw.

It was at that moment, as stormy pleasure gave way to soft, lapping waves of contentment that I realized how thirsty I had been all my life. Parched. That I had always been programmed to lust after something I'd never thought I needed until Lex caught my eye in the quad, strong and dangerous as an indignant goddess, and the urge to drop to my knees in worship had first claimed me.

Her hold on me gentled as I dropped my heavy head to her breasts, lying still and sodden between her legs. She stiffened slightly when I curved one arm around her waist and tentatively cupped the other one around the breast opposite the one that cushioned my cheek.

The moment she relaxed felt like a triumph.

Holding her was so different from holding Pierce. She was no less strong or powerful in her own right, but I loved the sloping topography of her curves and the sweet scent of her ridiculously soft skin. I loved how our bodies molded to each other instead of just mine to the hard edges of a man. Our flesh together made a kind of yin and yang.

Tears burned the backs of my eyes and spilled free from my lashes to streak down Lex's wet skin. They weren't tears of sadness, but of cleansing. The bath felt suddenly like a baptism, a welcoming to the very nature of who I was and who I was meant to love.

Lex used the pitcher of clean water to rinse the conditioner out of my hair, careful not to disturb me. Done, she gently collected and coiled the length of my hair on top of my head and fastened it with the wet velvet ribbon.

"Thank you," I whispered, the broken fragments of the words falling to her chest. "For saving me tonight, Lex."

Not just tonight, I thought, almost mad with epiphany. Part of me wanted to dance naked in wonder, hollering to the tree tops about how wonderful it was to know and acknowledge this side of me. But part of me was still afraid, no, *more* afraid, because now I had more to lose than my mother's regard or my reputation.

I was very much at risk of losing my heart.

CHAPTER SIXTEEN

"My bounty is as boundless as the sea,
My love as deep; the more I give to thee,
The more I have, for both are infinite."
—Shakespeare, *Romeo & Juliet*

Lex

"How did you know you liked girls?"

Luna's voice was worn with exhaustion and slumberous pleasure. It made me feel proud to know I'd given her that. Her first orgasm with a woman.

Of course, she didn't know it was my first time giving an orgasm to a woman, too. It felt too enormous to voice it, to acknowledge that I'd lost another first to her even though Morgan had taken such a milestone one from me last Halloween. It felt too much like healing to thank her for the gift she'd given me, too much like leaving my rage behind to acknowledge that she was saving me much more than I had saved her tonight.

"I knew I was gay like I knew the sky was blue. I never thought to question it until someone taught me to," I told her, giving her at least a small piece of honesty because she'd earned it with her easy trust in me tonight. To save her, protect her, and now, to cherish her.

"Who?"

"We lived in the mountains on a homestead without most modern amenities. An outhouse, animals to tend to if we wanted milk, cheese, butter, and meat. We had alpacas and sheep to card for wool and a rainwater collection apparatus for water. It was a very earthy lifestyle, and I didn't hate it, except it came along with a strict set of rules. No education outside the home, and the only books we had were the Bible, a practical guide to survival, my great-grandfather's old copy of *The Odyssey*, and a children's textbook my mum taught my brothers and I from until we were ten and old enough to help full time around the house.

"I felt caged from a very young age, which might seem strange because I had the run of our land and the forests around me. I'd escape into the trees and make up games for myself with imaginary nymphs and woodland creatures." Absently, I stroked over the bumps in Luna's spine, traversing them like I'd walked the mountains, peak after peak, from skull to tail bone. "The closest neighbor shared the forest with us, and they had two daughters. One of them was Penelope."

"Was she pretty?"

I laughed a little. "No, not really. But I was so used to men with two brothers, a father, and an uncle who passed through all the time. I think I was eager for femininity, and Penelope was so sweet, so kind and fragile. I was only seven, but I claimed her for my own. I think my parents thought I meant her to be my best friend, but even back then, before I had words to label her, I knew she was more than that."

"Do you think she felt the same?"

"Yes." I could still remember Penelope's big eyes as she'd asked me if I wanted to play pretend as man and wife. We didn't know better. We'd never been taught there could be two brides or two grooms. "But my father found me one day after I didn't come for evening chores and

I was cuddled with her in a hollow beneath a tree. He didn't like seeing us so close, even though it was innocent. He dragged me away through the dirt as I kicked and cried, promising me I'd never see Penelope ever again. Later, I heard him on the phone with her father. He called me a faggot and warned that Penelope was the same."

Luna shivered in my arms, and I pulled her closer to me subconsciously.

"What an awful man," she whispered.

"Yes, he was a tyrant. I think that's why he settled us all the way out there. So he could rule uncontested over his own little kingdom. My mum was the daughter of immigrant parents from Turkey, and when they died, she had no one left. Sometimes I wondered if she was truly happy with him or if she was just more scared of being alone."

"How did you get away?"

"I ran away four times before it took, and they stopped looking for me or calling the police," I admitted, remembering that final time, the triumph I'd felt squatting in the library overnight, hiding until they locked the doors at closing and left for the night. "Agatha Gorgon found me one day hiding in the supply closet when she was trying to close for the night."

"Grace, Effie, and Juno's mom?" Luna had her pointed chin propped on her fist so she could look into my face as I told my story.

The quality of her attention felt like sunlight on my skin.

"Effie is her adopted daughter from her first marriage. She got custody because her husband was abusive. Her second husband died in a car wreck two weeks after she had the twins. When she found me, she took me in without question even though she was already raising three kids on a librarian's salary."

"Wow, that's pretty amazing."

"She's an amazing woman," I agreed, my heart clenching at the thought of my chosen mother. "I wouldn't still be here without her."

"What do you mean?" Alarm seeped into her tone, and she grasped my chin between her wet fingers to force me to look at her. "Did you try to...were you suicidal after what happened to you last year?"

I shrugged, but the old ghost that haunted my soul gripped it tight in his fist.

"Lex," she said sorrowfully. "I'm so sorry. Will you...I'd love to hear about what happened to you from your lips if you feel comfortable sharing it with me? I would never share it with anyone else."

"I'm sure you know enough already. Someone attacked me the night of Halloween and left me to rot."

There was a long pause, crackling with intensity. My skin burned where it met hers, and I gave in to the compulsion to push her off and away. Luna went without hesitation, moving to the other side of the bathtub to rest her head, but she tangled our legs together so that we made a Gordian knot.

"Someone...or Professor Morgan?" she shocked me by asking.

I blinked at her.

"I was at home the following night so I could watch the new season of *Discovery of Witches* on Mom's Sundance account," she explained, keeping wary eye contact with me. "I heard her speaking to someone about what happened. That you..." She sucked in a deep breath. "That you said it was Professor Morgan who assaulted you, and you'd gone to his office to attack him in retribution the next morning."

"*That* wasn't my retribution," I murmured darkly.

It was her turn to blink. "So it's true?"

I stared at her steadily, unwilling to confirm it absolutely.

The truth was, even though that chasm in my chest where my heart used to be yearned to trust her, I couldn't bring myself to take the risk. I might not be seducing her solely to get back at Mina Pallas anymore, but admitting the full extent of my trauma was too much for me to confess to anyone.

Even myself.

"How can you stand it?" Luna asked after a moment, huffing out a breath that stirred a loose lock of red-gold hair from her pale cheek.

"What exactly?" There were too many burdens to bear from that single act. If she wanted honesty, she would have to be specific.

"How do you deal with people staring at you the way they do?"

"How do they stare at me?"

"Like they're hungry, and you're on the menu." For the first time since I'd known her, Luna's tone was filled with bitterness. "Like you're beneath them for what was done to you against your will, and they either want a taste of the leftovers or to throw you in the garbage."

It rocked me that she could see all of that so clearly. She was obviously more than just a jock. The way she could meet me quote for quote, spar with me, and do well in her honors classes. But this particular comment spoke to a deeper understanding. To an uncanny ability to see through the levels of bullshit to the outline of my real shape.

And that scared me as much as it intrigued me.

"I learned a long time ago to focus on how I look at other people instead of how they look at me. I have total control over one and none over the other. If I spent my life worrying about how people viewed me, I don't think I could ever love myself."

"Do you? Love yourself that is?" she asked, and I had the impression that she struggled with self-love too.

"Sometimes," I admitted, not adding that those occasions mostly played out when I was exacting vengeance on predatory men like Professor Morgan. That all my own shame and pain evaporated in the righteous flames of my fury as I made them pay only a sliver of the price they'd stolen from their victims.

Victims like me.

"Same," she confessed, fishing under the dissolving bubbles to find my foot and hug it between her palms. I liked that she seemed to need the contact, but I couldn't admit I needed it too. "You help, though."

"I do?" Now, that was shocking.

"I've never felt exactly...right in my skin. Like it was an ill-fitting coat or something. It got worse here at Acheron. Everyone seemed to buy into the same version of me before I even realized I was taking part in the illusion. I suppose I've never really taken the time to be deliberate about my life and who I am. Even before we spoke, when I first heard about what happened to you, how my mom could be so cruel about it...it started to change me. I began to think about myself for myself and about other things, like what happened to you, through my own scope instead of someone else's lens." She sighed, tipping her head back against the rim of the tub as she sank deeper into the water. "It's not a comfortable feeling to reevaluate everything you know, but I know it's good, you know? Progress. Like tears in a muscle making me stronger."

I think you're wonderful, I thought, the words rising tidal strong to the forefront of my brain. I wanted to hold her face too tight and tell her exactly that. Tell her I thought she was made of magic and moonshine as bright as her namesake. That I'd take her cool silver self over the golden one everyone made her out to be any day of the week and count myself the luckiest girl in the fucking world.

But I didn't.

I couldn't.

The words stopped up in my throat and clogged my airway so I could barely breathe.

I don't think I'm capable of love, but also, I might be falling for you.
I squeezed my eyes shut to stop the surge of affection and wildly

decided to replace it with an easier sensation.

Lust.

"Get out," I snapped, at the end of my tether.

Luna blinked at me as I stood abruptly, water and bubbles sluicing off my curves. Her cheeks flushed, eyes darkening.

"What?" she croaked.

"Out."

Without waiting for her, I stepped out of the tub and grabbed a towel, tossing another one on the stool beside the tub for Luna.

The air in my bedroom was cool against my overheated skin, and it helped to calm me down from the fever of angst and longing storming my blood. I went to the bed and tugged the covers to the end for something to do. By the time I was done, Luna had appeared in the steamy mouth of the bathroom, staring at me uncertainly wrapped in a towel with her wet hair dripping down all over her shoulders.

"I want to fuck you," I told her boldly, swallowing the fear that threatened to consume me.

She bit her lip, every inch of her pale skin flushed with heat from the bath, and heat, I hoped, for me. After a moment, she nodded. "Okay, I want that, too."

Oh.

Those words, so simple, unadorned, sheared through me like a hot knife.

"Drop the towel."

Her fingers trembled slightly as she reached for the knotted fabric, but she didn't look away from my gaze as she flicked it undone. I resisted the urge to take in her nakedness for the first time for as long as I could. An exercise in willpower. I wanted to make sure I was still in control of the ravening beast inside me, the only one that usually hungered for male destruction but which, at this moment, only hungered for her.

Luna lifted her chin just slightly, a physical dare for me to judge her and find her as wanting as she seemed to find herself.

At least I could give her that. Fuel for self-love. I could show her tonight how beautiful she was: skin, bones, and spirit. With my hands, my tongue, my teeth, and the words that fought to get loose on my tongue.

I let my eyes drop, and my gasp perfumed the three yards of space between us.

Rosy skin over strong, supple muscle. She had a natural curve at her waist, but no softness. Her abdominals softly sketched out in shadow, her hips firm and arms muscled. Her breasts were lovely, mouth-watering pink nipples naturally tipped up as if begging for my mouth's attention, and the apex of her lean thighs was covered in downy rose gold curls.

Arousal slapped me in the face, and I had to step back to brace myself against the wrought-iron footboard of my bed.

"I couldn't have imagined you more beautiful than this," I admitted, letting my tone soften to show her the depth of my hunger and admiration.

I felt almost woozy with lust.

My whole life, I'd wanted this. A woman to know like this: carnally, emotionally, spiritually. I'd dreamt of tracing curves and lines with my fingers, of being allowed to taste from the well between soft thighs, and the peak of a breast, the silken areola and the turgid nipple.

That I was being blessed with the opportunity to do so now, after everything that had happened to me, but also with this girl who made me feel almost clean and new again, nearly brought me to my knees.

So I decided to give in to the sensation and dropped to them.

"Come here," I demanded from my place of worship.

My mouth was so dry the only thing that would satiate my thirst was her.

Luna moved to me instantly, hooked on the line of my commanding tone. I fucking loved that about her. Her desire to submit to me, to please me. It made me feel ten feet tall and filled with unassailable power.

When she was within reach, I banded my arms around her hips and laid my brow against her flat stomach. After a moment, her hands found my head, the tips of her fingers winding through my hair.

Her bath-warmed skin was fragrant and soft as satin. I pressed a chaste kiss to her belly button. One to the blade of each hip bone. Another to the top of her groin. When I looked up at her through my lashes, her head was tossed back, eyes closed, and mouth open. After a moment, she looked down at me, wet hair unleashed from the ribbon to fall around her face.

God, she was gorgeous.

"I have to taste you," I told her, trying to keep the keen edge of my desperation from my voice.

It didn't seem to work. Her fingers flexed in my hair, and her flush deepened to a red turned golden by the lamplight, almost the same color as her hair.

"I want you to."

I closed my eyes to relish the permission and then bent my head to kiss just above her clit. The soft curls smelled musky and sweet, like honey and the spiced autumn wind. I moaned against her, pressing open-mouthed kisses down the sides of her inner thighs, closer and closer to her entrance.

"Lex," she moaned, fingers spasming in my hair. "Please."

"I'll give you what you need," I told her. "Just be a good girl for me. Spread your legs wider."

She adjusted her stance immediately, and I rewarded her with a husky laugh and a long, slow swipe of my tongue across her leaking slit.

"Ohmygod," she slurred, thrusting her hips forward to chase after the sensation.

I laughed again, and the sound unlocked a deep well of joy inside me I'd never known existed. I bent my head and feasted from her, clutching the dense swell of her ass in my hands to haul her closer to my mouth. My teeth scraped against her tender inner thighs, my tongue dipped into the heart of her, tasting the wet as it sprung from within her, and my lips sealed around her clit to suck, suck, suck until her knees softened and she had to cling to the footboard behind me to stay standing.

I gave her no mercy, and she didn't ask me for any. She surrendered to my savage intentions so sweetly, it lit me on fire. I could feel myself leaking through my wet underwear down my thighs onto my heels, where they pressed into my ass as I knelt.

She tasted like every fantasy I'd ever had. I'd been drunk with one kiss in the library. High after a single pass of her questing hand over the lower curve of my breast in the bath. And now, I was forever addicted from the moment she parted those thick thighs to give me access to the dark, wet heart of her.

The first time she came, she stopped breathing, legs quaking around my head, hands pulling too tight in my hair. The only noise she made was a strangled whimper seconds before she flooded my tongue with wetness sweet as agave nectar. I delved deeper, drunk on the taste of her as I drank every drop of her down.

"Lex," she cried softly when I didn't slow my ministrations, when I moved one hand from her ass to between her thighs to join my tongue inside her snug cunt. "Oh my God."

"Again," I demanded against the inside of her thigh before curling another finger into that tight heat and flicking her swollen, throbbing clit with my tongue.

She cried out then, louder and louder. We weren't home alone, but I didn't care. Part of me wanted to set up a speaker system in my room and play the sounds of her desire throughout campus so everyone could hear the symphony of pleasure I aroused in her. So everyone could know that Luna Pallas was mine.

This time, when she orgasmed, I fucked her even harder through it, fingers pressing into the front wall of her pussy, punishing that soft spot that made her wail and ride my face without one iota of shame.

When she came to and I was still kissing her sloppy, swollen folds, she moaned and tugged my face away from her. Before I could protest, she dropped to her knees in front of me, locked her hands in the hair over my ears, and towed me in for a brutal kiss.

Fuck, but it was sexy to hear her moans as she licked herself from my lips and sought more behind my teeth. She ate at me like a starved woman, like she would never get enough. And when she moved her desperate, sucking kisses down my neck to my chest, I didn't even protest when she shoved the cups of my bra under my flesh and plumped my tits in her hands. I loved the way she gazed at them, wild-eyed and drugged, like my breasts were a prize.

"So sexy," she breathed, almost to herself. "God, I could play with these all day. Worship them for hours."

She bent her head then, almost transfixed, bewitched. The moment her lips closed over my nipple, we both moaned in harmony. She licked and sucked and bit until my breasts were tattooed in hickeys and bite marks. The sight of them marked up by her almost threw me back to Halloween, to the way my breasts had looked brutalized by Morgan. But Luna seemed to sense my distress, and she pressed two gentle kisses to each peak before looking up at me.

"I love knowing I put these marks on you." Her voice was as

rough as sandpaper, her pupils totally blown out, eyes all black. "I love believing that my touch can erase anyone else's touch before it."

"Stop," I barked, unable to stand her kindness when I was already so vulnerable. "Don't do that."

"Don't do what? Worship you when you deserve to be worshipped?" she taunted, not mean but determined. "Love your body the way you deserve to be loved?"

I shut my eyes before the sight of her beautiful, earnest face undid me.

"You can close your eyes if it makes it easier, Lex, but we both know it's still me in this room with you. Me between your breasts. Me between your thighs." Her hand slipped through my folded legs and cupped my pussy beneath my underwear. Her fingers slipped on the well of wetness she found there, and we both groaned. "I know it's not enough to erase what happened to you, but I'm going to love your body until it's singing, and any thought of him is lost, at least for now."

I opened my mouth to spew venom, to remind us both I was a monster and not some young, naïve maiden, but Luna curled two fingers into my cunt, and I lost all sense for speaking.

She used her fingers to fuck me, harder and faster like she knew I needed it after the torture of making her come twice on my tongue. While her hand worked inside me, her mouth was busy at my breasts, sucking and licking them until they gleamed gold in the low light with the sheen of her spit. It was dirty and sexy and so feminine, having her pretty pink mouth on my tits and the lingering taste of her come on my tongue.

"Yeah, that's it, Lex, let go for me," she encouraged in a wrecked whisper as she moved to straddle one of my thighs and settle her wet sex against my skin, gyrating to bring herself pleasure even as she doled it out to me. "Come all over my hand."

"Only if you promise to clean it up with your tongue," I told her, one hand wrapping her hair around my fist while the other found her sexy ass and pressed her harder into my thigh. "Only if you come all over me again."

We both watched each other even though our lids were heavy with pleasure as we coaxed the other closer to the edge. My orgasm loomed, high and wide as a tsunami threatening to take me under. I resisted, panic skirting at the edge of my thoughts.

"Trust me, Lex," Luna panted, thrusting harder against my leg, her face pink and wet with sweat as she fucked herself and fucked me. "Come for me."

"Fuck," I bit out as her heel ground into my clit and stars burst across my vision.

"My God," she echoed, and a second later, she convulsed on top of me, her juices leaking down the sides of my thigh.

The utter delicious sight of her coming against my leg severed the last of my control in two like the swing of an axe. I fell apart, unspooling in her hand, losing myself to the bright, white wonder of pleasure searing through me. In that blissful haze, I forgot everything. Morgan. Mina. My parents. My seemingly irrevocable loneliness.

I forgot everything except her.

Luna, bright and alluring as the moon glowing above me, lighting my way through the dark.

"*Lux mea*." I realized I was chanting as I started to come to. "*Lux mea*."

My light, my light.

And when the tears came in a hot, frantic rush before I could cut them off at the pass, my light slid off my leg to sit on her rump and tug me into her arms so I could cry against her breast. She held me too tightly, but I didn't feel claustrophobic like I usually would have.

I felt cared for, protected.

Seen.

And even through the ferocity of my broken sobs, my mourning for every sexual touch that had come before hers, I whispered, *"Lux mea."*

My light that shines in the darkness.

CHAPTER SEVENTEEN

*"With his venom irresistible and bittersweet, that loosener of limbs, Love
reptile-like strikes me down."*
— Sappho

Luna

I woke up in the embrace of a woman for the first time in my life.
I also woke up smiling.

There was no disorientation when I opened my eyes even
though a hangover would have been warranted after my drinking the
night before. Just a calm, clear kind of awareness that had only ever
come after I practiced my morning meditation.

I knew it was Lex behind me, enfolding with her body like both a
blanket and a shield. Her limbs were heavy with sleep, her breath deep
and even as it stirred my hair over my cheek. I could smell her and a new,
different fragrance I recognized instantly as *us*. The aroma of salt-sweet
sex clung to the sheets. I buried my face in my pillow as a smile claimed
my face.

Last night had been…

I was a literature major, and I didn't have the words. Everything
seemed cliché. Could I say that sex between two women was life-

affirming? I knew there was no hope of procreation, but it still felt that way. Maybe because I'd never been more alive than I was under Lex's touch. Where Pierce had passed through me as if I was one of the ghosts that reportedly haunted this house, Lex seemed to excavate every inch of me, even the secrets that lay dormant beneath my skin.

Sex with Lex had been...yes, life-affirming. Yes, the best sexual experience of my life. Addicting, and that wasn't a hyperbole. I found my used and pleasantly aching sex throbbed when I thought of all the ways we'd explored each other throughout the night. Already, I was dreaming of having her again.

I'd always believed I was just one of those women with a low sex drive, but the truth was, I'd just been racing on the wrong track.

Everything about Lex appealed to me.

I loved her soft roundness. The weight of her heavy breasts in my hand, the way her ass bounced back under my questing fingertips. Her taste was so different in each place, a sensorial exploration I mapped with my tongue. Sweet, almost floral at her neck and darker, where her body curved—inside the elbows, behind the knee, in the crease of her thigh and groin.

I hadn't allowed myself to fantasize about sex with a woman, but if I had, I might have guessed it would be all softness and sighs. And we had that, sometimes, a unique kind of harmony. Moments when we pleasured each other at the same time, staring into the other's eyes and breathing the same breath. Moments when we felt like one person and still, wholly, honestly ourselves.

But there were also moments of roughness. Nails sharp against plush flesh, teeth like punctuation marks punched into straining muscles. Shouts and grunts and orders that softened my knees like butter and made me so wet I leaked down my thighs.

It was all hot, all wildly arousing.

I wasn't much of an artist unless you counted my hobby of photography, but it made me understand poets and painters. I wanted to trap this ecstasy in a portrait or print forever to relive again and again.

I allowed myself to bask in the morning afterglow for a long time, but eventually, I had to pee. We'd stayed up into the small hours of the morning, and Lex had done a lot of the heavier lifting—at one point, she'd literally hauled me up her body to sit me on her tongue—so I was careful not to wake her as I slid out of bed.

My clothes were still dirty, so I snooped through the antique, scarred wood chest of drawers until I found an oversized cream cable-knit sweater and a pair of tiny knit shorts that barely fit my more muscular behind. After using the toilet, I brushed my teeth with the same brush from last night and gave up on my mess of bedhead after a minute.

I had no doubt the Gorgon sisters knew exactly what Lex and I had been doing last night, so there was no point in trying to hide it. Besides, my lips were a raw pink from all the kissing, and I had three hickeys that made up a triangle on the right side of my throat.

The house was quiet as I walked past the second floor to the main, and I realized quickly it was because everyone was still in bed. The clock above the microwave said it was eight thirty in the morning, much later than I usually slept in, but it seemed the Gorgons were late to bed and late to rise.

I hesitated in the empty kitchen, unsure for the first time today.

My instinct urged me to make myself at home and start on breakfast. I was ravenous after all the sex, and the big bowl of fruit in the middle of the island countertop prompted me to make fruit compote for pancakes. It was a Sunday morning, and I didn't have practice until late that afternoon.

But...I wasn't really Lex's anything.

I wasn't even entirely sure she would say we were friends, though I hoped we were more.

The thought of leaving made my stomach cramp so badly, I winced and pressed the soreness with my fist. Real life awaited me outside of Charity Lane. My mother's disapproval. The whispers of my connection with Lex on campus and questions I didn't have the answers to.

I thought I was ready to come out. No matter what happened with Lex, I felt safe saying I was bisexual with a large bent toward women over men. But I didn't know how to cast myself in relationship to Lex.

All I knew was that I wanted to do this again.

The sex, but also spending the night, next time preferably without her having to take care of my stupidly drunk self.

Even more than that, I wanted to hang out with her. I wanted the opportunity to peel back more of those mysterious layers and have the honor of knowing the true Alexandra Gorgon. Not the one campus thought they knew, not even the one Lex pretended so often to be.

The real girl I'd held in my arms as she sobbed after we'd had sex the first time. The girl who'd been broken apart by experiencing sex in a good way after what that monster Dylan Morgan had done to her. She hadn't told me it was her first time since the incident, but she didn't have to, and it honored me that she trusted me enough to go there with me.

I wanted to know that girl.

I wanted to cherish her and protect her.

I wanted to love her.

And honestly, I was already more than halfway there.

So I took a deep breath and blew it out between my lips loudly before I opened the fridge to check if the Gorgons had buttermilk.

Forty minutes later, creaking footsteps alerted me to the first Gorgon girl coming down the stairs. A moment later, Effie appeared in the wide doorframe, looking absolutely gorgeous even though it was obvious she'd just woken up. Her curvy body was obscured in an oversized black tee that read "Sapphic Society." Her gold-kissed Afro was flattened slightly on one side, and her eyes were squinty as she peered at me for a long minute.

I flipped a heart-shaped pancake over in the pan without breaking eye contact with her.

Finally, she blinked and shuffled in fuzzy black slippers over to the dining table to scroll through her phone.

Five minutes later, loud stomping on the stairs heralded Grace, who bumped into the wall when she tried to turn into the kitchen. Her eyes were mostly closed as she moved to a cabinet to grab a mug. When she turned to go to the coffee pot, her gaze must have snagged on me because she froze comically.

"Huh?" she grunted, trying to widen her eyes by stretching her whole face.

"Good morning," I said with a cheery wave.

"Oh my God, what is that?" Grace muttered in horror.

"A morning person," Effie said from the dining room table without looking over at us.

"I've never seen one before." Grace shuffled closer to peer at me, and then, not happy with the results, she moved even closer and poked me.

"Did you have a good sleep?" I asked through my laughter.

Grace glared at me. "What's that racket?"

"You mean the music?"

"Yeah, that. It's too early for noise."

I laughed again. "I don't think it's ever too early for Taylor Swift."

"She's got you there, Grace Face," Effie rejoined. "Stop bitching and bring me a coffee."

Grace continued to blink at me dumbly, so I helped her by planting my hands on her shoulders and turning her toward the coffee pot. She grunted, in thanks or annoyance I wasn't sure, and helped herself to the fresh pot.

She'd only just sat down when Juno arrived silently in the doorway. Unlike her sisters, she looked a bit more put together with her blond hair in a neat braid and her trim body in a matching floral satin camisole set.

"Good," she said on a nod as she picked a huge black mug from the cabinet and poured herself some coffee. "It's only right you make us breakfast after you kept us up half the night."

I was too embarrassed to respond, so I ducked my head as I pretended the compote on the stove required my absolute devotion.

"What are you making?" Grace asked, looking a little more human.

"Pancakes with apple, pear, and cinnamon compote."

"Huh."

"Next time, make waffles," Effie ordered. "I like waffles."

"Or oatmeal with caramelized bananas," Grace suggested.

"Do you do smoothies?" Juno asked as she moved to sit with her sisters. "We grow kale in the garden."

"Luna isn't your morning line cook," Lex drawled, appearing so suddenly behind me that I gasped and dropped my spoon in the pot of compote. "Stop giving her orders, you ungrateful ingrates."

"How long have you been standing in the hall?" Grace demanded.

Lex shrugged a shoulder bared in the oversized, wide-neck black sweater she had on. It was cropped, so a sliver of her tanned belly was on display over the small triangle of her underwear as well as the long, lean lines of her legs.

I had to fight not to swallow my tongue as I looked at her.

"Long enough to hear you complain we kept you up all night." She flicked her middle finger at her sisters as she moved into the kitchen to grab her own mug and the electric kettle. "Ignore them, Lux. Those night owls never go to bed before two o'clock."

"You ruin all the fun," Grace complained.

"Aw," Effie drawled, but her smile was playful, not mean. "Lex and Lux, how cute is that, Juno?"

"*So* cute."

"I already made you a pot of tea," I told Lex softly as the sisters bantered when Lex made to fill the electric kettle. "Earl Grey, right?"

That stopped her in her tracks. Slowly, she turned her head to look at me, and I was surprised by the reptilian intensity in her unblinking gaze. The air between us quivered with it.

Then she moved so fast I almost couldn't track her as she dropped the kettle to the counter and lunged for me, dragging me by my shirt front into her chest where I landed with a thud against her breasts. Instantly, she banded her arms around me, tight as a boa constrictor, and bent to take my lips in a very thorough, very wet kiss.

When she finally pulled away, she was holding my entire weight up because my knees had turned to noodles.

"Good morning," she said against my damp mouth.

"Good morning," I echoed dumbly.

The smile she gave me was the best present I'd ever received. Wide, unguarded, full lips spread over straight white teeth.

"Try not to take my breath away in the morning," I muttered before I could help it. "It's too early to be dumbstruck."

She laughed, another gift, this one lasting even longer. The sound was throaty and low, a perfect match for her husky voice. I pressed closer to feel it move through her and into me.

"You made my family pancakes?" she asked softly when she was done.

I nodded, still a little enchanted and unwilling to look away from a

Lex this easy and free.

It was heady to think I had something to do with this uncharacteristic levity.

"Thank you," she said before kissing my nose.

Actually *kissing my nose.*

I stood there reeling as she turned on her heel like nothing had happened and fixed her tea before joining her sisters at the table.

In fact, I stood there so long Grace said, loudly enough for me to hear clearly in the kitchen, "I think you literally kissed her stupid."

That broke me out of my trance long enough to throw a kitchen towel at her head.

I left after pancakes even though I was reluctant to leave our happy little bubble. To my intense pleasure, Lex seemed just as unhappy to see me go, and she kissed me breathless on the front porch before sending me off with a promise to meet me in Mathieson Library that night to work on our Tragedies papers together.

The closer I got to my apartment on the other side of campus, the more dread invaded my heart. The morning sunlight was now obscured with gray clouds that seemed like a portentous warning.

I should always listen to pathetic fallacy.

Because I was walking by the Walking Stick Café when Flora and some of the hockey and soccer guys swung out the doors immediately into my path. As soon as they saw me, I was surrounded.

"You know, he's in the hospital because of you," David spat in my face, looming over me with every inch of his six-foot-four height. "You stupid bitch."

I blinked up into his furious face, frankly shocked by his vitriol.

David was on the football team, but he and Pierce had always been friends, and we'd had a nice rapport.

"Who?" I asked because it occurred to me that I hadn't thought to ask who had assaulted me when I was passed out last night.

God, that seemed like years ago.

"You know who," David roared, jabbing his finger so close to my face that I flinched instinctively backward.

"Beckett," Flora said from just behind David. "It was Beckett, Luna."

My first response was horror. Beckett was one of the top D-men on the hockey team and one of the most popular guys on campus. The fact that Lex, who everyone seemed to fear or hate, had beaten him up would not go over well for her.

And when Beckett was healed, I had no doubt he'd make her pay.

"Fuck," I cursed, even though I usually refrained.

The situation deserved it.

"Fuck is right," David growled even though Andrew tried to pull him back. "You goddamn ruined his season. He has a concussion that'll take him out for weeks."

"*I* didn't give him a concussion," I pointed out, my shock fading into indignation. We were drawing a crowd, but I didn't care. "And I won't feel bad that a man who was taking advantage of me when I was *passed out* can't play hockey for a few weeks. Worse things have happened. One of those being he *tried to take advantage of me when I was passed the fuck out*."

I was panting by the end of it, anger coiling in every inch of me until I felt seconds away from striking out.

"Lex Gorgon was probably lying about it," Flora said softly, pushing past David to take my hand. "She's like *crazy*, Luna. Beckett wouldn't do that to you."

To you.

But she thought he might do it to someone else?

"Lex didn't make anything up. You can ask Haley and a girl named Bryn, too. They were both there and saw what he was doing."

"Did they also see that bitch attack Beckett?" David asked through his teeth.

"She was protecting me," I argued. "You would have done the same for one of your friends."

"Yeah? That crazy bitch is your friend?"

Why did people always make women out to be crazy? Lex was probably the most levelheaded woman I knew, especially considering the trauma she'd been through. A man would never be called crazy for beating someone up who was endangering one of their friends. Only a woman was never allowed to be violent, not even when it was justified.

"Yeah, she is," I said loudly, jutting my chin into the air and crossing my arms over my chest.

"Yeah?" he sneered. "Or is she more than that? Are you fucking that slut now? She went through all the guys who'd have her on campus, and now she's slumming with girls."

My stomach clenched around the pancakes, threatening to expel them. What could I say without outing Lex? Without outing me?

But how could I lie about this big beautiful thing lighting me up from the inside out.

"Luna isn't gay," Flora said, rolling her eyes at the idea. "But seriously, why the hell would you defend that witch?"

Witch. Bitch.

I wished I was both at that moment. That I had the ability to curse them for their horrible insensitivity.

"Lex was assaulted on campus, Flo. How can you call her names?"

"Everyone knows she's a slut."

"Like Taya?" I asked, my lips peeling back over my teeth as I took a step toward my old friend. "Seriously, Flora, are you so desperate for male attention you'll turn your back on women to impress them?"

Flora's blush was instant, a red traffic light.

I ignored it and stalked forward until I was inches from her face. "How can you live with yourself speaking about a woman who was taken against her will? Do you have zero empathy? This is why victims don't speak out. This is why abusers get away with it. Because of weak women like you who refuse to acknowledge what makes you uncomfortable."

"You make me uncomfortable," she lashed out, juvenile but effective because she'd always been good at cruelty. "Why are you defending her against your own friend, huh? Maybe David's right, and you are sleeping with her. Are you a dyke now, Luna?"

For one long, suspended moment, I thought about backing down. Tucking my tail, burying my secrets and my truths, and getting the fuck out of there. I didn't like conflict. I was the peacemaker, always the mediator and resolution seeker.

Some of that was just in my nature, but some of it came from years of blindly obeying my mom or any person with authority over me. I'd basically backed myself into a cage and locked the door.

But I wasn't going to do that anymore.

Being with Lex, knowing Lex and the enormity of her strength had helped me tap into my own reserves.

I would not let anyone, even someone I'd once thought was a friend, speak so hatefully around me, let alone *about* me or someone I cared about.

So I shrugged a shoulder the way Lex would have and said, "Yeah, Flo, if being attracted to women makes me a dyke, you can call me that. It's not an insult because liking women isn't a crime. And yeah, I like Lex Gorgon. She's the best woman I know because even when people throw hateful, ugly words at her like you just did to me, she holds her head up high and doesn't give a damn. I'll never be even half the woman she is, but I'll spend the rest of my life trying to be."

Flora gaped at me. "You're choosing her over our friendship?"

I laughed, but the sound grated through my throat and came out mean. "Yeah, I am. Because a friend would never call me a dyke for being bisexual. A friend of mine would *never* call a victim a witch or a bitch. A friend of mine would never side with a guy who felt me up while I was unconscious. But it's not about choosing her over you. It's about choosing to stand up for a victim instead of siding with a bully. It's about choosing *me* and who I want to be."

"You're disgusting," she hissed, her fury eradicating any of the goodness I knew she had inside her to give. "You probably think those criminal Man Eaters are actually doing some kind of good, don't you?"

"No," I argued even though I hadn't given much thought to the vigilante group who'd attacked Jerrod and the fraternity. "You can't meet violence with violence without starting a war, but this doesn't have anything to do with them. This has to do with you and me, and why you can't handle the fact that I was attacked by Beckett or I might like girls."

"I can't handle it because it's not right, and neither, apparently, are you," she snapped. "To think we've had sleepovers together. Maybe you did to me what you're saying Beckett did to you, and I don't even know it."

It was a toxic combination, pride and rage. I knew she was just lashing out because I'd made her look bad and maybe even hurt her feelings. So I didn't let her splash any more fuel on my fire. There was no point in letting this go on any longer.

I stepped back, glared at David, and nodded at a few of the other guys who had stood silently by while those two tried to hassle me.

"I didn't beat up Beckett, but I'm not sorry for what happened to

him if it means he'll think twice before doing something like that again."
I spoke calmly, but inside, I was quaking, the tectonic plates of who I
was shifting uneasily into new positions. "And if you have anything to
say about me being bisexual, keep it to yourselves. I don't comment on
your sex lives, so don't comment on mine."

David opened his mouth to spew something nasty, but to my
surprise, Ricky, one of the soccer guys I'd partnered with last year in my
Jane Austen seminar, stepped forward to clip him with his shoulder.

"Shut up, Dave." He pushed past him and stopped at my side to
offer his arm like some kind of old-fashioned gentleman. "Can I walk
you home, Lune?"

I blinked up at him, shocked by his show of support. Moved by it. I
cleared my throat to test my voice but decided not to risk it and nodded
instead. Ricky's grin was wide and kind as he slotted my arm through his
and propelled us forward past his crew and my old friend, Flo, without
looking back.

"What you did was kick-ass," he said after a few minutes of
comfortable silence. "You'd think in this day and age people wouldn't be
so fucking harsh and judgmental. My little brother is gay, and the shit he
has to put up with sometimes makes me rage."

"I, um, I just discovered I liked girls too, so it's new to me," I
admitted shyly.

He knocked me with his hip and grinned. "Well, props to you.
Takes a lot of guts to put yourself out there like that. I'm sorry they were
such assholes. I know you've got other friends, but if you ever wanna
grab a coffee or study together, I'm your man."

"Thanks, Ricky," I said as warmth moved through me. It was a nice
reminder that not everyone was a judgmental prick. "I think I'll take
you up on that."

"Just be careful, yeah?" he said as we approached my apartment.

"David, Beckett, and those guys...they hold a mean grudge, and I wouldn't put it past them not to let this thing go."

A shiver of fear wormed its way down my spine, but I nodded mutely instead of responding because on the steps of the house stood my mother.

And she was not pleased.

Ricky seemed to sense that, too, because he stopped on the sidewalk before the pathway and whispered, "You want me to hang around?"

I grinned at him, genuinely moved by his kindness. "No, but thank you. I'll be texting you about that coffee, though."

"Do it," he urged, then patted my arm, shot one lingering look at my mother's formidable expression, and sauntered back down the street.

I sucked in a deep breath to brace myself before starting up the walkway. I'd just faced down Flo and David, but my mother was an entirely different and terrifying beast.

CHAPTER EIGHTEEN

"Come and be my girl. To feel your face and hear your footsteps, I'd give the world."
— Sappho

Luna

"Luna Athena Pallas," Mom seethed the instant I got close enough to hear her. "Get your butt in the house right now."

I avoided eye contact as I moved passed her. Lex might have given me the courage to face common bullies, but the force of Mom's anger was still enough to cow me.

The door slammed behind us, and before I could turn, Mom was grasping my hand and whirling me to face her. Her face was mottled red with rage, teeth bared like an animal about to tear my throat out.

"Didn't I tell you to stay away from Lex Gorgon?"

Fuck.

I was swearing a lot today, but all of it felt warranted.

"Yes." It surprised me that my voice didn't break.

"And you disobeyed me?" she hissed, eyes flashing. "It was a simple request, Luna."

"No, it wasn't. I like Lex. I don't want to stay away from her."

"You goddamn *will*," she roared, slamming her hand against the hall wall so hard that a photo of us at my high school grad fell to the ground but didn't break.

"Why?" I asked, letting her anger fuel me instead of crushing me the way it usually did.

I was twenty-one years old. I had a scholarship to Acheron and a trust fund left to me by my grandparents. I was a smart, capable woman and didn't need my mother to make my decisions.

"Because I fucking well said so," she shouted. "Lex Gorgon is a menace."

"To you, maybe," I countered. "I don't know what she's got on you, but she terrifies you, doesn't she?"

"Don't be ridiculous. I just don't want my only daughter associating with a girl known for her promiscuity and ill-kept rage."

"Why would I be scared of her rage when I grew up with your temper?" I argued, gaining traction now, giving years of latent resentment a voice. "For my entire life, you have told me what to do, Mom. Is it so horrible if I want to make my own mind up about some things?"

"Not this," she said, pointing at me like a witch with a ready hex. "You don't think I tell you what to do for your own benefit? Think about where you'd be without my advice. Nowhere."

"Maybe not here, but I would have been okay. Maybe I'd be at Cambridge or Oxford, maybe I wouldn't be playing field hockey six days a week, and I'd spend that time working at a bookstore or library, taking a photography course even though 'it's a silly hobby.'"

"Don't talk back to me, Luna. Not about this. Take your photography class if you want to, but do not see Lex Gorgon again, is that understood?"

"What if I say no?"

The silence that followed was the eye of the storm. I knew no matter what came next it would be chaos, an utter collapse of everything I knew before. But I was on a roll, tumbling down a slippery slope I could only hope ended in being a better me.

"Then you're out of here," Mom said finally, so soft and silken, her words like snakes in the grass coming for me.

Only, I wasn't afraid of snakes anymore.

I'd faced Lex's Timber rattlesnake, kissed the serpents on her thighs, and sucked a bruise onto the snake's tongue that licked her carotid artery on the side of her neck.

"You'd kick me out for being friends with her?" I confirmed, trying to swallow down the surge of hurt like bile on the back of my tongue. "Are you serious, Mom? She's just a girl."

"She's the devil," she snapped, "and she's trying to take me down!"

Ah, there it was.

The truth.

She wasn't scared of what Lex would do to me, but her.

I'd always known Mom was selfish, but it was as obvious and unchangeable as the sun or the moon in the sky. I'd never thought to take umbrage with it, never thought about how unfair it was of her to put herself first again and again. We'd moved every few years growing up so she could take new jobs at universities across the country even though it meant making friends was difficult. I learned to cook when I was eight, so I could make dinners for us both when she got home late from work. She never went to my field hockey games even though she liked to brag about my awards, and she forced me to do mother/daughter photo shoots every year so she could add to the collection of faux domestic bliss on the table behind her desk in her office.

I was just a part of her illusion to having it all. Something meant to be seen, not heard like some throwback to children from the eighteen-hundreds or even the fifties.

Well, no fucking more.

"Don't you think Lex has more things to worry about than whatever you think she's after you for? She was attacked on campus, and she had the courage to return. How can you hate her for that?"

Mom opened her mouth to say something, then curled her lips under her teeth to stop herself.

Something ominous churned in my belly.

"Unless...you actually did something to warrant her anger," I murmured.

Lex was filled with rage, I knew that. I thought most of it was directed at Professor Morgan, a little to men who thought they were above consent, and women who judged her for what had happened on Halloween as if it was her fault.

But...I remembered the ugly anger in Mom's voice as she'd spoken about what happened to Lex and her conversation with Professor Morgan. Suddenly, it was all cast in a different light.

Mom had never been a dumb sheep blindly following the lead of others. She didn't believe Morgan hadn't raped Lex.

She knew he had.

And she was trying to cover it up because a scandal at Acheron while she was president would hurt her chances of achieving her dream of being president of Cambridge University.

The pain of the truth arrowed through me so sharply I lost my breath.

"You knew what he'd done," I breathed, tears pooling in my eyes as I stared at the woman who'd given birth to me and realized she was a dangerously selfish creature. "You hushed it up so it wouldn't affect your candidacy at Cambridge."

Mom stared at me with cold eyes. "Don't be ridiculous, Luna."

"Don't fucking gaslight me, Mom."

"Language."

"Fuck your language," I shouted, stalking closer, so enraged I couldn't see straight. "Are you serious right now? Did you know about the others too? About what Jerrod Ericht had done? And the Delta Alpha fraternity that was in the paper this morning?"

She stared at me thin-lipped, hands fisted at her sides.

"You knew," I whispered.

I'd read enough books about heartbreak and listened to enough songs, but I'd never truly known what they meant when they referred to it until then. My heart very honestly felt as if it was about to shatter. The anvil of truth had knocked into it with such force I lost my breath. My hand clamped over my breast as if I could catch the pieces as they started to break off painfully inside me like shards of glass.

"Mom," I whispered. "How could you let this happen?"

"The girls were compensated for what happened to them," she gritted out. "Don't be so dramatic."

"What, so they were given hush money?" My stomach cramped so hard I folded in half over it. "Jesus."

"This stays between us, Luna. I'm your mother, and you owe me your loyalty."

My laughter tasted as bitter as poison on my tongue. "No, no, I don't. You just threatened to kick me out of the house because I wanted to be friends with a girl whose very existence threatens you. Well, guess what, Mom? Lex has already taught me more about integrity and being true to myself than you ever did. So if you want to give me an ultimatum, fine. You just made the choice disgustingly easy. At this point, I'd choose anyone over you."

I turned on my heel to walk away from her, going to the door to the staircase leading to my basement suite.

"If you leave, Luna, you won't be welcomed back," Mom warned me, stalking after me so she could loom in the open doorway, the light at her back making her all black with shadow.

"Okay," I said even though my heart was still breaking off piece by piece, and I just wanted to go to a cool, dark corner and cry. "Bye, Mom."

When she slammed the door on me, I didn't even flinch.

I packed some clothes and toiletries into a suitcase and then, because I couldn't part with them, I put my favorite books into another one.

It was only when I closed the door behind me, laden with suitcases, my book bag, and the remnants of a broken heart for the mother I'd always loved, that I realized I didn't have a single clue where to go now.

I could have gone to Haley's place. She had been my best friend since twelfth grade, and she always had my back. But she lived in a cramped apartment with her sister and her sister's boyfriend. I could have gone to Pierce's, but I was insecure about the news of my bisexuality inevitably reaching his ears. Of course, I'd come out to him already, but I wasn't sure what he would think about my relationship with Lex, and I couldn't bear to be questioned about things I didn't have the answers to.

So I went back to Charity Lane.

Or maybe all of those things were just excuses, and I wanted to go back there. I liked the creaky, character-filled house. I liked the Gorgon sisters with their easy repartee and quirky, sassy kindness.

And I liked Lex most of all.

Still, I hesitated on the landing outside the front door that had a new wreath on it, this one made of little pumpkins because Halloween was just ten days away. I didn't know what Lex would do or say when she opened the door to find me with suitcases and no place to stay.

I wouldn't know until I took another risk in a long lineup of risks for a Sunday and knocked on the door.

So I did.

A moment later, it swung inward to reveal Lex. Her hair was piled on top of her head and secured with a plaid scrunchy, thick curls dangling down her neck and framing her beautiful face. She was wearing the same sweater as this morning, but she'd put on a short velvet black skirt and dark tights. There was a half-eaten fig in one hand and an old copy of Sylvia Plath's *The Bell Jar* still open and raised as if she'd been reading as she walked to answer the door.

She was so achingly lovely, I forgot everything as I drank her in.

"Lux?" she said, cocking her head to the side. "Did you borrow more than my sweater this morning, and I didn't notice?"

I looked dumbly down at my suitcases, and everything surged back into my brain. I swayed a little under the force of it. Lex stepped forward instantly, steadying my elbow with a frown.

"Hey, are you okay?"

I opened my mouth to say something, but a sob burst forth instead.

"Hey, hey," Lex murmured, wrapping me up in a hug that smelled of dark earth and crushed violets. "What happened?"

I just pressed my nose into her throat, into the same place I'd sucked a hickey last night where a tattooed snake kissed her pulse point, and I wept.

Lex held me, murmuring little platitudes into my ear. Eventually, when I shivered as the wind picked up and whipped dead leaves around our feet, she pulled away to unpeel my grip from the suitcase handles so she could drag them inside herself. Once that was done, she pulled me by the hand into the hall and closed the door behind her.

Grace and Effie stood in the hall, watching us with worried eyes, but Lex only shook her head and led me past them up the stairs to her attic bedroom. She had been studying on her messy bed, but she moved everything aside and then pressed my wooden body onto the mattress.

"Okay, can you tell me what happened now?" she asked, sitting beside me to frame my face with her hands.

I bit my lip so hard I drew blood.

She wiped it away with her thumb and sucked it into her mouth.

My heart shivered, and my groin pulsed.

God, I felt bewitched by her.

And knowing that, I felt a little steadier.

I hadn't left my mom because of Lex. I'd left because I'd discovered I was living with a woman I couldn't respect. But Lex had been a part of making me realize that and a surge of warm gratitude washed through me, cleansing away some of the gunk in my heart.

"It's only been like two hours, but I feel it's been two days," I admitted wearily. "I ran into some old friends on the way home, and they confronted me about how you beat up Beckett and about...about our relationship."

She frowned. "We didn't act romantically when I went to get you last night."

"Well, you did beat someone up for groping me."

"He deserved it."

"Oh-kay...so it had nothing to do with me?" I asked, peeking at her through my lashes.

She sighed. "Of course it did. I usually have better control over my temper than that. Seeing you that way with him looming over you...I snapped."

"Because you care about me?" I dared to ask, holding my breath as I searched her face for the answer.

She stared right back at me, gray eyes hooded.

My lungs started to ache, and black spots whirled across my vision, but still, I didn't breathe.

Finally, she sighed and reached for my hand to place it against her breast, over her heart. "I don't have much in me to give anymore, Lux, but yes, I care about you. I wouldn't be able to bear your touch if I didn't, let alone crave it the way I do. I wouldn't be able to show you glimpses of the pain shredding my insides to bits every day if I didn't trust you to be good to me."

"I care about you, too," I said, a little too eager, a little too free, but I didn't care.

She made me feel that way. Giddy with liberty.

"I told them I cared about you, too," I admitted. "I told them they were bullies for how they talked about you, and I told them...I told them I was bi."

Lex's hand flexed over my own. "You didn't owe them that."

"No, but I owe it to myself if that makes sense."

She rubbed a thumb over the back of my hand. "Yes, it does."

"They didn't take it well. Practice later will probably be awkward because I called Flora out on her bigotry, but I'm glad I did it. I've been silent and easygoing my whole life. It felt good to take a stand."

"I'm glad," she said, smiling a little. "I wish I could have seen it. I bet you were magnificent."

"I tried to channel my inner Lex Gorgon."

She laughed, and the sound almost made everything better.

But then I remembered why I was there with suitcases.

"My mom was waiting for me when I got home. The news about last night had already reached her. She knows everything that goes on around campus...I should have known she knew the truth about what happened to you." Tears pooled in my lower lids and started to drip again, one by one down my cheeks. "I just never thought she could be so...so selfish and cruel."

I was so locked into my own sorrow that I didn't really notice the way Lex stiffened.

"She forbade me to see you again. She said you were out to get her like you were some vigilante in a superhero movie trying to take her down." I laughed weakly, but Lex didn't move a muscle.

"She knew, Lex, about Jerrod Ericht and Delta Alpha. She probably knows about half a dozen other incidents on campus, and she's been sitting on them because she's too focused on her fucking career." I shook my head, still horrified by it, still processing. "Anyway, she threatened to toss me out if I didn't agree to stop being your friend, but I left of my own volition. How could I stay in the same house with her knowing what I know now?"

Lex didn't have an answer for me, but I didn't need one. I shifted to face her fully, kneeling on the mattress and threading my fingertips through the sides of her hair.

"Can I stay with you until I get a more permanant situation figured out? I-I have other places I can go, but I want to be here. With you."

Lex swallowed hard, once, twice and then cleared her throat. "If people are already talking, it won't be good for your reputation to stay with me."

"It's a bit late for that. I basically told people I like you. I didn't speak for you, though, so I can still go, and no one will think we're together. Just that I have a crush."

"No." Her hands cupped over mine on her face. "No, I want you to stay. I...well, thank you. No one but my sisters have ever stood up for me before."

I tipped my forehead to rest against hers. "I'm team Lex Gorgon all the way."

She didn't laugh the way I wished she would, but what she gave me was even better. Her kiss was chaste, a soft brush of her lips against my own.

I tightened my hands in her hair, desire sparking in my blood. "I want to fuck you. Can I?"

Last night, Lex had taken the lead, but I wanted to lay her out now and explore her. I'd just cast off so much of the weight holding me down. I wanted the chance to experience this lightness inside me. I wanted the chance to love her without the yoke of my mother's expectations and my reputation around my neck.

I wanted to flex these new muscles and enjoy who I was fighting to become.

Lex hesitated, fear pinching the corners of her mouth.

"I've never been so attracted to anyone in my life," I whispered to her as I placed a kiss on the corner of her full mouth and then another on the hinge of her jaw. "I can't imagine ever getting enough of you."

She moaned lightly and let me slowly press her torso back against the bed. I moved slowly so I didn't spook her because I knew one wrong move would send her sprinting away like a spooked mare. She watched me with wary eyes as I peeled off her tights and underwear and then unzipped her skirt. I left her sweater on because I could see she wasn't wearing anything beneath it, and I wanted to give her some security.

Joy cartwheeled through my chest when she let me place her ankle on my shoulder, spreading her open to my gaze.

God, but her pussy was pretty.

The skin around it was soft and utterly smooth, a dusky gold that felt like silk. I watched as it slowly bloomed, wet and open as I bit her big toe and then sucked kisses up the length of her leg. When I reached those kissing snakes, I traced their forked tongues with my own and then followed the path of their twining bodies up her thigh with my mouth and hands.

By the time I finally reached the apex of her thighs, she was glistening and as fragrant as honeysuckle.

I never would have thought I could find a woman's sex so absolutely arousing, but the sight of Lex splayed open like that, gorgeous and trusting, almost undid me.

I shifted her leg over my shoulder as I lay between her thighs, one hooked over my back so she was forced wide open. I rested my cheek against her groin and used one hand to pull at the top of her sex, exposing her swollen clit from its hood. My mouth watered at the sight, but I teased her with the soft back and forth of my thumb instead of using my tongue.

She writhed, but I pinned her still with the hand on her mound and increased my tempo.

"Luna," she groaned, her hands diving into my hair to hold a little too tight.

My own pussy spasmed, and with a moan of surrender, I bent to taste her.

The tangy-sweet flavor of her exploded across my taste buds, eradicating my control. I sealed my lips around the soft swell of her clit and sucked, abusing it with hard lashes of my tongue.

Lex shouted, back bowing off the bed, hands tugging me even closer to her sex.

I loved to feel her so greedy, to know it was me bringing this woman pleasure.

I could have worshipped her for hours, teasing her mercilessly, but I was too driven by the need to feel her come apart on my tongue to hold out. Two fingers dipped into her grasping entrance, a little more slipping inside her tight hold each time.

"More, more, more," she chanted, bucking against me.

"Goddammit, Luna. Please."

"Just because you asked so nicely," I practically purred, and then I hooked those fingers inside her and pumped hard, hard enough she thrust her head into the mattress and cried out in ecstasy.

"Yes, yes, yes," I encouraged as she tightened around me, and her clit throbbed madly under my tongue. "I want you to come and force me to lick it all up."

That was all it took to finish her. The idea that I wanted her to control me, to dominate me. I'd never loved the idea of power play before, but with Lex, I loved it when she took me with that fired intensity. Even though I was the one making her come, we both knew it was because I wanted to please her, worship her.

Be owned by her.

She broke open, her leg shaking on my shoulder, her pussy clamping so tightly on my fingers it almost hurt. I bent my head and sucked every inch of her clean with a desperation that made me dizzy.

When she was clean of cum but shiny with my spit, Lex dragged me up her body by my hair and sealed my mouth with a ferocious kiss. She raked her teeth over my lower lip, thrust her tongue against my own until I felt like the entire world was spinning around us.

She pulled away, panting against me, and her eyes were so black they sucked me in like a hole through the galaxy. "I want to fill your mouth with me again. My flesh, wet for you, my name aching on your tongue as you beg. I want to be everything you taste and breathe and speak. I want to be the only thing on your mind because you're the only thing on mine, and that's the best fucking gift you could give me. Get on your back, Lux. I'm going to fuck your face now and then after you've made me come, I'm going to make you scream my name."

I groaned loudly, completely uninhibited as I automatically obeyed, rolling to my back. This was different than being obedient to my elders all my life. I was taking my power back in its own way by choosing to submit to Lex. And I did it not only because it made me hotter than anything I'd ever done before but also because I knew she respected me. That she wouldn't want me so keenly if she didn't admire me, too. It was just who she was. She was homosexual and sapiosexual, and it made me feel like a goddess to know I satisfied both cravings in her.

When she climbed onto my face and her fingers gripped the headboard, the view up her curvaceous body was so fine it made my mouth water in anticipation.

"When I come, drink it all up," she ordered, looking down at me with gleaming, dangerous eyes.

I sealed my mouth to her leaking sex and did exactly as she bid.

And later, when I was flat on my back with my legs over her shoulders as she kneeled on the floor and fucked me with her mouth and fingers to three orgasms, each one harder than the last, I knew with a certainty I felt in my bones that I'd made the right choice that day.

Not just to be with Lex, the girl I was perilously close to loving.

But to be *me* for the first time in my life.

CHAPTER NINETEEN

"I pray you do not fall in love with me, For I am falser than vows made in wine."
—Shakespeare, *As You Like it*

Lex

The pain of my own deception grew like an abscess in the wall of my stomach day by day. I could not hide from my false intentions when the woman I'd set out to seduce in order to destroy her mother was now living in my house and sleeping in my bed.

What a strange irony it was to regret exactly what I worked for and wished to happen.

I felt...out of sorts whenever I caught Luna's look of loss in the moments she thought I wasn't watching her. Staring out the kitchen window, she'd cup a mug of coffee in her hand like it would bring her comfort. Gazing into the distance at the library when we were studying as if her mom were calling to her from across campus at a radio frequency only she could hear.

The truth was, I had never felt like a villain before now.

My violence and cruelty were targeted against those who had already made themselves monsters. I could find a perverted kind of righteousness in exacting justice against those who deserved it.

The problem was, Luna didn't deserve this.

Any of it.

Losing her mom in an ultimatum I'd provoked.

Tarnishing her reputation because she'd confessed to being in a relationship with me.

Falling for me when I'd essentially lied to her from the beginning. And she was, falling for me.

I knew because she was dragging me down with her.

I watched as she walked around the European Sculpture exhibition in The Met with her hands behind her back as if she were handcuffing herself from the temptation of feeling the cool marble beneath her fingertips. She was a tactical woman, always brushing her fingers over my skin, toying with my hand while she highlighted a text, rubbing her foot up my leg under the table when we went off campus one night to eat, and leaning against me anytime we sat down or stood together in a lineup.

Even on the train in from Connecticut, she'd claimed the window seat then completely cut herself off from the view by leaning against the wall to drape her legs over my lap. She handed me my copy of *The Bell Jar*, closed her eyes, pulled my left hand between the cage of her own and demanded I read to her.

It stirred me how comfortable she seemed to show me affection in public. Walking down the streets of New York holding her hand felt akin to walking down some kind of red carpet. I felt proud and honored by her.

Which of course, made me feel sick and evil in equal turn.

I was starting to feel like Dr. Jekyll and Mr. Hyde, two definitive sides of me at war with each other. I'd never be able to quell the violent rage inside me without having my vigilante outlet, but it was at elemental odds with the part of me that loved Luna's soft touches and silken kisses. I hadn't been scared since Halloween, because what could be worse than the crimes Morgan had committed on my body? But when Luna looked at me like I hung the moon, a different kind of fear took root in my soul.

A fear that I might survive without the rage. All I had to do was focus on her light in the darkness.

"Hey, grumpy." Her sweet voice cut through my brooding thoughts seconds before I felt her arms wrap around my waist and her lips pressed to the green and black snake on my neck. "What's the matter? It was your idea to come here."

I tilted my head to give her better access to my throat and simultaneously glared at the older man staring at us through the arms of a statue across the hall.

"This one always makes me melancholy," I said, gesturing to the statue I'd been standing in front of for the past five minutes.

It was true, too.

The statue of Perseus holding Medusa's decapitated head.

"Why?"

The sigh that unwound from my lips spilled heavily to the ground. The release felt like a relief. That I could bury some of my story, some of my emotional baggage, in the myth of another woman who was horrifically wronged.

"Do you know much about the myth?" When Luna shook her head, I continued, "Medusa was a beautiful virgin priestess in the goddess Athena's temple. One day, Poseidon took notice of her beauty and decided to take her against her will in the temple. When Athena found them, she punished Medusa by turning her into a monster with snakes for hair and a gaze that turned all men who looked at her to stone."

"That's horrible," Luna breathed, staring at the sculpture with frank horror.

It pleased me to see her so undone by the injustice. I knew she was a soft-hearted woman, full of sympathy for those less fortunate, but I was beginning to understand that there was no hardness in her heart. No space for the anger and revenge that seemed to dominate my own.

Still, I tested her.

"It is. At least Medusa was made into her own weapon of revenge. I like to think she took at least a little pleasure in her curse, turning men who sought her out as a prize into immortalized tributes to their own greed."

"No," Luna said, gazing into the eyes of the decapitated head as if she could reach through centuries and read her original intent. She stepped forward to give in to her natural temptation to touch and brushed her fingers along Medusa's cheek. "I bet she was terribly lonely."

"She had sisters."

"Okay, but she was still stuck. Athena imprisoned her in this body and made it impossible for her to connect with anyone new ever again." She looked over her shoulder at me, and there were tears in her pretty green eyes.

That chasm in my chest yawned open a little wider. My hand pressed to the pain even as I looked away from Luna, unable to stand the agony of seeing the empathy in her gaze.

"Yes, well, life is often unfair."

Luna caught my hand as I went to turn away and tugged me into her front. Her fingers delved into the hair over my ears so she could hold me still and force our gazes to connect.

God, she was pretty.

I let myself wish for a single second that she could be mine.

Not just now at this moment, but forever.

But I hadn't thought beyond my next plan for revenge in so long that I didn't even know what that dream of the future would look like.

"You can brush off what was done to you like it doesn't matter, but it does," she said gently, thumbs brushing over my cheekbones.

"College-aged women are three times as likely to be sexually assaulted. One in three women is raped, and those are just the cases reported. Most women are convinced not to report the crimes against them, or they are too ashamed to do so." I shrugged but felt brittle, like one wrong move would make my fragile bones shatter beneath my skin. "It's not so uncommon."

"Don't use other people's suffering to minimize your own, Lex." Luna's fingers tightened in my hair as she leaned forward to press her forehead to mine. "It's okay to hurt. It's okay to be human."

My lips formed a snarl before I could remind myself she wasn't the enemy. I couldn't convince my body that she wasn't trying to attack me, though, not when my heart started to sprint through my chest.

"You don't know what you're talking about." I wrenched away from her and away from that damned statue, stalking across the room to the headless marble trio of the Graces.

"I could," Luna argued, calling after me. "If you let me."

I was grateful we were mostly alone because I was perilously close to losing my cool.

"Alexandra." My full name in her mouth sounded like a poem. I had to close my eyes against the urge to claim it. "You can share your pain with me."

"It's all I have left," I growled without turning to look at her, my shoulders hunched at my ears, my nails digging deep wells into my palms. "Excuse me if I want to keep something for myself."

"Okay," she said after a long moment. "I just thought it might be a...relief to share the burden."

I turned on her there, my teeth bared, eyes burning in my skull like twin coals. "You couldn't handle it, Lux. Don't you get that? This anger burns in my chest like some eternal torch. This armor I have to wear every second of every day because I can't handle even a single drop of more pain or I'll overflow and drown in my own rage and hurt."

I lunged for her, snapping my teeth at her neck, but she didn't flinch.

"Do you want to be tainted with all this anger?" I demanded. "Do you know how close it comes to crushing my bones to dust beneath my skin?"

She held perfectly still, her throat exposed to my snarling mouth, one hand carefully braced on my hip. I could see the throb of her pulse beneath the pale skin, and my mouth watered with desire. There was something blatantly vampiric about my longing to suck her bright aura inside my hollow shell and allow it to bring me back to life.

"I'd like to help you move beyond it," she said quietly. "I'd like to help you see the future instead of looking backward at the ugly past."

"Oh?" I sneered cruelly. "And what does my future hold that's so worth looking forward to?"

"Me," she said, so quick, so easy that, at first, I thought I'd imagined it. "Maybe a future with me."

It was me who froze then, both horrified and utterly beguiled by the thought.

She shifted slowly as if I was a wild animal she was afraid to startle. Her hands went to my hips, fingertips slipping beneath my sweater vest to press into my warm skin.

And her eyes were as green as freshly watered earth, lush and verdant. I wanted to plant myself in that healthy soil and watch how I could grow.

"You want to be a professor of the classics, right? Well, I've always wanted to go to Cambridge. I visited when I was a girl, and I thought *yes*, this is where I need to be. We could go to grad school there. Live in a little stone cottage with two cats and more books than furniture. I'd wake your lazy bones up in the morning with kisses to your pulse points. Here," she said, pressing a kiss to the snake's flickering tongue over my carotid artery. "Here." Another to my wrist, which she lifted tenderly to her lips. "And while you were still half in a dream, I'd move my kisses to your pussy and make you come on my tongue. You'd go to your classes, and I'd go to mine, but every night we'd come home to each other.

"A simple life, maybe," she breathed against my lips. "But it feels like a dream to me."

And me, I wanted to say but couldn't.

Even the last few days waking up beside this girl with sunset red hair and a smile even while she slept was too much to bear. The idea of more, of *forever*, staked me through the heart and threatened to kill the monster I'd become.

Desperate to end the conversation, I moved to the bare-chested female statue beside us and lifted my hands to her breasts.

"If you wake me up, I'd put you to sleep," I continued her fantasy but perverted it. Stripping away the emotion and cranking up the lust. "I'd start with your sweet breasts."

My hands cupped the statue's chest, my fingers circling the space where her nipples should have been. I watched as Luna's mouth parted on a heavy exhale, and her eyes went dark.

"Just my fingertips until you begged for more. Then I'd lick and suck the swells, love bites like love letters written just here." My hands rubbed over the cool marble. "Only when you were writhing would I finally take your nipple into my mouth. I wouldn't be gentle, Luna. I'd nip and bite and gnaw until you were swollen and red and whining like a greedy girl for more."

"Lex," she whispered, rubbing her thighs together in the little velvet skirt I'd let her borrow because I liked her in my clothes better than I liked wearing them myself.

I didn't stop.

My fingers cupped the statue's breasts, then smoothed down over her hips to frame the hidden apex beneath the marbled folds of fabric.

"Would you beg me for more?" I taunted, watching as Luna chewed at her pink bottom lip, leaving it slick as the slit between her thighs. "Would you ask me nicely?"

"Yes," she agreed. "I'd beg."

I loved her shamelessness. Luna had been with a woman for the first time in her life for all of a few weeks, and she'd totally embraced it like she seemed to embrace everything that came at her. With total enthusiasm, warmth, and a complete lack of reservation.

It was the antithesis of how I operated, which maybe explained why I was so enthralled by her.

"Are you wet for me?" I asked, leaving the statue so I could replace its cool feel with Luna's soft warmth.

Her pupils were blown, so dark in her face like black holes sucking me in. When I carefully wound her long hair around my fist, her lips parted as she started panting.

"Let me check," I murmured, slipping my hand up the inside of her skirt, playing along the line of her thigh-high stockings, the same ones I rolled up her legs that morning, and then finally cupping her sex. The damp heat was obvious against my palm. "Such a dirty girl for me."

"Can we leave now?" she asked, already begging, and I barely had my hand on her. "Please."

"I thought we'd see the Ancient Egyptian exhibition too," I demurred.

She rocked her hips into my hand right there in the middle of The

Metropolitan Art Gallery. "*Please*, Lex."

Triumph sluiced through me, washing away the remnants of clinging bitterness our argument about our futures had stirred in me. For a second, I let myself marvel at the magic of Luna Pallas, before I reminded myself what this thing between us had to be.

Revenge plan B.

And Luna Pallas was only a delightful cog in that wheel.

When all was said and done, she'd be lost to me, but somehow that made more sense than her absurdly wonderful idea of spending forever together.

I left Luna napping in bed after I thoroughly fucked her and forced myself to go about my business instead of indulging in a lazy evening with her.

The moment I descended the stairs, I was glad I'd done so because Rhea and Dahlia were in my front parlor drinking tea with my sisters.

"What's this?" I asked, immediately moving to Rhea, whom I'd been friends with before we'd been assaulted.

She opened her arm to me, her cheeks damp and lips trembling as she hugged me to her side. "Sorry to bother you, Lex."

"You're never a bother," I promised, dropping into a crouch right in front of her instead of taking a chair at the table. Her hands were cold and too thin in my own. "What's up?"

Tears swelled and broke in her lower lashes before cascading down her cheeks. "I know I said it would be enough, but it's not. I thought... I mean it felt good—*feels* good—to know Jerrod was publicly humiliated and exposed as a rapist, even if the school didn't do anything about it, but I still feel this..." She ripped her hand out of mine to curl it into a fist over her chest, mute with the weight of emotion on the back of her tongue.

"Chasm?" I filled in, feeling a phantom pain in my own brutalized chest.

She nodded, tears flinging off her jaw.

I looked over at Dahlia, one of the girls who had been assaulted and filmed by the Delta Alpha fraternity. "And you?"

"It's the same," she whispered brokenly.

Effie offered her hand across the tabletop, and Dahlia took it like a lifeline.

"I'm working on changing things around Acheron, but it takes time," I admitted bitterly.

My sense of helplessness was kindling for my voracious rage. It ate at the feeling until my skin was ablaze.

"I know. I don't mean to sound ungrateful," Rhea protested, taking my hands again, a little too tightly in her earnestness. "You've done so much for me. I don't think I would have had the courage to do anything about Jerrod myself."

"You focus on your healing, okay? I'll worry about stopping Jerrod and his ilk."

"It's just, sitting on my hands doesn't feel right either," Dahlia interjected. "I have all this energy inside me, and without a place to go, it just beats up my insides."

"We were thinking maybe we could help?" Rhea asked, and she was so pretty, I didn't doubt she usually got her way.

Happily, I was so enchanted by Luna, it was easy enough to stick to my guns. "I don't want you in any more danger, let alone punished for taking action against these guys. My sisters and I know what we're doing."

"How?" Dahlia had the balls to ask, looking at my sisters sitting mutely around the table, their bold personalities under wraps to give room for these two healing hearts.

I looked at Effie, who shivered slightly before answering. "My birth father was unwell. He attacked our home when we were just kids and took me away with him. The police found me two weeks later, but...well, it left scars both literal and metaphorical. Our mother taught us to be strong and capable, not just in mind but in body."

"We've been enrolled in one martial arts class or another since we were seven," Gracie told her with a little smile. "We know how to protect ourselves."

Rhea looked at them and then down into my eyes, searching for something. "I don't know how to protect myself."

I opened my mouth to say I'd keep her safe but stopped before I could speak. Was that even a promise I could keep? Maybe to Rhea and Dahlia, but what about the four other girls assaulted by the Delta Alphas or Taya, who was also assaulted by Jerrod? What about the girls who texted HELP to our burner phones? Could I stand sentry for every single female on Acheron's immense campus?

The simple answer was *no*.

I was only human, however much I wished to be a god.

The extent of my rage could take down a grown man, but could it take down every predator in the vicinity of this institution? And what happened when I graduated next year? What of those girls I'd made promises to so they could sleep easier at night? Would their nightmares return?

"No, you don't," I agreed, squeezing her hand. "Do you want to know how?"

Rhea shuddered, but Dahlia answered immediately, the word a single, angry bark. "Yes."

"Yes," Rhea echoed.

"Okay." I sucked in a deep breath to brace myself. Could I take this on? Between classes, Luna, and my plans for President Pallas and Professor Morgan, did I have more in me to give?

I remembered Agatha saying to me once, when I first started living with them, that the true sign of strength is not how hard you can punch but how much you can carry. I wondered at the endurance of my heart and decided I wouldn't know if I didn't try.

And this was worth taking on.

"I'll teach you," I promised, and that felt better, teaching them to fish so they could eat for a lifetime instead of giving them fish so they could eat for a day.

"Us too," Juno said instantly, overlapping Gracie's words of, "Hell yeah."

Effie grinned, slow and wicked. "Whoever said the Man Eater Crew had to be a group of four?"

CHAPTER TWENTY

"How can you hide from what never goes away?"
— Heraclitus

Luna

I found the first snakes when I was reading on a bench in the commons a week after I'd moved into Charity Lane. My body was sprawled over the damp wood even though it was really too cold to linger outside anymore. Lex's secondhand copy of Sylvia Plath's *The Bell Jar* dangled from my fingers, and my gaze was fixed on the massive oak tree towering above me. I was procrastinating by thinking of different words for the variety of colored leaves still clinging to dark branches: *russet, ochre, honeyed, golden, tangerine*. My lexicon was running low when my gaze skirted down the trunk and snagged on a carving in the wet wood.

Two snakes, twisted together in a figure-eight pattern, each eating its own tail.

It was instantly memorable. The message stark. Eternally eating its own tail, forever making the same mistakes but surviving. Life and death. Balance.

I swung off the bench, dog-earing my place in the book. The wood was rough and cool beneath my fingers as I traced the symbol. Beneath it in small, precise numbers was carved 4357.

It was a curiosity, but I had too much going on to dwell on it. Living with the Gorgons was interesting, to say the least. They stayed up late studying or playing cards or reenacting scenes from their favorite plays dressed up in silly clothes they kept in a trunk in the hall closet. The night before, we'd done the fight scene from *Romeo and Juliet*, Gracie a cutting Mercutio and Lex a righteous Romeo. I'd been Tybalt, dressed in a frilly, old-fashioned shirt and riding boots that were two sizes too big with a tree branch from the oak tree outside as my sword. I'd laughed so hard my stomach still hurt.

Nights with Lex were spent without much sleep, but I managed, caffeinated by the sheer pleasure of exploring this side of me and a new side of her. When it was just us in bed, she laughed sometimes and told me stories about her time with Agatha and the girls in Richmond before they'd all decided to apply to the same university. Every day I spent with her, I fell deeper and deeper, and I wondered when I would hit the end or if I'd just keep falling. If that was what it was like to be in love, to feel like your heart was expanding every moment you spent with the object of your affection.

My mom had left fourteen messages on my phone, but I hadn't returned any of them. I intended to, at some point, but I still needed time to process. I just couldn't figure out how to reconcile the woman who'd raised me to be a strong, independent feminist with the monster who was okay with hushing up sex crimes on campus.

And then there was the team. Flora had formed her own little posse who glared at me each practice and said nasty, derogatory things about my sexuality and gender every time I got too close to them. Mostly, I didn't care, but our disunity led to us losing our first game of the season on Friday night, and that wasn't okay. I had to figure out what to do about it, but it was probably the lowest item on my priority list.

Mostly because I'd started paying attention in Professor Morgan's class.

He had two clear favorites, a pretty brunette by the name of Felicity who seemed to be a loner on campus, and an Indian girl, Rebecca, who I knew from a few of my lit classes. I got closer to them as they got closer to him.

Felicity was a loner because she suffered from severe social anxiety and even when she agreed to go for coffee with me, she asked if we could do it at her house, away from other people. She was sweet and shy, blushing when I asked about Professor Morgan. They had tea twice a week in his office, and didn't I think he was dreamy?

Rebecca was harder to get to know. She had a group of good friends, and she worked two part-time jobs to make ends meet because she was an orphan and paid her own way through school. I met her at the Penny, where she worked the night shift three times a week. Between serving other customers, she told me that Professor Morgan kind of gave her the creeps. Still, he was talking about offering her a space as his research assistant next year, and she was desperate for the money and status that came with it.

At first, I couldn't find a connection between them.

If he was targeting girls, why Lex, Felicity, and Rebecca—all different ethnicities and personality types?

But then, I remembered what he'd told my mother that evening when I'd eavesdropped outside his office.

Lex is no one.

No one.

All three girls came from very humble backgrounds. If he did sexually harass them, Felicity didn't have the social currency or bravery to fight back, and Rebecca quite clearly couldn't afford to blow up her life with a sex scandal when she was already working so hard to get ahead in life. Lex, too, fit that mold. A foster child there on the grace of scholarship money without any prominent friends or family connections to cause a fuss.

Rebecca was the reason I started to put the dots together about that snake symbol too.

"Don't worry about me," she'd told me. "I know he's a bit of a creep, but I carry pepper spray with me everywhere, and I have the number if I ever need to text it."

"What number?" I'd asked.

She'd slid a torn piece of paper across the table to me. "Have it, I can grab one somewhere around campus, but I already have the number programmed in my phone, anyway."

It was the same four-digit code I'd seen on the tree in the quad. 4357.

"Where did you get this?"

She frowned at me, waving a hand as she moved away to another table. "They're all over the place if you look around."

She was right. There were posters on bulletin boards in the hallways, in the Walking Stick Café, and the Penny. I found a chalk drawing of the snake ouroboros on the sidewalk by the lake front and a spray painting of it on the side of a dumpster next to the cafeteria.

When I looked up the number online, I learned the number spelled out HELP.

I was still thinking everything over, trying to uncover the mystery because it felt somehow important when I got home from the library that Monday night and the house was empty.

Effie was on the student council, so she often had late-night meetings, and Gracie was part of the theater troupe on campus, so I wasn't surprised she was gone, too. But Juno and Lex were usually home by then, studying or reading or debating current events.

Something at the back of my mind squirmed, but it was too slippery to catch in my grip.

I was too restless to study, so I paced the living room and then the dining room and kitchen. When I grew bored of that, I made my way into the library on the main floor. I didn't spend any time in there because it was mostly Juno's domain, the big desk taken up by computer monitors and technical equipment that didn't make any sense to me because I was old-school enough to like longhand notes and typewriters.

I spun in the big red leather chair behind the desk and kicked my feet up on the table, accidentally dislodging the computer mouse.

The screen came awake with a little whirr, and the black screen snapped to a different image behind a passcode prompt.

I stared at it, jaw slack, open mouthed.

The desktop wallpaper depicted two snakes twined into an infinity eating their own tails.

The same symbol I'd found around campus.

Without letting myself think too hard about it, I dug my phone out of my pocket and looked up the article in the school paper about Jerrod Ericht and then the Delta Alpha fraternity. In the photo of Jerrod with the poster stapled to his chest, I could just make out a small tangled symbol next to the Man Eaters sign off.

There was no mention of it at the fraternity house where twelve members had been found two weeks ago tied up in their basement with illegal sex tapes they'd made of assaulting other students, but I knew it had been there somewhere.

It was the Man Eater Crew's calling card.

That was how they knew who to target in their vigilante crusade.

I sat back in the chair, breathing heavily even though it didn't seem to bring any air into my lungs.

I hadn't given much thought to the Man Eater Crew. I had enough going on in my life, but now that I'd turned my mind to it, an anchor of fear sank deep in my gut.

What kind of people would think it was okay to take the law and justice into their own hands this way?

Who was brave and angry enough to take on grown men and bring them to their knees?

I swallowed the bile on the back of my tongue and closed my eyes.

There was only one answer I could think of and she had the school motto painted above her bed in looping script, "*Veritatis et acquitatis tenax.*" Persevering in truth and justice.

I sat there numbly for a very long time. Long enough to puzzle things together until I got a sense of the whole picture.

And that picture didn't look good for Lex.

Or for us.

It was two in the morning by the time the front door opened and the clatter of shoes announced the Gorgon sisters' arrival home.

Juno found me first, startling when she came through the doorway to find me sitting in her chair in the dark.

"Hey, Lunar Eclipse," she said slowly, sensing the heaviness of my mood. "What're you doing in here?"

"Have you heard of the Man Eater Crew?" I asked woodenly.

She blinked.

I noticed she was wearing all black, and something was protruding over her shoulder where it was obviously strapped to her back. It looked like the handle of a baseball bat.

That anchor of dread in my gut dragged my heart down along with it.

"Where is Lex, Juno?" I asked quietly.

As if summoned, she appeared behind Juno. If she was surprised I was awake or that I'd taken up vigil in Juno's office, she didn't look it. Instead, she merely pulled her sister back by the shoulder into the hall and then stepped around her into the office and shut the door. It was dark, the only light spilling over me from the computer monitor and lighting the room with a dull, neon glow.

"What is it, Luna?" she asked softly, but it wasn't a gentle tone. More like a dangerous lure goading me into a trap.

"Are you and your sisters the Man Eater Crew?"

She didn't say a word or move a single inch. I wasn't even sure she breathed.

It took me a couple of minutes to realize she wasn't going to answer, and something in my sunken heart began to quake.

"I don't know why I didn't think about it until now." I laughed at myself, the sound hollow, almost coughed out of my throat. "Maybe I was too much under your spell to really notice. How can you do this, Lex? You're...you're terrorizing people."

"Terrorizing?" she said in that same quiet, frightening tone. "You mean like Morgan terrorized me? Like Jerrod terrorized Rhea and your friend Taya? Like the Delta Alpha boys terrorized five different girls over the past few years and fucking *taped* it?"

"You could have turned them in," I said, my stomach churning so hard I thought I'd be sick all over Juno's computer. "You don't have to be a monster to take down monsters!"

"You don't know anything about it."

"I know enough," I argued. "I sleep beside you every night. You think I'm not awake when you cry out and wake up screaming? You think just because I haven't been violated, I can't imagine the horror of it and the way it must haunt a person? I *can see* the way it haunts you, Lex."

"Yes, well, now I'm haunting them." Her smile was a wide, dim white wedge in the darkness like the Cheshire cat's floating, menacing grin.

"Why did you come back?" I asked even though I knew the answer like it was written in blood on the walls.

"I refused to be buried at the scene of the crime. I had to come back."

"You had to come back to get revenge," I surmised, feeling numb and robotic like my body didn't even exist. "To get vengeance on everyone who let you down that day."

Lex blinked at me, that slow, reptilian blink that freaked everyone out but me.

"Don't you see?" I begged, desperate for her to see beyond the red-tinged glasses of her own hatred to the painful truth of my words. "You're still letting him control you. I know he hurt you. I know what he did was...was inconceivably evil. But you cannot heal by causing him or others like him pain, Lex. That's not how it works."

"How do you know that?" she asked, not mean, just chewed up with her own anger and hurt and crazed bitterness. "The only time I feel peace is when they're suffering."

"Numbness isn't peace."

"It's not numbness." She snapped her teeth at me, once, twice, like a rabid wolf. "It's fucking joy. It's filling the emptiness in my chest with white-hot rage. It's being drunk on the rightness of seeing them feel even a slim margin of the pain they've meted out. It's being high on the fumes of their bewildered fear. Seeing how the mighty have fallen and at *my* feet, the feet of a victim, the feet of someone they held in so much contempt."

She stepped forward, and I could see the whites around her eyes. "The man we exposed tonight put his girfriend in the hospital, Luna. In the fucking hospital because he decided he needed to fuck her up to get his rocks off. You think that's okay?"

"There are other ways," I said, but at the moment, faced with her like this, a maenad drunk on the wine and revelry of revenge, I wasn't sure what those would be. A part of me even felt that primal drumbeat luring me into the dark, into a place where women could revel naked and fearsome around a fire, powerful and free. Dionysus' maenads had been coined "the raving ones," but were they raving, or were they just unafraid? "What you're doing...it's illegal, Lex. Not to mention morally wrong."

"There is a warrior lying dormant in every woman," Lex argued, hands and spittle flying through the air, hair kicked back like writhing serpents. "A defense mechanism born over centuries of abuse and oppression. Triggered like *that*." She clapped an inch away from my face. "You can't know what it's like to shed the soft skin, that sheep's cloth, and become your true self. Both a woman and a wolf. Something with teeth and more aggression than society allows women to have.

"You can't know what it's like!" She almost roared the words, pounding at her chest. "You have to pass through fire, be crumbled to ash, and if you survive, only then can you be reborn with the teeth and claws you need to move on. Do you deny me the right to my defenses after everything? Do you hold me in contempt for my rage when rage is the only thing that gets me up in the morning? Would you refuse my need for vengeance when I was not the only one to suffer his disgusting attentions?"

"The police," I tried, but my voice was weak, warbling under the waterfall of tears falling down my face. "The university. The law."

"They ignore us!" she screamed, the scream of a banshee, of a woman wailing for her lost soul. "Would you have us be alone and suffering? If we are wolves, should we not become a pack? Something to be feared by others, to give comfort to our own?"

"I don't want you to be alone," I whispered, anguished by her anguish.

It was then I knew how much I loved her. Because her pain, so acute, brutalized my own soul as if it were her own.

Because her heart had become more precious than mine.

I wanted to offer her salvation like some kind of priest, but the truth was, she didn't want it. So what was I supposed to do?

"Not this," she hissed, and I realized I had asked that last question aloud.

"'The rarer action is in virtue than in vengeance,'" I quoted softly because other people's words had always helped me before and no one was more eloquent than Shakespeare.

"So you want me to sit on my hands when your mother and this whole damn institution does nothing about the crimes going on beneath their very noses?"

"No, not that. But there are other ways. Start a support group, set up a chaperone system for girls who go out alone at night, submit an article to the paper. 'An eye for an eye will only make the whole world blind.'" I quoted Gandhi because when in doubt, who wouldn't listen to his wisdom?

Apparently, Lex.

Her entire body seemed coiled tight as a snake about to strike, the clack of her nails on the countertop akin to the rattle of a serpent.

"You want to quote to me? 'Being against evil doesn't make you good.'" She spat Hemingway's words like venom. "You have to take action, Luna. It's not enough to stand by and let these things happen. Willful ignorance is not bliss. It's cowardice."

I opened my mouth to say something, though I wasn't sure what. I'd started out being on the right side of the issue, but I was increasingly feeling like the villain here.

"You want to know who's a coward?" She sneered, and there was none of the Lex I knew in her face, only a predatory monster. She planted her hands on the desk and leaned close. "Your mother."

I reared back. "I know she—"

"Why hasn't any of this blown up larger than *The Delphi*, Luna?" she asked bitterly. "A group of vigilantes on a college campus exposing men for their sins? That's salacious stuff. Newsworthy. Why is Jerrod still enrolled here? Why was *I* punished when Professor Morgan was the one to take so much from me?"

"No," I said because I knew where this was going, and I wanted to stop it.

Lex barreled on. "Your mother. She knows everything that happens on this campus. Everything. If you think she doesn't hush this shit up, you're a fucking idiot."

I flinched at her words but tried to swallow the hurt. "And you think beating up young men will change that?"

A quivering silence like the faint rumble of the earth heralding a catastrophic quake.

Foreboding swept through me, a sudden chill.

"Lex..."

She bared her teeth at me like a cornered animal. "She deserves everything coming to her."

"What are you going to do?" And then, my stomach cramping so hard I fought the urge to gag, I whispered, "What have you done?"

She canted her chin into the air just like she'd done that day in the quad when I'd noticed her, like she was daring anyone to come at her. Now, she was daring me.

"I'm taking away everything she loves," she said, her voice dead, dead, dead. "Acheron..."

No, no, no, I thought madly, knowing I was about to be hit by a freight train but unable to move out of the way.

"And you."

"And me." The air punched out of my body. My bones cracked and disintegrated on impact, and I felt like I was bleeding out all over the red chair, all over the ground. I looked down at my chest in a daze, startled to find I was physically whole.

It was just my insides crumbling to dust.

I didn't have any more words for her. What could I say?

Why did you have to go so far?

How could you have drawn me into this awful game of revenge when I did nothing to no one?

What was I supposed to do with this betrayal when I *loved* her? When she'd changed me, and I had no idea how to go back to what I'd been before?

I just sat there quietly falling to pieces, and Lex just watched me.

"Okay," I said finally, long after the computer had gone dark and plunged us into absolute blackness. "Okay, then."

I got up, surprised my bones would hold me, and carefully walked around the desk on the far side of Lex so I didn't have to get closer than necessary.

"Lux—" she started.

I was at the door, pulling it open, hall light flooding over my face like salvation. I held up a trembling hand to stop her, waited a beat to make sure I wouldn't start crying, and then moved out into the hall.

I closed the door softly behind me.

No one bothered me when I went to Lex's attic room, the room I'd come to love so much. I got to say goodbye to Chrysaor, who slithered to the glass to stare at me morosely as I collected my things.

I got to leave without seeing the Gorgon sisters or the monster that led them.

When I looked back at the shadowed Victorian house from the end of the walkway, I realized that Charity Lane was haunted.

By the ghosts of the Gorgon sisters' pasts, whom they allowed to possess them.

I shivered as shadows moved behind the curtains, and I got the hell out of there before I was crying too hard to see where I was going.

CHAPTER TWENTY-ONE

"But surely for everything you love, you have to pay some price."
—*Agatha Christie*

Luna

Pierce let me crash on his couch. He offered me the bed, but I didn't want the memories of us between the sheets. Not when all I had left of Lex were memories I wanted to cherish, untainted by what came before. She'd done me so wrong, broken my heart intentionally like a hammer to Spode china. Yet I loved her still. I loved her for showing me the path back to a version of myself I wanted to be.

Brave, bold, free.

Pierce didn't get it. He was angry for me, forever my champion, and he wanted to storm over to Lex's house and give her a piece of his mind. Given what I knew now of Lex, her anger, and her abilities, I didn't think that was a good idea.

In any case, I was distracted.

Not just by heartbreak but also by a burgeoning sense of injustice stirring in my own gut like twisting snakes.

I couldn't stop thinking about her bitter, anguished words.

Both a woman and a wolf. Something with teeth and more aggression than society allows women to have.

Would you have us be alone and suffering? If we are wolves, should we not become a pack? Something to be feared by others, to give comfort to our own?

You have to take action, Luna. It's not enough to stand by and let these things happen.

For four days after our confrontation and breakup, I stewed in the residue of her anger and righteousness. Through some kind of osmosis, I found myself increasingly unable to stand my own inaction.

Lex had chosen anger and cruelty in her pursuit of truth and justice.

But that wasn't the only option.

I could do something without becoming like her.

Like them.

Like my mother.

My stomach problems got so bad that I was swallowing Tums like they were candy and losing my breakfast almost as soon as I finished it.

But that stopped the fifth morning when I woke up in Pierce's apartment and decided, finally, to do something.

It started with a phone call to my mom's assistant, who was happy to tell me Mina would be busy all evening with a faculty dinner in town. I went to my classes, ate lunch alone in the cafeteria, blind to the whispers about me and the fact that none of my field hockey girls deigned to sit beside me, and then, when the sun fell to a ribbon of gold on the horizon, I set off to do something courageous—heroic—for the first time in my life.

It was the week before Halloween, but a wintry wind cut through campus, stirring up little whirlwinds of dried leaves and cutting through layers of wool and cotton until even my bones seemed to shiver. I huddled up in my tweed overcoat and cut through the quad with purpose, ignoring the looks from Flora and her lackeys as I prowled by where they congregated, gossiping together.

"Pervert," she spat at me, and her friends twittered.

It rolled off my back, barely felt.

Loving Lex, touching her body and enjoying the way we had brought each other pleasure wasn't perversion. It was something like worship, something holy that I felt all the way through to my spirit. I felt bad for Flora that she didn't understand that.

Clearly, she'd never been in love.

Clearly, something about my own easy acceptance of this aspect of myself threatened her.

Part of me, the same part that crushed on Draco Malfoy and loved Lex Gorgon, wanted to go to her then and offer help. Offer kindness and unconditional acceptance to see how my old friend might grow and evolve under the sunshine-like alchemy of love in the human heart.

But I had bigger things to worry about.

I stood outside my old house for a long time after I arrived. It was a stately home befitting the president of Acheron, meant to hold faculty parties and visiting professors with a steeply gabled roof and huge mullioned windows under stone arches. I wanted to burn it to the ground.

The viciousness of the thought took me by surprise. I was a pacifist, a harmony-seeker, and a peacekeeper. Not the vengeful demon I'd thought could love me.

But I couldn't shake the tempting image. The house burning, plumes of smoke and ash clogging the bitter cold air, reducing this status symbol of my mother's to cinders.

She didn't deserve it. Lex was right.

If she was really hushing up scandals on campus to better her own career, she deserved to be stopped and stripped of her glory.

Unease stirred in my heart as I thought about what Lex might have planned for her, though. Mina Pallas was a lot of things, but she would always be my mother, and I would always be the kind of daughter who instinctively thought to protect her. I just had to find a way to bring her misdeeds into the open and keep her safe from the Gorgon sisters' wrath.

She hadn't changed the locks, and she wasn't home. Why would she think her own daughter would turn against her? After years of obedience, she probably assumed my latest, uncharacteristic act of rebellion would be as short-lived as the Anglo-Zanzibar War. I wondered if she waited each night at the kitchen table for me to come home with my tail between my legs, begging for absolution and forgiveness for defying her.

Well, I'd come home, but it wasn't for forgiveness.

I knew my way around her home office, the code to her computer, and it didn't take me long to find the emails.

Mr. & Mrs. Ericht. Professor Dylan Morgan. Chief Inspector Daniels. Paul Chambers, Dean of Student Life RE: Delta Alpha.

All the receipts I'd ever need on this innocuous hard drive.

I copied them all to a USB drive, put it in a spare envelope, and wrote the name and address carefully on the front. The literature student in me couldn't resist finding a copy of a book I knew Mom housed on one of her shelves. I ripped a page from the volume and scribbled a quick note there before adding it to the envelope.

I sucked in a deep, shaky breath as I locked up and walked to the corner post office box to drop it inside. If I did this, it would end the most important thing in my mother's life.

Was it worth it?

What allegiance did I owe to a woman who'd seduced me just to twist the knife in the back of her enemy?

None, I decided, but that didn't mean I didn't owe allegiance to the women who'd been wronged by Mom's ambition.

It didn't mean I was exempt from doing the right thing.

The envelope dropped into the open mouth of the metal box and fell to the bottom with a hollow clang.

"Hey, Luna."

I spun around, hand to my thumping heart, to see Beckett standing there, flanked by two friends from the team. I couldn't remember either of their names because Pierce had never liked them much, preferring to limit his interaction with Beckett when he could, and certainly with his lackeys. The trio wore matching looks of something like excited violence.

I recognized the expression from Lex's own face when she'd spoken about her acts as a Man Eater.

"Oh, hey, Beckett. You startled me."

"Yeah?" He stepped forward, crowding me against the mailbox by leaning to brace a hand on either side of me. "You should be careful. There's a violent group going around campus beating people up."

My laughter was forced, a yip like a distressed animal cornered by a predator. "I think I should be okay. It seems like they're only targeting men. I'm sorry, by the way, about what happened to you. Lex, um, she was just concerned."

Even as I apologized, I hated myself for giving in to my ingrained need to say sorry for the way *he* had treated me. Was it biological or learned behavior that made women feel guilty so often for actions taken against them, especially when they weren't deserved?

A sneer curled his lip like the edge of a villain's mustache. "You should be sorry." He gestured to his bruised face. "I'll be out for most of the season with a fucking concussion because of your attack-dog bitch."

"She's not mine," I argued with a little smile, trying to charm him even knowing I'd fail. Lex was the seducer and the warrior. I was just good girl, bland girl Luna Pallas.

"Sure seems like she's yours." He leered at me, eyes lingering over the exposed wedge of my chest in my blouse and open coat. "Does she make you come harder than Pierce? That why you left him for the slut? I bet she's good with her mouth. Maybe I'll have to put that to the test."

"Don't." The word whipped across my tongue with such force, Beckett actually reared back a little, a minuscule flinch that filled me with power. I dug deep, trying to find that wolf Lex had spoken about buried in the heart of every woman. "Don't threaten her and don't threaten me. Step back, Beckett. I have friends waiting for me at the library, and they're going to wonder where I am."

He laughed and didn't move. His breath wafted over my face, minty clean like he'd popped a mint because he'd known we would be this close.

"What friends?" he taunted. "Even Luna Pallas isn't popular enough to withstand the taint of hanging out with Lex Gorgon." He leaned even closer, tongue touching the corner of my mouth before I could throw my head back and away. "Has she taught you how to please a man? Maybe I should take you for a spin. See why Pierce put up with you for so fucking long."

"Back off, Beckett," I warned, hands fisting together, anger thrashing like waves against the breakwater I'd reinforced in my gut. I was precariously close to losing what calm remained, and I wasn't naïve enough to think I could take on Beckett and two guys from the hockey team without being seriously injured. "I'm not dating Pierce anymore, but we're still friends. He will be furious with you if you hurt me."

"Yeah, he would be furious if you were hurt," he repeated slowly, something dark flaring in his eyes. Fear skittered through me like bugs fleeing the coming apocalypse. "Absolutely fucking furious."

He laughed, a mean, grating sound that scraped across my nerves and made me break out into goose bumps.

"So we'll make it seem like Lex did it," he decided, wickedly triumphant as he slammed a hand into the center of my chest, pinning me against the metal box.

"She'd never hurt me," I argued, trying to wrench out of his hold by kicking at his shins.

He held fast, a happy smile on his face. "No one will believe that. Lex Gorgon is a fucking pariah on campus. Everyone hates her already. I'm just going to give them one more reason."

I struggled hard, pushing against him with all my might so I could twist out from his grip. It worked, miraculously, and I was able to bring my knee up to hit him in the nuts. His breath escaped him in a rush, and I used the opportunity to *run*.

A lifetime of field hockey had made me fast, but unfortunately, the two hockey players were fast too.

I yelled as one of them tackled me from behind, trapping my arms at my sides so when I fell to the sidewalk, I did it fully on my face. Pain exploded like shrapnel through my head, and even though I fought to stay aware, blackness surged up to meet me, and I passed out.

CHAPTER TWENTY-TWO

"We are healed of a suffering only by experiencing it to the full."
— *Marcel Proust*

Lex

I was lying in the Ancient Greek section of the library between row D-E reading *The Oresteia* in the same position Luna had found me in weeks ago when I'd first set the stage to seduce her.

The idea seemed so laughable now. She was the one who had seduced me in the end. No, not seduced. *Captivated.* I was so in her thrall that even days after she'd stormed out of my house, I couldn't stop thinking about her. I'd walk into a room and catch the phantom scent of her. Check my phone way too often to see if she'd texted. Study the selfie we'd taken in bed one morning, her smiling face pressed to mine, my mouth softer than I'd seen it in months, my eyes heavy-lidded with residual pleasure from the orgasms we'd traded when we woke. She had one hand pressed to my opposite cheek, holding me to her like I was... like I was precious.

I hadn't been precious to anyone like that ever.

My sisters and Agatha loved me, but this was different.

This was a woman who'd wanted to put me first.

And I'd fucked it all away.

My sisters tried to talk to me about it, but I refused. What words could I find to explain the chaos of pain sweeping through me at all hours of the day? How I felt hollow again, brittle and on the cusp of shattering. The combined weight of the assault and breaking my own heart—Luna's pure fucking heart—was *this* close to dragging me down to a place I knew in my bones I'd never recover from.

So to slow the inevitable fall into a dangerous depression, I threw myself into my causes.

On Tuesday, I hosted my first self-defense lesson at the college gym. Rhea and Dahlia had invited friends. Taya had shown up, much to my surprise, with a few friends from the field hockey team, including Luna's best friend, Haley, who watched me intently the entire session, and my sisters had invited even more. Forty women all packed into the exercise room, willing and eager to learn how to defend themselves from predators.

For that hour, and that hour alone, I'd felt free of the sick anchor of despair in my gut.

They trusted me to help them. To teach them. To protect them.

Even though I caught fear and some disgust in a couple of their expressions, it didn't matter. I didn't need them to *like* me. I just needed them to be safe so they never had to experience what I had.

My revenge plans for Mina Pallas were coming along. I'd persuaded Professor Diana Strong, the only faculty member to stand up for me after I was assaulted, to write a signed statement testifying to the fact Mina had hushed up two sexual scandals on campus that she knew of.

One of which involved Professor Morgan and an ex-student Juno had finally tracked down.

Tessie Baker lived in Oregon now and worked at a women's shelter in Portland. When I reached out, she ignored my calls and emails until I finally divulged I'd been assaulted by him too and just wanted justice served.

She'd called me back then, and she was on standby to help however she could.

Another wolf to join my pack.

As for Professor Morgan, I'd approached one of his current "favorites" Rebecca, who agreed to collect as much evidence as she could about his activities without putting herself in too much danger.

Both of them would lose their jobs.

For Mina Pallas, maybe that was enough.

But not for Dylan Morgan.

He'd taken my goodness and corrupted it all to dark, dangerous desires. Desires for payback that extended far beyond the end of his good reputation. From what I'd been able to cobble together, he'd been assaulting his students since he was a student himself, TAing during his Master's program at Ducat University.

He deserved pain.

Horror.

Madness.

Fear.

All the things he'd made so many women feel under his attack.

I'd avoided him on campus for so long because I knew if I saw him, I'd be unable to resist. I'd storm up to him, take his handsome face between my hands, and snap his fucking neck.

And that wouldn't do.

No, I wasn't going down for his death. Not the death of a monster.

After all, in the Greek mythology I loved so well, no one was ever punished for killing the monster. They were rewarded. Perseus with Medusa, Jason with the sea monster, Hercules and the Hydra.

My reward was to end Morgan and live on, free and unencumbered by the threat of him.

So breaking his neck would never do, and I knew exactly what would.

I just had to be patient.

Everything was going to plan. After months of scheming, of training and yearning for exactly these outcomes, I should have been on top of the world.

Instead, I felt like I was being buried alive.

All because of a girl with pretty rose gold hair and eyes the color of Slytherin green.

I dropped my book open on top of my face to smother myself in the comforting scent of parchment and dragged in a deep, shuddery breath.

"Lex."

I tipped my head back, the book sliding off my nose and falling with a thud to the ground. Effie stood in the aisle, and even viewed upside down, I could tell something was wrong.

So wrong.

I swiveled to my feet in an instant, fists already curling closed to fight.

"What happened?" I asked, but my heart was already dropping into my belly, sizzling in the acid buildup.

"Luna," she said in two broken syllables, and just like that I was punched out of my body, all physical sensation forgotten, just a shell of a woman. "Someone attacked her."

I didn't stop to ask who, to wonder where, to plan to fucking *end* whoever had dared to lay their hands on my beautiful, pure Luna.

The only thought in my head was her.

Getting to her.

Saving her.

"Where is she?" I said, but my voice was wrong.

Dead.

Because whatever was struggling to stay alive inside me would perish the moment I discovered she was anything but okay.

"At Phoebus General Hospital."

I was running before I could even think about it, surging by my sister, book and bags forgotten on the floor between D-E in the Ancient Greek section.

She didn't try to stop me. She was my sister, so she wouldn't have tried. Instead, she tugged my hand and ran beside me all the way downstairs to the parking lot where Grace and Juno already waited in the idling car.

I could have cried then, but I didn't because my gratitude was so sharp it felt like another knife pinned through my heart.

I didn't remember the trip to the hospital, and I was getting out of the car before Gracie had even come to a full stop. The admin nurse at the front desk directed me to a waiting room on the fourth floor, but no one would give me any information beyond that. I stalked back and forth across the linoleum, boots thumping, pulse racing, my brain empty of everything but the thought of Luna like the moon hung in a dark night.

At one point I was aware of Juno moving to walk in tandem with me, a metronome beat beside me.

"What happened?" I asked, the question falling from my lips like a gasp.

"She was walking near President Pallas's house. A neighbor said they came across her lying in the street, beaten badly." Juno hesitated when a whimper leaked through my mouth. "Lex, word on campus is *you* did it. After she broke up with you."

Shock barreled into me so hard, I missed a step and fell forward into a wall. Juno caught me by the wrist and tugged me into her arms, holding me loose but close.

"What?" The word punched out of my chest.

I curled my fingers tight around Juno's biceps, but she didn't flinch, and her gaze was all warmth, all tenderness as she repeated, "People are saying you beat her, Lex."

"I..."

The idea seemed so absurd, so impossible that it took me a moment of struggling to realize how plausible it might sound to people. Lex Gorgon, the outsider, the slut, the angry lesbian. Was it so much of a stretch to think someone like the woman they thought I was would beat her own lover?

Was it even much of a stretch to think about the anger I had inside, constantly on vigilant lockdown like a high-security prison, exploding out of me as violence?

No, it wasn't.

No one knew the truth about my feelings for Luna because I'd never deigned to show them how much she meant to me.

How she meant *everything* to me.

How she was the best part of every day, of every single part of me, and I would no sooner hurt a single hair on her head than I would cut out my very own heart.

Yet I had hurt her.

Irrevocably, unabashedly.

I'd set out to hurt her and then fallen in love with her. It didn't get much more Shakespearean than that, but for the first time in my life, I loathed the comparison.

I loathed myself.

In all my anger and my rage, I'd hurt the only person who was blameless in this entire fucking mess.

And now she was lying in a bed somewhere in this maze of a hospital, probably alone and hurt and scared.

Possibly because of me.

A high-keening wail pierced through my throat and into the air.

"It's okay," Juno said, the prettiest lie. "We'll get it sorted out."

As if summoned by karma, Mina Pallas appeared over her shoulder flanked by two familiar policemen.

I turned to stone in Juno's arms.

"Alexandra Gorgon," Mina greeted silkily as she sauntered toward me in her silk blend trousers and designer blouse, heels clicking like snapping teeth. "How dare you show your face here after what you did to my daughter?"

"I would never—" I paused to choke back a sob, forcing myself to stand tall and firm even though my insides were collapsing. "I would never harm Luna nor did I."

"You're capable of anything," Mina said, waving her hand in dismissal. "That's why these nice officers are here, to take you into the station for questioning." She stepped forward, forcing Juno to let me go and step away. Only then did she get close enough to whisper in my ear. "I told you not to fuck with me, Lex. Let this be a lesson you stew on in prison on aggravated assault charges."

When she pulled away to smile almost serenely into my face, triumphant in the knowledge that she'd won, I felt...bewildered.

"What kind of woman are you that you cheer for another woman's downfall?" I whispered, falling apart but genuinely curious. "How can you perpetuate violence against women and sleep at night?"

"I take a sleeping pill," she said flippantly, tossing her hair as she turned so it flicked me in the face.

The slumbering rage in me flickered under the debris of despair in my chest, tempted to grab her by that hair and sink my fist into her perfectly groomed face. But that would have been playing into her hand.

That would have been proving to her and all the others on campus—including Luna—that I was just a vessel of violence and vengeance without a conscience or morals.

So I stood there, mute and dumb, as the cops approached and took me away for questioning. Away from Luna.

Every step away from her felt like a razor blade to the heart she'd regrown in my chest, but I refused to cry because I didn't deserve to cave into self-pity when I'd inflicted the pain on myself.

CHAPTER TWENTY-THREE

"It is better to conquer yourself than to win a thousand battles. Then the victory is yours. It cannot be taken from you, not by angels or by demons, heaven or hell."

—Buddha

Lex

"Hi," I said, "my name is Lex."

"Hello, Lex," everyone echoed, a ritual we'd taken from other help group meetings and applied to our own.

It had been three days since Mina Pallas had the police drag me out of the hospital for questioning and forbade me from visiting Luna.

Three days of agony.

But if the breakup with Luna had taught me anything, it was not to stew.

If I let the emotions overtake me...well, it felt like I'd die, and I wasn't sure I meant that metaphorically.

The first thing I did after the police were forced to cut me loose due to lack of evidence was organize the first meeting of Acheron's new Women's Sexual Assault Support. The group was sponsored by Professor Diana Strong, and it was surprisingly, and heart-breakingly, well attended. About twenty girls sat around the circle in blue plastic chairs, all of them staring at me with none of the usual anger or fear. They all looked...hopeful.

Hopeful because they believed hearing from the most infamous sexual assault survivor on campus might help them work through their own trauma.

Truth be told, I didn't want to talk about it.

Of course, I didn't.

I never did.

To speak about the act of destruction Morgan had doled out to me was to open along the seams of tender scars and reopen the wounds. It was to be blooded and flayed in front of other people, in front of strangers. My track record reputationally wasn't stellar, to say the least, and it made bile rise to the back of my throat to have to prostrate myself like this before these twenty women.

There were only two reasons I was doing it.

One, Rhea and Dahlia had helped me realize that violence against our attackers just wasn't enough. Like anything, healing needed a multipronged approach. So along with the self-defense classes my sisters and I held once a week in the gym, we'd also decided on this.

A group.

A safe place for survivors to come together and mourn what had been taken from them. To celebrate each other for our little steps forward beyond the trauma that threatened to drown us in darkness. To be together instead of alone. A pack of women wolves unafraid to show their teeth.

And two, I did it for and because of Luna.

She'd been right, as much as I was loathe to admit it, when she said my overwhelming fixation on vengeance had left me in some kind of thrall to my abusers and my trauma. How would I feel when all was said and done, justice served cold and mean to everyone who deserved it? Empty. Because even though I'd come back to Acheron, risen from the ashes of who I'd used to be and reformed myself as something stronger, crueler, I'd done so based entirely on the principle of revenge. Who would I be without it?

A vessel without fuel stalled on the side of the road of my life.

So I was here, standing in front of twenty people eager to hear my story.

Rhea was there, and Dahlia, Taya, and some of the other girls from the Delta Alpha attacks. A few I didn't know at all, my sisters, Professor Diana smiling supportively, and finally, Bryn.

All women who could understand some of the seething mess of darkness in my chest chasm.

"On Halloween last year," I started, clenching my fists so tightly my nails cut crescent moons into my palms. The pain helped to ground me. "I was assaulted by a man I thought I could trust..."

Telling my story for the first time, start to end with only a few gasping pauses when I felt like I was drowning, wasn't just hard.

It was excruciating.

I carved the words out of my own scarred flesh and offered them to the group like a blood sacrifice.

I couldn't look at any of them as I spoke, instead fixating on a poster of the school production of Shakespeare's *The Merchant of Venice*. Under other circumstances, I might have laughed seeing it there, but as it was, I couldn't have dreamt of a better focal point.

When I was done, there was one pure moment of absolute quiet. Not silence; there were still the sounds of thighs rubbing, bottoms shifting, someone picking at their nails and another sucking in a heavy breath. But quiet, like I'd dropped a bomb in the middle of the room and everyone was dead in the aftermath.

293

But then, a single whisper.

"Thank you, Lex."

I kept staring at the poster, and I didn't recognize the voice.

Then another. "Thank you, Lex."

And another and another until the whole room was filled with the echo of gratitude.

Finally, I wrenched my eyes from the scales drawn on the poster and looked around the room at the faces of the women who were thanking me for telling them a horror story.

Many of them were crying, either triggered by my words or empathizing with them. One girl was nodding like she didn't even realize she was doing it, a bobbing head of emphasis, and another was almost vibrating with intensity, her eyes locked on mine like I was her touchstone.

And then there were my sisters.

Gracie was staring at me already, and the moment my gaze touched hers, she mouthed, *You're kick-ass.*

Effie pressed a hand to her heart, saying, *I love you.*

Juno was the one who started clapping.

And then I was crying, great gasping sobs that hurt my chest, but I still managed to gasp, "Okay, thank you, everyone. Who wants to go next?"

I was walking home that night when my crimes caught up to me. Uncharacteristically, I wasn't paying as much attention to my surroundings as I should have been. I'd spent the last few hours in Mathieson Library writing a paper for my Tragedies course, which of course made me think of Luna. She hadn't been in class the last three days, but I heard through the grapevine that she'd been discharged from the hospital with a broken nose, a concussion, and a sprained hand. She was staying with her ex-boyfriend, Pierce Argent, and I tried not to let the knowledge burn a hole in the lining of my gut.

As if conjured by my thoughts, the big hockey player appeared from behind a tree as I walked down a narrow lane behind Piedmont Hall to get home. He was an affable-looking guy, blond and wholesome like a Midwestern farm boy, but with the perfect features of someone who might try to make it on the big screen. I'd never seen him around campus with anything other than a smile. It was one of the reasons I hated the idea of Luna with him so much. Because it made so much sense for them to be together. Two lovely, kind-hearted smiling blonds like a couple out of a fucking J.Crew ad.

Only, Pierce Argent wasn't smiling now.

And he wasn't alone.

His kind—popular kids, jocks, douchebags, take your pick—were never without their entourage.

The only one I recognized was Beckett, the one who'd had his hand up Luna's shirt when she was passed out at that party. Dark satisfaction moved through my veins like the warmth from rich wine when I saw the fading bruises on his face. It was only the last year of searching for signs of threat and violence that alerted me to the bruising around the knuckles on his good right hand. I wondered idly who he'd gotten in a fight with. He sneered at me over Pierce's shoulder.

I raised a brow and stopped walking, casually adjusting my book bag on the edge of my shoulder so it would be easy to drop if I needed to fight. There was a can of bear spray in the inside pocket, and the silver rings I wore at the base of four knuckles on my right hand made wonderful makeshift brass knuckles. Fear skittered up my spine, but just enough to bring clarity.

I wasn't the same trusting girl I had been last year, and I knew how to fucking defend myself. It would be hard, one against the four strapping hockey guys facing me down, but anger made for explosive fuel.

Only Pierce looked angry enough to set even me on the back foot.

"Lex Gorgon," he said, the words grinding out between his teeth, square jaw clenched so hard I could see the tendons pop even in the low light of the antique street lamps.

"Pierce Argent," I said, adopting a little gesture like I was tipping my hat to him. "To what do I owe the pleasure of this late evening chat?"

He seemed startled by my ease. I doubted he was used to a woman being unfazed by his presence, especially when he was weaponizing his size.

Six foot two or three to my five foot eight was a significant difference.

But I didn't care.

I was just closer to his tender bits.

"You destroyed her," he said finally, gathering the tattered edges of his anger to him like a shroud as he stepped forward. He wasn't so pretty with the sneer on his lips. "First, you fucked her, then you fucked her reputation, and to top it all off, you fuck her up? She has a concussion and a goddamn broken nose."

I continued to stare at him implacably. I wasn't going to turn myself inside out to show him the wounds and old scars. He didn't deserve to know anything about me, let alone the extent of my pain.

It only made him angrier, which wasn't a surprise. In my experience, men were always annoyed when women didn't give them an emotional response, which was ironic, because they also often complained when we did.

"Are you a goddamn monster?" he seethed, stepping closer again so only two yards were between us. "Do you even have a heart? Luna is a good person. How could you do that to her?"

Of course, I hadn't beaten her, but a part of me ached as his words connected because I had hurt her nonetheless. I'd used her shamelessly to bring pain to her mother, and I hadn't even apologized for it. It didn't matter that I couldn't get close enough to her to try. I should've rented a damn airplane to fly the words in the sky (even though that was so far out of my budget, it wasn't funny).

Maybe a little part of me felt I deserved his aggression, the promise of violence like the scent of sun-baked metal on the air. I dragged it deeply into my lungs and watched as he took another step forward.

"I didn't touch a hair on her beautiful head," I said finally, and the words throbbed in tandem with my heartbeat. "But I did hurt her. You're right. She didn't deserve it."

"You're damn fucking right," Pierce agreed, looming over me, his huge shoulders blocking out the light behind him so his face was all in shadow.

It threw me back to that night in the woods when I'd come to as Morgan hauled me over his back into the woods behind his office. When he dropped me unceremoniously to the ground, he'd only been a dark impression in the nighttime forest. Pierce was like that now, and it made me tremble despite myself.

I recognized the coiling of energy in his body as he collected his strength to lash out at me, but I didn't move.

I was paralyzed with old fear and this persistent need to take punishment for the way I'd hurt Luna. Wasn't he her champion? Shouldn't I pay a price the way I was forcing Mina Pallas and Jerrod Ericht and the Delta Alpha frat and Professor fucking Morgan to pay one?

Oh.

His hand was at my throat.

I'd thought he would punch me, but instead, he squeezed and lifted, dragging me to my tiptoes. I hung limply, fighting the urge to defend myself as adrenaline flooded my bloodstream.

Take it. You deserve it.

The voice in my head sounded exactly like Professor Morgan's.

Air squeezed out of my throat like the remnants of toothpaste forced from a tube and soon, black spots danced across my vision, eating segments of Pierce Argent's pretty shadowed face. It felt like he would decapitate me with those big male hands, popping my head off my body as simple as *that*, a cork from a bottle.

It was then panic kicked in. He could hurt me in retribution for Luna, but I wouldn't allow him to take my consciousness from me, not when I was surrounded by unknown men intent on harm. I couldn't live through another sexual assault. My soul was already scraped to the bone, and I knew it would disintegrate entirely in another acid bath of pain and shame.

I lifted my shaking hands to his on my throat and pressed in. Tears as hot as fresh brewed tea scalded my cheeks. I imagined the scent of jasmine in my nose and wanted to gag.

I braced myself to fight, ready to kick out, but the strangest thing happened.

He dropped me.

One second, he was holding me half suspended, and the next, I was falling to my knees coughing, his body retreating a few steps back in my periphery.

"What the fuck, Pierce?" someone demanded, his anger sharp and indignant. "You barely fucked the bitch up."

A long sigh. "I can't beat up a girl, Beckett."

"She fucking deserves it! She's a goddamn *bitch*."

"Yeah," Pierce agreed. "But so are you and you don't see me beating you up, do you?"

"Fuck you," he spat, and through my watery, unfocused gaze, I saw another figure moving toward me. "I'll do it myself, you pussy."

Pussy.

Like having one was weak.

When pussies delivered babies. When women dealt with pain every single month that wracked their wombs and their minds with dark, sharp hurts. When the clitoris had four times the nerve endings than the head of a cock.

Pussy, I thought, and that old anger, subdued by the shame of what I'd done to Luna, flexed and uncoiled, hissing in my belly. I imagined the snakes tattooed on my skin writhing into wakefulness, ready to spring.

I cupped my hands over my face as if couldn't get up, as if I was as weak as this fucking asshole thought all women were.

When he got close enough, steps heavy and fast with momentum, I reared up like the strike of a cobra, darting inside his reach, using the entire weight of my body springing up from the ground to land an uppercut to the underside of his square chin.

Pain burst through my knuckles at the massive impact of the hit, but it transmuted to fierce, vibrating triumph a moment later as I watched the big bully sway on his feet. His eyes were unfocused, mouth slack and dumb. I pushed into his chest with a single finger and grinned when he fell straight back, landing on the grass beside the path with a heavy thud.

Pierce and his two other buddies stared at me with slack-jawed shock.

One instinctively moved forward, probably to defend his now-out-cold buddy.

But before he could, there was a loud *whoop* of noise.

And then another.

And another.

Coming from the shadows between buildings, from behind trees.

A moment later, dark shapes appeared, running down the path toward us on either side.

I rocked to my toes, hands loose fists at my sides, prepared for anything.

What a shock it was to realize *I* wasn't the one under attack.

Black-clad bodies of women materialized in the low light as they surged around the men. A flash of fishnet-covered thigh. A swish of a leather skirt. The gleam of a metal baseball bat as it descended and hovered threateningly by the head of Pierce Argent.

They were dressed like the Man Eaters, but I would have recognized my sisters anywhere, even in black ski masks and war paint.

These weren't them.

"Are you okay?" one of them asked me, staring at me through uneven holes cut in the fabric of a balaclava.

The others waited, in position to attack, but restrained like attack dogs at the end of their chained leashes.

I nodded, a little dumbstruck. "I'm fine."

My voice was threadbare from the strangling, but it seemed to be enough to pacify their leader. She stalked up to Pierce, clearly reading that he was in charge, and got in his face, made tall enough to do so by the heeled shit kickers on her feet.

"I expected more of Pierce Argent," she hissed. "Keep your dogs on a leash and let the rest of your buddies know we're patrolling campus now. It won't be so easy to catch someone unaware and vulnerable anymore."

Pierce swallowed thickly and dragged a hand through his hair so it stuck up like a little boy's. He looked young and weary, a kid past his bedtime.

"I'm sorry," he said to me reluctantly, eyes flashing to me and then to the ground. "The guys riled me up, and I was already pissed off with you, but that's no excuse. I shouldn't have put a hand on you."

I lifted my chin in the air and stared at him for a moment before I conceded, "I understand your anger. What I did to Luna wasn't right, and neither was what you did to me. I think we can call it even."

He pursed his lips like he wanted to say more, then hunched his shoulders, thrust his hands in his pockets, and jerked his head at the two quiet friends beside him.

"What about Beckett?" one of them had the guts to ask.

Pierce snorted. "Leave him."

And they did, walking through the narrow space the warrior women made for them and then disappearing down the lane and around Piedmont Hall.

As soon as they were gone, the leader turned to me, and after a moment of consideration, she pulled off her mask.

Dahlia's smile gleamed like a knife's edge in the light.

"Hey, girl," she said, chipper and giddy. "You sure you're good?"

I blinked at her. "What the hell is this?"

Another woman took off her pink balaclava and grinned at me too. "We thought we could help."

I blinked again and wondered if the seconds without oxygen had affected my reality.

Dahlia laughed lightly and moved forward to take my hand in her own. She swung it back and forth between us, like two kids on a playground. "We wanted to make a difference like the Gorgon sisters have. I mean, we know we're not at the point where we can like find the monster in the dark as it were. But we can patrol campus. We can make girls feel safe after dark."

Another girl moved closer, and I realized it was Rhea, all done up in black face paint. "Juno set us up with some burner phones, and we're making new posters. If people want a chaperone home, they can text, and whoever is available can escort them."

I wasn't breathing right.

Pierce had done something to my throat, permanently damaging my airway because I could not get enough oxygen into my lungs.

"Lex?" Rhea asked, concern crumpling her fierce joy. "Are you okay? Should we take you to the hospital?"

I shook my head so hard it hurt, but it helped to clear some of the fog.

"Why?" I asked even though it was oversimplified.

Why hadn't I thought of that?

Why did they decide on this plan of action?

Why were they so brave and good?

Dahlia squeezed my hand and cocked her head earnestly, like she couldn't understand how I didn't see it.

"What do you mean?" she asked. "We did it because of you."

"I mean, yeah," Rhea agreed. "If you can come back to your crime scene and protect other girls from what happened to you, so should we, right?"

This was what I had wanted without ever being able to articulate it. For all the lonely, traumatized women who bore scars to come together to heal, yes, but also to protect each other. A pack of female wolves on the prowl.

And they'd done this because they were inspired by *me*?

Lex Gorgon.

A nobody and then a slut, a bitch, a fucking monster.

How could someone like me have inspired such a beautiful, empowering movement?

Tears pricked the backs of my eyes, and for the first time in so long I couldn't even remember the last time, they stemmed from happiness and awe.

"Thank you," I told them as the rest of the girls crowded around me. *Thank you for being better than me and doing right by us all.*

They all collapsed into happy chatter, energized by the adrenaline of their confrontation with the hockey players. They pet me, touched me, bouncing on their toes and talking over each other. I listened a little, but really, I tried to catch my breath and absorb the magnitude of love I felt surging through me. Love for them, but also, for the first time in a long time, a little love for myself too.

And all I wanted to do in the wake of this massive moment was go to Luna and thank her.

If I could stand down Pierce, inspire sisterhood in traumatized women, and come back to the setting of my nightmares, couldn't I find the courage to ask for forgiveness too? Couldn't I find the courage to make myself vulnerable enough to love someone, really love them with all of my scared heart and broken soul?

I found that I could, and I knew exactly the first step I had to take if I had a hope of winning back the pure heart of Luna Pallas.

CHAPTER TWENTY-FOUR

"In order to be effective truth must penetrate like an arrow — and that is likely to hurt."
— Wei Wu Wei

Lex

The first step in winning back the heart of Luna Pallas was contacting Bryn.

"Are you sure?" Her face had been an odd flux of concern and excitement. It made me like her even more, to know that despite her own desire to see my story shared, she didn't want me to hurt.

She obviously didn't get that I was used to living with pain.

I met her mother, the famous Quinn Harper, that very night at a quaint but expensive restaurant in town. She was just as impressive as I'd imagined, yet something in her air put me at ease. This was a woman who took her job seriously, who would do justice to my story because she wanted to do justice for women everywhere. This was someone I could trust as much as I ever trusted anyone.

As much as I should have trusted Luna.

Four days later, I was on my way to meet Quinn to read over her preliminary draft of the article when I decided to stop at our mailbox because the arm was lifted on its side. I'd applied for early admission at Cambridge for a MPhil in Classics, and I was waiting with bated breath for the letter that would seal my fate.

That wasn't what I found in the metal box.

My fingers curled around a rectangular envelope, and when I pulled it into the light, I instantly recognized the loose, looping script of Luna Pallas.

Alexandra Gorgon, it was addressed with our Charity Lane information beneath it.

I tore the paper open with my teeth, and a USB drive fell into my palm along with a scrap of paper torn out of a book. It was the title page of a retelling of Medusa from a collection of mythology I recognized by Marios Christou.

And scribbled on it in that flowery handwriting was a note from the lover I'd betrayed.

Lex,

"Veritatis et acquitatis tenax."

Persevering in truth and justice.

I know you've taken Acheron's motto to heart in your crusade against the men who threaten women on campus. I know you think it's admirable and just, and maybe it is. But it's a Band-Aid over a bullet hole. If you want to stop the problem, cut it off at the source. This should help your cause, and maybe, it'll help heal your heart. I think it's a good one buried beneath all the hate.

Luna

My fingers cramped around the page, tearing one corner. Carefully, fingers trembling, I smoothed it out on my tights-clad thigh before folding it carefully into a square and tucking it in my pocket.

Luna's goodness, even and especially in the face of my own selfish fury, made my heart ache and throb in my chest. I felt like the Grinch must have, the goodness of others fertilizing his fallow heart until it grew three sizes. I rubbed at the pain as I walked to meet Quinn, but I relished it too.

Because I was healing, and it had more to do with Luna and her unflappable example of kindness than it did with the beatings I'd handed down to vile men on campus.

Although, it did have a little to do with that too.

When Quinn inserted the drive in her computer, I knew Luna had torn out a section of her own heart in order to heal mine.

She'd turned in her own mother.

The scores of emails not only condemned Mina Pallas for obstructing justice but they also implicated Professor Morgan.

"This is it," Quinn said, excitement ripe in her cultured voice. "Mina Pallas exchanged bribes, for fuck's sake! This changes everything. It's the justice you and the other women deserve."

And it was.

Written right there in black and white.

Combined with testimony from the Delta Alpha victims, Taya, Rhea, and even Professor Strong, this article was the iceberg we needed to take down the entire *Titanic*.

So why was I sitting there in the quaint pub feeling hollow as a reed?

"Where did you get this information?" Quinn asked, clicking through emails, the blue light of the screen giving her smooth skin a sickly cast.

"My—" I choked off what I was going to say because Luna wasn't my girlfriend. Had she ever been? Whatever we were to each other, it was over now. "A friend."

Quinn side-eyed me. "A friend close to the president, obviously."

I inclined my head, my nails clicking against the side of my mug of

Earl Grey.

She sat back in her chair to study me properly. "You know, we should call a press conference for the morning I publish the article, Lex. This will blow up in Acheron's face. A scandal the likes of the 'Varsity Blues' admissions scandal and the sex scandal at Harvard a few years ago. Only this one also involves a group of vengeful women led by a girl in an actual snake mask…" She laughed, but it was a bitter little hiccup. "Hell, they'll probably make it into a Hollywood blockbuster starring Margot Robbie."

I winced. "I'll be glad for the publicity, but only because things need to change. Acheron is a dream to so many women. It shouldn't turn into a nightmare when they set foot on campus. The story doesn't need to be sensationalized. It's bad enough as it is."

"Hey," she soothed, reaching over to pat my hand and rolling with it gracefully when I instinctively pulled it out of reach. "I understand, Lex. This is real life. This is journalism. I promise I take this very seriously."

I nodded because too many things were in my throat to speak, like a badly clogged drain.

Quinn had Bryn's sensitive gaze but a thin, expressive mouth. She studied me, and her mouth wobbled like a child's hand-drawn line. "You've lost a lot to this place. You'll feel better when we've taken some of it back."

I nodded again because what could I say?

My victory against the nightmares that haunted me was looming on the horizon and the only thing I could focus on was Luna. Because the truth was, the light of victory seemed dim compared to the light she'd brought into my life.

"Are you ready for this?" Quinn asked, a little sharp, a general reminding her soldier to be ready for war.

I sucked in a deep breath, curled my hand around Luna's folded note in my blazer pocket, and nodded. "I'm ready."

Dawn poured across Acheron's autumnal campus like skimmed milk, the light pale and thin with the coming winter, the sun a silvered icon in the cloudy sky. The air was cold enough to sear through my lungs and plume in the air from my warm mouth as I walked through the empty quad on my way to Hippios House. The grass crunched with frost beneath my loafers, and the soft drizzle of rain limned my hair and tweed blazer in fuzzy wet. It was pathetic fallacy, the mimicry of the afternoon I'd first connected with Professor Morgan on this very path when I'd dropped my books, and he'd deigned to pick them up.

A shiver climbed my spine, painful as ice picks against each vertebra.

My sisters had wanted to go with me, at least as far as the wooden door to the warm hall, but I'd forced them to stay away.

The hero in the myths I loved so much always completed the final mission alone, and today was the day I was wrapping up all the loose ends of my past so I could finally face my future.

The door creaked as I pushed it open and hot air rushed out to embrace me. It smelled of damp stone and coffee grounds, the early-bird professors caffeinating themselves as they began morning preparations for classes. Professor Morgan had always been an early riser—in his office when it was still dark and quiet outside. It had surprised me back then, but it didn't now. Predators were usually creatures of the night.

His door was closed when I stopped before it, but I could see the stripe of light glowing at its base, and the sickening fragrance of jasmine tea seeped from beneath it. I fought the urge to gag, pressing a firm hand against my stomach as I sucked in a deep breath. The newspaper rustled under my arm as I adjusted my stance, shoulders back, chin canted high. I wasn't religious, so I couldn't pray for strength, but I believed in history and mythology and all the strong women of the past. I channeled from them then: Joan of Arc, Cleopatra, Artemis, Harriet Tubman, Marsha P. Johnson, Ruth Bader Ginsburg. All the women who'd faced their fears and championed their causes and been examples to every woman ever after. I was just a girl, not worthy of immortalization, not without her flaws. But this was my crusade, and I was going to bring it all to a crashing close.

I knocked on the door in time with my heart against my rib cage, and when his voice called out to enter, I thought for one wild second that I might die right then and there of fright.

Don't go in there, my sanity screamed. *Run, run, run.*

But I wouldn't, because if I ran, someone else would be victim to Professor Morgan, and that was blood I felt on my hands, tacky and warm.

So I turned the cold handle and pushed into the heart of my nightmares.

The office was completely unchanged.

The palatial wood desk was littered in papers and books, a steaming mug of that jasmine tea perched precariously on an uneven stack of texts about Homer. The same velvet chair, decompressed by many bottoms sitting in its center, and the same carpet where my mug had fallen to the floor. The acrid taste of that spiked tea bloomed on the back of my tongue and I almost gagged again.

Please, I begged myself, *make it through this without a panic attack.*

I thought of Luna, the taste of her sweet mouth over mine and the fragrance of all that sunset gold hair, and it calmed me enough to look at the professor behind the desk.

He was still handsome. What a dangerous illusion. Dark hair waving away from his broad forehead, wide shoulders encased in one of the blazers he liked with the clichéd suede elbow patches, tanned throat exposed in the open collar of his Oxford shirt. He looked at me as if I was a monster looming in his doorway, snarling mouth dripping foam, hands bloodied and clawed.

It made a genuine smile curl my lips like scissors to a ribbon's end.

He was quick to blank his expression, but that momentary flash of terror was enough to buoy me. He'd known I was coming for him, and the idea of him living with that venomous anticipation made me hungry for more.

"Hello, Dylan," I greeted, pleased with the slick ease of my voice. "How are you?"

He blinked, his gaze somewhere beside my head as if he thought I could turn him to stone with my gaze. "What are you doing here, Lex?"

"Oh, did you think I wouldn't visit?" I mocked, moving forward to take that seat, *my seat*, as I had many times before. "You used to love when I stopped in for tea."

Every inch of his body was coiled with tension. I watched as he forced his stiff fingers to clasp in an uneasy approximation of casualness on his desktop.

"Why are you here at Acheron?" he amended. "You're not wanted here. You must know that."

"Oh, I don't know about all that," I disagreed. "I know President Pallas doesn't like me much anymore. And there's you, of course."

"And the rest of the students who know you for the slut you are," he added, viciousness edging into his tone. He was remembering himself. His maleness and power. A professor and a man faced with a female student who had no control over him.

Yes, the snakes hissed in my belly, *relax. No matter what, we're coming for you.*

"We both know I was a virgin when you raped me." The words fell flat between us, used bullet casings without any punch.

Morgan's face twisted with a sneer before he could curb it. "Rape implies you didn't want it. I know you wanted me. You *needed* me."

"I needed a friend," I agreed, surprised my ribs hadn't collapsed under the hammering of my heart. My palms were so slick with sweat, they left handprints on the fabric on my skirt. "I needed a mentor. I didn't need what you did to me and neither did Tessie Baker."

Surprise broke open across his face, and I grinned at him, feral as I closed in on my prey.

"Oh yes, I know about Tessie. I know you lost your old job because of rumors of misconduct with students. I know you used your pull with Mina Pallas to get tenure here. I know so much about you, Dylan. How you take your coffee in the morning, what time you get into your car to drive to work, the girls you're grooming—Rebecca and Felicity—the safe deposit box you rent at the bank, and the gun you keep in a safe in your bedroom closet."

He was breathing heavier but holding still as a deer who knows a wolf is somewhere downwind of him. He wanted to flee but didn't know how without inciting a chase.

"I know everything about you," I repeated, then took the copy of *The New York Times* out from under my damp armpit, uncoiled it, and tossed it on the desk. The headline stared up at him in bold typeface. *Sexual Misconduct at the Heart of Acheron U.* "And now, so does everyone else."

He snapped the paper up, cruel fingers ripping the edge of the fine newsprint as he devoured the short introduction to the article before he flipped to the full article and read that. I watched with voracious greediness as his skin blanched and his jaw tightened, muscles popping into relief.

Professor Dylan Morgan, I knew the article read, *was accused of sexually assaulting a third-year undergraduate student, Alexandra Gorgon. Instead of properly investigating the potential crime, the president of Acheron University, Mina Pallas, placed Alexandra on academic probation for two full semesters. The student in question was only reinstated due to pressure from her lawyer. This is one of many hushed-up sexual scandals that resulted in frustrated students taking matters into their own hands. A vigilante group, masked women known as the Man Eater Crew, began to patrol campus and expose supposed sexual assaults to public scrutiny. Still, the university failed to act.*

It went on to list more details about the other sexual assault cases, about illustrious Professor Dylan Morgan's shameful history, and the email exchanges between Mina Pallas, the Acheron Chief of Police, and wealthy alum who paid off their children's bad acts.

In truth, I had the whole thing memorized.

So I knew exactly which words were running through his head as horror, fear, and anger—*so much anger*—played out over my enemy's face.

Finally, he crumpled the newspaper into a ball, the loud crinkle of parchment and smack of his big hands coming together the only noise in the room other than his harsh breath.

"You fucking bitch," he growled, slamming the paper to the table as he lurched out of his chair to loom over his desk. His eyes were as black as they were that night he'd drugged me, taken me, beaten me, and stolen so much from me. Nearly everything.

Fear burst like a firework display in my chest. The metal tang of adrenaline coated my tongue and teeth. My blood pumped so hard I thought it might burst from beneath my skin.

But somehow, I stayed in my chair.

It was the only way to get some of the poison in this abscessed wound out of my system for good. I had to absorb the fear like a lance, the pain and the horror of it, so I could purge it all here in this room of my nightmares and hopefully, leave the majority of it behind me.

"You think going to the papers is going to do anything?" he continued, all bared teeth and angry flushed cheeks. He wanted to murder me. I could see it in every angle and plane of his big body. If he could have gotten away with it right there and then, he would have snapped my neck. "You think anyone will believe a little no one from nowhere with a bad reputation?"

"You gave me that bad reputation." I didn't recognize my voice. It was cold, carved from the ice and stone my body had alchemized into after his assault. "Nothing you say will change the fact that you did this to me. To Tessie. To yourself. I'm blameless here."

It felt good to say that.

Blameless.

The word that never seemed to be directed to me. As if we were polar opposite sides of two magnets that could never meet.

I was flawed. I had made mistakes. But nothing in my life had made me responsible for what Dylan Morgan did to me. Not my good looks, not the way I dressed, not the fact that I'd even befriended him.

He was the monster.

So why had he *never* been punished as one?

"You think what I did to you then was so bad?" he asked, seething and boiling with anger. He rounded the desk faster than a blink, and suddenly, he was caging me in that fucking velvet chair, his body all around me. Bile rose in my throat, and I thought I would vomit into his face. It would have served him right, but I couldn't allow myself to show any of the weakness surging inside me.

I refused to let his perception of me as weak and meek become a reality.

I would be brave because I deserved justice.

I could be brave because I finally knew how much love I had at my back. My sisters, Agatha, the girls in the group, and the girls in the new Man Eater Patrol Crew.

The love of Luna Pallas, even and especially when I didn't deserve it.

So I could do this, look into Morgan's cold, furious face, a god in this world of academia, whereas I was a mere mortal, a peasant. I could look into his face with this dynamic, and I could fucking *smile*.

Because nothing he said would change the acts I'd taken and the ways I'd been changed because of what he did.

"What I'm going to do to you for speaking of it will be so much worse," he taunted, and there was actual delight in his expression, like the idea of violating me again, breaking me apart until I died, was a fantasy of his. "You stupid cunt. You could have just walked away and lived a normal life. Instead, I'm going to ruin your future."

"Too late," I said, and thank God or whatever force was out there that my voice was steady. I could smell the jasmine on his breath, and I wanted to cry. "I ruined yours first. You can't hide from this, Morgan. It's public now, what you did, and you'll have to pay for it."

"Men like me don't pay for shit," he goaded, and then his hand was on my throat.

My neck was still sore from Pierce's attack, so the contact instantly shot pain from the roots of my hair to the ends of my toes. My vision darkened, narrowed, and I thought I might pass out from the fear.

But then there was a firm knock on the door.

A *rap, rap, rap* that echoed the wild pounding of my heart.

I sucked in as much breath as I could when Morgan tightened his fingers. "Today," I gasped. "They do."

I curled my hands into his over my throat, nails digging so deeply I could feel the skin *pop* and warm blood pool against my flesh.

"Get off me," I breathed.

His fingers tightened.

Another knock. "Professor Morgan? Open the door."

Panic etched itself under the lines of angry strain on his once handsome face. "You cunt," he repeated, like calling me names would fix anything.

I wrenched his hand off my throat, leveraging my entire weight with my back against the chair to peel his fingers off.

"This isn't even the end," I said, voice threadbare but victorious. "Losing your job and your reputation isn't enough. What you did to me will haunt you like it's haunted me. I hope you know one day, I'll kill you."

He reared back and backhanded me so hard, stars and black holes burst across my vision, and I slumped sideways in the chair.

Another knock, another demand, this one firmer, to open the door. Just as the officers outside warned they were coming in anyway, I turned my cheek to face Morgan's mottled face, and I smiled, blood smeared across my teeth, tangy on my tongue.

I wiped my hand across my split lip and let him see the wolf he'd forced out of my skin.

"I'll murder you, Morgan," I whispered, a promise, an oath I had no problem making and signing in the blood he'd spilled from me. "When you least expect it, you'll be gasping for breath on the verge of death, and you'll know it was me."

Three officers burst through the door and, seeing me, bloodied and slumped, raised their guns.

"Dylan Morgan," Officer Ponce, the same idiot who'd dragged me in for questioning twice before, glared at the professor with more than professional dislike. "You're under arrest for two counts of sexual assault and battery."

Professors, the same from that morning after Halloween a year ago, crowded in the doorframe to watch the mayhem as I sat primly bleeding in my chair as Dylan Morgan was finally punished for his crimes.

I closed my eyes against a surge of riotous tears and let out a slow controlled breath before whispering a quote from *The Merchant of Venice*, "'and they shall feel the vengeance of my wrath.'"

Because the truth was, falling in love with Luna had made me realize there was more to life, and me, than revenge, but it hadn't fundamentally changed who I was.

I was a monster, not just by circumstance at the hand of Dylan Morgan, but now, I realized, by *choice*. I would always be something with teeth and claws, hunters chasing me through the woods and prey racing from me through the bush.

Maybe there was more than the choice between a victim and a monster after something happened to a person like what happened to me, but I didn't care.

I'd chosen to be monstrous, and Luna had shown me that even monsters could have hearts and morals, too.

Even if they were a little crooked.

CHAPTER
TWENTY-FIVE

"To fear love is to fear life, and those who fear life are already three parts dead."

—Bertrand Russell

Luna

I was at field hockey practice even though I wouldn't be cleared to play for another three weeks. Still, I was the captain so I should be there even if I couldn't participate, and I was bored of wallowing in my pain and misery. I was a happy person by nature, probably because my mother was a complainer, and I'd relentlessly honed myself into an optimist to contradict that negativity. It didn't matter now if I was a counterweight to her or not because I'd cut her out of my life. She'd seemed surprised by my resolve, by my anger, when she'd visited me in the hospital. A momentary rebellion, she'd said of my recent behavior, a blip she was willing to forgive me for if I smartened up and moved home.

Even drugged up, my entire face throbbing from Beckett and his buddies' beating, I found the resolve to stand up to the most important person in my life.

"It's not a blip," I'd told her, tongue thick and dry as a piece of leather in my mouth. "Just like your behavior isn't. I know you've hushed up more than just Lex's assault, Mom. Ironically, you didn't raise a girl who would be okay swallowing that truth. These girls deserve justice, and *you* should have been the one to give it to them."

"This is because of that *girl*, isn't it?" She'd sneered, lips peeling back over capped white teeth. They had none of the sharpness of Lex's canine smile, and I had the thought that Mom had never stood a chance against her vengeance, even if I hadn't helped take her down. "Awarding her a scholarship is the biggest mistake I've made in my life."

I laughed hollowly, then winced as it ached in my ribs. "Oh, Mom, there is so much wrong with you that you believe that. And it's as much about Lex as it isn't. She helped me realize some things that were so close under my nose I couldn't see them. Things about you, yes, but also about me. I think I'm gay, and I think I'm good. That is, a good person. Lex helped me see both of those things, and I'm glad she did."

"Don't do anything stupid here, Luna," Mom warned, a flash of something like fear in her eyes. She reached out to touch my face, her fingers cold and shaking. My throat closed up because I wanted desperately to feel she was giving me comfort and genuine love, but I knew well enough to doubt her intentions. She was and always had been about herself. "You don't want to ruin our lives, do you?"

"Our lives? You mean your life. I'm not the same person as you, and I'm not your puppet," I asserted, dominance flooding through me as surely as the drugs through the IV. "Now, get out."

She hadn't. Instead, she'd railed at me, voice growing shrill enough to draw the nurses into the room. When she refused to leave at their behest, I had the awful/awesome pleasure of seeing her escorted out by security.

And I'd lain there alone in my hospital bed, badly roughed up, brokenhearted, but alive in a way I hadn't been since I was a child.

The blood pumped fiercely through my veins, and my vision was clear despite the drugs.

I'd chosen my path, captain of my own destiny, and decided against the easy journey in favor of the one that felt right.

When Pierce found me, I was crying, but I smiled at him through the tears to let him know I was okay. He didn't buy it, but he didn't have to. He was my friend, so he let me have my dignity, and he didn't push while I recovered in his apartment even though I could see how angry my circumstances made him.

Lex didn't try to contact me. Relief and despair tangoed in my gut, driving me crazy as I tried to recover as quickly as possible from my concussion and sprain. Even when Pierce came home one night, dull-eyed and shaking, and admitted that he'd started to strangle Lex in retribution for how she'd treated me. I didn't reach out and neither did she. What Pierce did was horrible, but I could see the way it ate him up inside. He reminded me a little of her at that moment, his heart in the right place but his acts made bestial by a white-out surge of fury. He apologized to me as if I was the one he'd put his hands on, begging for absolution. I gave it to him because, in his own way, he'd been my champion through everything. The only one to love me wholly and unselfishly however I came.

But I suggested he apologize to Lex again.

In fact, I was struggling with the urge to do the same. I'd declined every visitor who'd made an attempt to see me after the assault, too depressed to do anything but curl up on Pierce's couch and rewatch *Pride & Prejudice* a hundred times. So, I hadn't known about the rumors swirling that Lex of all people had been the one to beat me up for breaking up with her. Pierce hadn't asked me to validate the gossip before he'd gone after her, thinking I would cover for her out of pride or shame. By the time I set the story straight with Pierce and the rest of my friends, the false gossip had already made the rounds.

Still, the knowledge that Lex had been hurt because of me, even indirectly, hurt almost as much as my physical wounds. Knowing that people were so ready to believe the worst of Lex because being raped had irreparably tarnished her reputation also made me reconsider the hard stance I'd taken about her vengeful activities. Mostly, because I felt the violent urge to go out and hit every single person who'd ever spoken badly about her.

I was thinking about this as I sat huddled on the bleachers in my quilted parka, mouth tucked behind the high neck and the cashmere scarf bundled up around my throat. It was calming to watch my teammates run drills and now, stretch together in a tight little clutch. Flora and Haley both kept casting me little looks, but I couldn't read why, and I didn't really care.

I'd numbed my heart to help along its recovery after Lex.

Both the pain and the brief flares of hope were too much for me to bear.

Because a little part of me couldn't help wondering if Lex loved me back despite her prior intentions. If she was just scared to make herself vulnerable, to me or anyone, after what had been taken from her. If I shouldn't have just a little more empathy and grace, a tiny bit of patience.

Maybe she'd come back.

Maybe she'd fight for me like she fought for so many women before me.

Every day that ticked by without her wore away my resolve and sank me further into despair.

The first person—woman—I'd fallen in love with heart and soul, and I'd only been her pawn.

"Luna?"

I looked up from my thousand-yard stare to see Haley fidgeting with her hockey stick, rocking it back and forth between her hands. Her cheeks were flushed from exertion, and she looked pretty standing there in her little blue skirt with her trim thighs on display, pinked by the cold air.

She caught me looking, and the stain on her cheeks darkened.

I found myself cocking my head, a gesture reminiscent of Lex. "Hey, Hales, what's up?"

"I know I already told you this, but I'm sorry for what happened to you," she said, the words moving so quickly through her mouth they jumbled together. "I'm sorry I haven't been a better friend. That...well, that I didn't take care of you better at Flo's party, and that I just kind of abandoned you when I found out you were with Lex Gorgon."

I hadn't thought she'd abandoned me, but maybe that was because I had been so focused on Lex and the new, extraordinary feelings she stirred in me.

"I was tied up with my own stuff," I assured her with a soft smile. Haley had always been soft and kind, sweet cheeked and younger looking than her age. Being mean to her was like kicking a puppy. "Please don't worry about it. You've always been a good friend."

"I could have been better," she insisted, stomping her cleated foot a little so the metal bleachers echoed. "I, uh, I know a little of what you were going through, and I wasn't there for you. It makes me feel like an ass."

"What do you mean?"

She sighed, sucking on the end of her ponytail, a nervous habit. "I mean, I'm bi, too. Or I don't know how you identify, really. But I'm bi. And I've known since I was a kid, and I had a crush on Demi Lovato *and* Dylan and Cole Sprouse."

"Oh," I said because, for a second, I was shocked. "Why didn't you tell me?"

She shrugged. "I don't know. I don't really tell people, I guess? And then, you were suddenly gay or bi or in a relationship with a woman and not just a woman but *Lex Gorgon*. And you were just so easy with it, you know? You stood up for yourself, and you were brave and bold and happy with Lex even though people gave you shit." She shrugged again, a little helplessly. "I guess I was a little jealous."

"Lex is beautiful," I allowed with a teasing grin because I could tell these words had cost her.

She laughed, a little yip of surprise. "Yeah, well, you'd have to be blind not to know that, but that's not really it. I think I just thought it was cool and wild you could adjust so quickly. It made me feel a little inferior like I should be doing more as a bi woman. Like not telling people meant I was a bad bisexual."

I sighed, and it felt good to release some of the ugly tension in my chest. The bench was cold as I patted the metal beside me, and I waited until she took a seat before I said, "I'm pretty sure there is no wrong way to be a bisexual woman, Hales. You have to do what makes you comfortable and what makes you happy. You don't owe anyone anything you don't want to share. But I know how you felt because I felt the same way about Lex. Looking at her, so fearless and herself no matter that people hated her and reviled her? It was intoxicating. I guess I just channeled a little bit of her bravery and got addicted to the feeling."

"Yeah, I can see that." She nodded slowly, then knocked her knees into mine. "Maybe I can borrow some of that bravery."

"Anytime," I promised. "I'm no Lex, but I learned a lot about myself from her."

"Can I ask why you broke up?"

I bit my lip and ignored the cramp turning my stomach into knots. The sun was rising higher in the sky now, warm fingers of light trickling down my face. "I was a casualty of war," I said finally with a grim smile. "Sometimes I think the war was worth my sacrifice, but mostly, I just felt used."

Haley reached out to squeeze my knee. "I'm sorry, Lunatic. For what it's worth, the only time I ever saw that woman smile was when she looked at you and thought you weren't watching."

Warmth moved through my chest, flooding my lungs so I couldn't breathe for a moment.

My phone started buzzing in my pocket, and I was glad for the distraction.

"Hello?"

"Lune," Pierce's panting, excited voice came over the phone. "Lex is giving a press conference in the quad. Have you seen *The New York Times* this morning? She did it."

"Did what?" I asked, but I was already standing, tugging Haley's hand to take her with me.

"She exposed them all."

The conference had already started by the time Haley and I jogged into the fringes of the crowd. Lex stood in front of the podium flanked by the Provost and a handful of other women, including Professor Diana Strong. She was dressed in her requisite black ensemble: a short skirt over sheer dark tights, chunky heeled boots, a cable knit sweater over a button-up visible beneath an ankle-length black overcoat that flapped in the cold breeze. Her hair was a riot of curls writhing like serpents in the wind, mimicking the bright green and black snake tattooed on her neck. Bold and confident, her face a little pale to my trained eye but firm with resolve. It was my first time seeing her in over a week, and the impact of her beauty was like a punch to the solar plexus.

Haley steadied me with a hand on my lower back.

"Are you okay?" she whispered close to my ear.

Lex saw me then, pausing almost indecipherably in her speech as our gazes caught and snagged on each other. Those stone-gray eyes flared and narrowed as they took in how close Haley was to me, holding me almost. I thought she would be angry, lips flatlining, jaw tightening. Instead, her mouth went soft and supple as it did before we kissed.

"What did I tell you?" Haley whispered again. "Hundreds of people before her and the only one she sees is you."

I shivered so hard my teeth rattled, but I didn't look away from Lex. Not even when I realized what she was saying.

"As my lawyer said, I will not be taking any questions after this, but I wanted to make a statement in order to finally and hopefully clear the air on Acheron's campus. Last Halloween, I became one in five women sexually assaulted on a college campus, according to the statistics from the nation's largest anti-sexual violence organization. It happened here on this campus, first in the office of a well-renowned professor, and then again in the forest, where he left me like a carcass. Maybe, if this had been an isolated incident, I could have held my tongue. But it became increasingly obvious to me as I spoke with other students that sexual assault was rife and frequently covered up by the people in power at this university. People like President Mina Pallas, who threatened my academic standing and future if I continued to accuse my assaulter of his crimes. People like Professor Morgan himself, who has a history of assault that was covered up by the university because of the funding his popularity brought to the school."

She paused, eyes moving from me to sweep over the crowd before finding me again.

I felt trapped in that gaze, solidified by the power of it.

Listen to me, she seemed to whisper just for me. *I'm doing this because you taught me it was the right thing to do.*

I swallowed thickly.

"Thanks to the investigative journalism of Quinn Harper, the monsters lurking in the shadows of Acheron University have been brought into the light. A police investigation has been instigated into the actions of both President Pallas and Professor Morgan along with a few other faculty and board members who were complicit in these cover-ups. All I can ask for now is that the university reconsider its sexual violence policies. Escort systems set up for women walking alone after dark on campus, a hotline to call in misconduct, and most of all, a 24/7 support system for victims of sexual assault. Speaking from experience, it is not easy to return to the scene of a crime and flourish on the same path you were taking before. If we want students to succeed, we need to destigmatize being a victim of sexual violence and provide a safe place for them to seek help. I was lucky enough to find my own support system on campus, friends and a girlfriend who helped me see that I was worthy of love even when I felt like I couldn't get past my trauma."

Her eyes glistened, but no tears fell. Voice strong, shoulders squared, that chin canted at an angle like a pugilist daring to be punched, she looked exactly like that first day I'd been drawn to her in the quad. My heart hammered so madly that I was light-headed and swaying on my feet. Each beat seemed to tattoo the same words into my flesh: *I love you, I love you, I love you.*

And I did.

I loved this beautiful, brave woman standing before everyone and opening a vein so they could see how damaging what had happened at Acheron was. I loved her strength and her feminism, even her viciousness and rage. I loved that she could also be soft and romantic, sweet as strawberry wine.

And I loved that little old *me*, Luna Pallas, had helped her battle back her demons so she could take the entire system on.

"I hope this is the first step in many toward making this campus, and every campus across the country, a safer place for students, especially women, to pursue their dreams and higher education. Thank you very much for your time."

There was a flurry of flashes and murmurs as the photographers and reporters closer to the stage hastened to capture the last moments of Lex Gorgon making her stand. I watched as she stepped away, and her lawyer replaced her at the podium to take questions. Diana Strong slipped an arm around Lex's shoulders and squeezed.

Lex didn't look at me again.

And when I went to look for her through the crowd after the conference was done, she had disappeared.

"What are you going to do?" Haley asked, having wedged through the crowd beside me. "You know she was talking about you."

I did know.

But I didn't know exactly what that meant or what she wanted. Being thankful for my part in taking down my own mother was one thing. Loving me and wanting to be with me was another matter entirely.

And for the duration of our relationship or whatever you wanted to call it, I'd been the one to capitulate, to float on the tide of Lex's magnetic currents. This time, I wasn't going to seek her out. I wouldn't make it easy for her.

Some things were worth fighting for, yes, and Lex was one of them.

But so was I.

And I would not be with a woman who wouldn't put me first. I'd spent a lifetime with a mother who couldn't and wouldn't do that, and I refused to let history repeat itself.

If Lex wanted me, she'd have to come for me.

CHAPTER
TWENTY-SIX

"Keep your face always toward the sunshine and shadows will fall behind you"
— Walt Whitman

Luna

It was finally Halloween.

A year since Lex's assault.

It was impossible not to think about her as I went about my day. It was a Friday, so thankfully, I had classes to distract me, but she wasn't in our shared Tragedies class, and her absence bothered me.

Was she okay?

How could she be okay on a day like today? Even with all her demons punished, they'd inflicted wounds that would never heal. Still, it heartened me to think of Dylan Morgan behind bars. They'd collected a sample of his DNA and matched it to the sample they'd taken from Lex when she was issued a rape kit at the hospital the day after her assault. He was awaiting trial, but there was no doubt he'd be imprisoned for what he'd done.

My mother was another matter. She'd officially resigned as president of Acheron University before they could formally fire her, and the offer from Cambridge had been quickly swept off the table. The house we'd lived in on campus was now the home of the new interim president while the selection committee searched for a permanent replacement. Mom had moved back to California to take a job at a small community college in her hometown.

I only knew this through the grapevine. We hadn't spoken since I told her to get out of my hospital room, and after she'd found out my role in her disgrace, I didn't expect to hear from her ever again.

It hurt. No matter how awful I knew her to be, she was still my mom *and* my dad, my only living blood relative. She'd done terrible things for personal gain and used me like a puppet, but there had been good moments too. Bedtime stories cuddled up in her big comfy bed, hot tea shared at the kitchen table while she helped me with my homework. Christmas mornings, Easter Sundays, and Thanksgiving dinners, just the two of us.

I relished the memories because I knew I'd never have those moments again. It took some adjusting, realizing that a person who had shaped me and raised me to be a woman I was proud of could also be a villain in so many other people's lives.

The truth was, the loneliness was hard to bear.

I'd always been popular, surrounded by my peers and boyfriends, my mother and her colleagues.

Now, after Lex, I'd lost a lot of my old friends like Flora and Courtney and their lot. I still had Pierce, but he was seeing a new girl and spent a lot of his time out of the apartment with her.

I'd also lost Lex and her sisters.

Even though we'd only been together a short time, the loss was considerable. I'd felt more at home on Charity Lane with the Gorgon sisters than I ever had anywhere else. Their close bond, theatricality, sense of fun, and romanticism called to my own heart, and it panged whenever I thought of them.

Needless to say, in the few days since the press conference and ensuing shitstorm on campus, Lex hadn't come to claim me.

The strange thing about heartbreak was that it wasn't a single hammer hit to the organ. A one-time shattering. It was ongoing. A withering with time, a flux and contraction of fruitless hope paired with the bitter reality of unrealized dreams dying slow deaths.

It hurt the most.

Because I'd seen a future with Lex so clearly in my mind's eye, more clearly than I'd ever seen my future alone.

Long nights staying up too late listening to Debussy and Bach, studying until our vision blurred before taking out our restlessness on each other's soft bodies. Mornings in the den of her bed, cocooned from the world together, her husky voice soft as she read to me from Homer and Sappho. Applying to Cambridge together. Getting a dog one day, or maybe a cat. Having kids if that was what she wanted, and suddenly, I conjured an image of a little girl with Lex's dark curls, and my heart quivered with longing.

I sighed as I sat on the window ledge in Pierce's apartment kitchen. A single lamp illuminated the space, highlighting my total loneliness.

Halloween on a Friday night and I was alone in an apartment that wasn't even mine.

Music played softly through the speakers, and combined with the book in my hand, I was trying to stay busy. But not even the words of Shakespeare, Lex's favorite *The Merchant of Venice*, could keep me entertained.

Click.

I startled, looking through the window to see if a bird had landed on the ledge, but nothing was there.

Click, click, click.

Little pings against the windowpane.

I dropped the play into my lap and pressed my face to the icy glass so I could look down at the ground four stories beneath me.

A woman stood in the glow of the streetlight. All in black, she looked like a living shadow, totally obscured even in the warm glow.

A shiver worked light fingers down the knobs of my spine.

I knew it was Lex.

The tangled mess of emotions knotted in my stomach rose to lodge in my throat. My fingers found the glass as if I could reach out and touch her.

Beside me, my phone buzzed.

Lex: "O that I were a glove upon that hand, That I might touch that cheek!"

I grinned despite myself at the quote from *Romeo and Juliet*.

Luna: I thought you didn't enjoy the romantic plays.

Lex: I didn't enjoy a lot of things before I met you.

I touched my fingertips to the screen as if to make sure the words were real. My chest ached and throbbed, a warning and a yearning all at once.

Don't go back there, my voice of reason screamed. *Don't go back to a woman who might not ever be capable of loving you back.*

But the voice was garbled in low under the rush of blood in my ears calling me to go to her.

To go home to her.

Lex: I know I don't deserve it. I know the moon belongs in the sky far from my earthly desires and horrors, but would you come down to me, Luna? I have things I want to say to you.

I bit my lip so hard blood bloomed on my tongue. My fingers were moving across the screen before I could tell myself to stop them.

Luna: Okay.

I was moving then, quickly so I couldn't second-guess myself. Adrenaline brought me to my toes as I raced through the kitchen for my thick wool coat and boots, then I grabbed my scarf and twirled it around my neck. I paused to look at myself in the mirror, noting the bright spots of color in my freckled cheeks and the luminous excitement in my green eyes, close to glowing. I looked enraptured, even with the fading bruises from Beckett's fists, recklessly following a siren's song, uncaring of the danger of drowning in the dark depths of the sea.

I shook off the fear and left the apartment, closing the door loudly behind me as if it would trap my concerns inside.

The air was cold and clear outside, a slap to the face, urging me to wake up and think straight. I ignored that too.

Because Lex was there, that shadow in the lamp light. The girl in black I'd met in the library, the bold rebel I'd seen across the quad, the beautiful girl I'd fallen in love with.

"Hi," I said, a little breathless, my word a hot plume of air between us.

I bounced on my toes and wrung my hands together so I wouldn't go to her.

She moved closer until I could see the paleness of her silvered eyes and the dark arched brows above them. I wanted to trace them with my fingers, run my thumbs over the edge of her cheekbones, and drag her mouth to mine to remind me of the way she tasted.

She seemed so much like *mine* standing there in front of me it was hard to remind myself she wasn't.

Maybe she'd never even wanted to be.

The thought doused me in cold water like nothing had before, and I took an instinctive step back.

Lex took another forward, face firm with resolve.

"Hello, Lux," she murmured low and quiet, the way one would

speak to a spooked animal.

I fidgeted. "Why are you here? Are you okay? Do you need something?"

A little smile like the flicker of a snake's tongue. "Hush for a moment. Let me look at you. It's been too long, and I'm too greedy to speak before I get my fill of you."

A shiver that had nothing to do with the cold.

"I haven't been sleeping well," I explained with a flap of my hand to explain why I looked bedraggled, not even half as gorgeous as her.

"Mmm," she hummed, rocking back on her feet a little. "Well, we'll have to see if we can change that. No matter anyway, you look absolutely divine to me."

Absolutely divine.

How could anyone resist someone who thought that of them?

She offered me her gloved hand, then frowned when I reached forward without thinking to accept it in mine. Clucking her tongue against her teeth, she pulled back to tug at the finger of each glove with her teeth and remove them. Then stepping close enough I could smell the bruised violet scent of her, she carefully worked the leather gloves over my own hands before chafing them between her own.

"Always so cold," she teased softly.

I'd never seen her soft, not an ounce of tension in her face, not a coiling of muscle anywhere in her long, curved form. I realized she was a predator making herself small for me, exposing her belly in a show of submission. An animal kind of apology and one that suited her.

I gulped hard as she tangled her hand with my own and tugged me forward down the path.

"Will you let me show you something?" she asked, even though she was already leading me away. Even though she had to know the answer was and probably always would be *yes*.

336

I peered at her as we walked. "How are you, though? Today, I mean."

She squeezed my hand. "Better than I've been in a long time. It's not a bad day, love. It's a day of celebration."

"Because you got your revenge?"

She stopped so suddenly, I slammed into her shoulder, and she had to steady me with both hands on my hips. Her face was utterly somber, black and white in the shadows and moonlight.

"Because I got *justice*," she amended firmly, shaking me a little. "I got justice because you helped me see beyond the simplicity of revenge."

"Is it enough for you, though?" I asked, and there was one of my fears buried in those words.

Will you be able to move on now?

Will you be able to accept goodness in your life now that the monsters have been vanquished?

Do we get a happily ever after, or is this like those myths with only tragic endings?

Her gaze scoured my face as if committing it to memory. My heart thumped so hard it made it difficult to breathe.

Her sigh unwound between us, tickling my throat.

"For now," she admitted, shifting her hands up my sides inside the open flaps of my coat until she could cup my cool cheeks. "One day, I'm going to kill him, though."

I blinked. "What?"

Her thumbs shifted to my temples, fingers digging through the sides of my hair. She brought me closer to speak the words hotly against my parted lips. "One day, when Morgan is out of prison, and he thinks the nightmare is over, I'm going to kill him."

When she pulled back, I was blinking madly, mute with shock.

"I'm not joking, Luna," she said, each word carefully enunciated so

I couldn't mistake her meaning. "I learned a lot of valuable things from you. How to be a better person, how to seek justice for everyone and not just myself. How to put things to rest so I can finally figure out how to look forward. But at the end of the day, there is no changing who I am inside. How what happened changed me irrevocably and eternally." She took my hand and placed it on her chest. I could feel the calm beat of her heart, and it steadied my own. "I'm never going to be as good as you, and I don't want to try. The person I am, I believe Morgan should die for what he's done, and I'm okay with being the one to see it through to the end."

A heavy pause, just the beating of two hearts falling in tandem.

"The question is," she whispered, leaning forward to place her forehead against mine so all I could see were those gray eyes like twin moons. "Are you okay with it?"

"What do you mean?"

"I mean, are you okay with loving a woman who is capable of hunting monsters and killing them if they deserve death?"

"Is this a habit you're going to make?" I asked, following instinct instead of the rational voice in my head telling me all of this was wrong. "Killing predators?"

"No. But I'm going to kill this one."

"Are you going to keep beating up students as the Man Eater Crew?" I could understand her complicated need for Morgan's death. He'd raped her, destroyed her reputation, and threatened her future. But the others? They were bad men, but I didn't think they deserved vigilante justice when the cops would do.

"No," she admitted, tugging at my hair in a soothing way. "Some of the girls who were assaulted started a Man Eater Patrol. I've been teaching them self-defense, and they're offering chaperone services now. We even have a sexual assault survivor's group. I spoke at the first meeting, and I was able to do it because I knew you'd be proud of me for sharing my pain and helping others." A pause, shimmering with fear and hope, emanating from us both. "Are you?"

"Oh, Lex," I said on a gusty exhale, finally moving to hold her back, wrapping my arms around her waist to bring us flush. "You should be proud of yourself for what you've done, regardless of how I feel."

"I do, but I need to know..." Her hands turned to claws in my hair, nails digging into my scalp a little too sharp. "I need to know if you can love me even after everything I've done."

"Why?" The word tasted like blood in my mouth, like I'd carved it out of my heart.

"Because I'm so in love with you I can barely breathe," she admitted, voice breaking, eyes filling, like the dam had finally broken, and emotion was rushing in through the scorched earth of her fallow heart. "I'm so in love with you that every day without you is almost more agony than I can bear, and I've been through a lot. I need you, Lux. You're the light in the dark for me, and you always will be. I can't promise to be easy and good after this. I think I'll always be a little feral, a little violent, and a little afraid. But I'll do everything that is within my power to be worthy of you if you still love me. If you want that future with me that I thought was too good to be true."

I didn't realize I was crying until I opened my mouth to respond and salt burst on my tongue, tears running between the grooves in my teeth.

"I love you," I told her, and the words felt like an explosion from my chest, the loosening of an arrow shot from heart to heart. "I love you, Lex, and it might be wrong, the beatings, killing Morgan, turning in my own mom, but I don't want to have a life without you in it. So I guess I'd rather be a little wrong than empty. I'd rather be with you than anyone else in the world no matter how good they might be."

"Really?" she said, a little gasp like a puncture wound in a balloon.

"Really," I agreed, holding her tight because I felt like I would float away. "I feel like I was born to love you, and I can't believe anything about that is wrong."

I barely got the words out before she was kissing me.

No, not kissing.

Devouring.

Eating me up like she'd die if she didn't consume enough. Her tongue in my mouth, her teeth over my lower lip nipping and opening that split I'd put there earlier so my blood bloomed between us. It felt like a blood oath, a promise to be together no matter what darkness came, until the end of our time on earth.

"I love you," she murmured between sipping at my lips. "I love you."

I closed my eyes and gloried in it, kissing her back with all the desperation in my heart.

"I'm sorry," she said, a little choked up, coughing the words. "I'm so sorry for hurting you. I won't do it ever again."

"I know," I soothed, kissing her tanned cheeks, her mauve eyelids, her lush red mouth, a paint by colors I filled in with my lips.

We stood there for a long time, touching and kissing until our lips were swollen and our breath came in ragged pants. Finally, she hugged me, wrapping me up like delicate tissue paper in the box of her embrace. I felt so cared for, so seen that tears sprang hot and fresh to my eyes again.

She kissed them off my cheeks with smiling lips.

"Can I show you that something, now?" she asked.

I nodded, too overcome to speak.

She beamed at me. *Beamed.* Brighter than a full moon overhead and twice as glorious.

I followed a little dazedly behind her as she led us through campus to the edge of the woods behind Hippios House. Only when she started into the darkness did I hesitate, but she just shot me a reassuring smile and tugged me forward.

I didn't understand at first.

It was dark and cold, each tiny creak and murmur frightening me not just because it was Halloween but because this was where Lex had woken, forever changed and broken that morning last year.

"Lex," I started to protest.

And then I saw it.

The glimmer of light through a gap in the trees.

Followed quickly by the bass of strong music, thumping through the forest floor into the soles of my shoes.

We stepped around a few more trees, and suddenly, we were in a clearing, everything bright and clear. A huge bonfire crackled red and yellow in its center, casting orange light and dancing shadows over the women gathered around the edges. I recognized Taya and Haley, heard the distinct cackle of Gracie over the noise, and the low murmur of Effie somewhere nearby. All women, all gathered with drinks in their hands, some dancing, others chatting, every single one of them at ease and smiling.

"Like maenads," I whispered, wondering if it was real.

Lex grinned at me, pulling me close to her side and tucking an arm around my hips. "Exactly. Wild and free, dancing together. I thought it was the perfect way to celebrate. Not just the annihilation of monsters, but the start of something safe and strong for women at Acheron."

The warmth of the fire seemed to leap through me, surging hot through my veins.

"Do you know all these girls?"

Lex nodded, a proud little smile around her mouth. "Yes. They're

my all-women wolf pack, I guess. They're all a part of the Man Eater
Patrol or in the support group with me. They've all been through
something and come out the other side."

"Just like you."

"Just like us," she corrected, kissing my temple.

"Good, you're here," Gracie crowed, skipping over. "I think it's time
to dance."

Lex looked at me, and I realized I was her touchstone, the
grounding rod for the lightning force inside her. What a gift, what a
responsibility, one I'd bear happily for the rest of my life.

I smiled at my girlfriend and then at the sister she'd given me.
"Yeah, I think it's time to dance."

And we did.

Scores of women dancing around a bonfire, drinking and laughing
and yelling loudly just to hear our voices raised in tandem against the
dark sky. And I knew as we writhed and seethed around the flames like
hissing snakes, like beautiful, dangerous creatures, that our ending wasn't
the tragic kind.

It was a well-earned, hard-fought happily ever after.

EPILOGUE

"I have found the paradox, that if you love until it hurts, there can be no more hurt, only more love."

—*Daphne Rae*

Luna

FOUR YEARS LATER

Lex was gone for three days that winter. I didn't go with her. She told me it was the end of her (anti)hero's journey, and she needed to do it alone. Also, if anything went wrong, she didn't want the blame to fall on me.

I knew nothing would go wrong. In the years we'd been together, life had blessed us with luck and joy as if the fates knew we'd suffered enough for now and we deserved a break.

Dylan Morgan was released on parole on a Tuesday. Lex left on the Wednesday, and when she returned on the Saturday, it was done.

The last dark deed to end a dark story.

The story went like this.

Morgan went for a walk in Cockasponet State Forest two days after he became a free man. Maybe he wanted a breath of real fresh air after

years in jail for his crimes. A sentence too short for the severity of his
heinous acts. Maybe he wanted to stretch his legs, or maybe he wanted
to search for some young female hiker alone on the path, eager to assert
his dominance and terror again.

Who knows.

They did report that Dylan Morgan was on an unpopular trail in
the depths of the forest when he had the misfortune of coming across
the den of one of North America's mostly deadly predators.

A Timber rattlesnake.

The details were unclear, but after sustaining four bites to his
person, Morgan must have lost consciousness and died sometime in the
following four days before he was found off trail by another hiker.

Lex arrived home the day before he was found.

She flew in and out of Boston for a conference there on the
works of Socrates. No one looking would have been able to track her
movements after dark when Dahlia lent her a beaten-up Honda that she
drove through the night hours to reach the state park. No one would
have known that she'd connected with Morgan in an online chatroom
two years into his prison sentence and that he'd agreed to meet
Hermione Rogers that Sunday morning at the trailhead.

No one could have known that Haley had been taking care of
Chrysaor or that Lex picked him up on the way to meet the man who'd
almost ruined so much for her.

I was there waiting at Heathrow when her plane landed, holding
a bouquet of lilies because they were funeral flowers, and I wanted to
show Lex in every way I could that I loved her. I supported her. Not just
through the good times, where she smiled easier and laughed freely, but
through these times as well, when dark vengeance surged through her
system and demanded its own retribution.

The smile she gave me was full of gratitude and relief so stark it nearly took my breath away.

When we returned home, I kissed every inch of her body and sucked each of her fingers as if I could pull the taint of blood off them with my tongue. She'd cried afterward for the first time in a long time, gentle rolling sobs as I cradled her against my chest.

But after, she'd seemed lighter even against my own body, bones purged of leaden marrow, cleansed so clean she seemed to float.

The next morning dawned gray and drizzling, but most days in England were clouded and damp, and I'd adjusted to the bone-chilling air after three years in Cambridge. Lex liked to tease me about my copious layers—today I was in a cashmere turtleneck, thickly knit fisherman's sweater the same color as my eyes, an overcoat, a massive scarf, and a beanie pulled low over my ears—but it was necessary even in late October, especially because my girlfriend insisted on spending time outdoors.

"Come on, Lux," she called to me, humor rich in her husky voice. "It's practically balmy out."

I watched as she raked the leaves in the yard of our small but also adorable stone cottage. Her movements were brisk and efficient, yet there was still a graceful sensuality there. In the four and a half years since we'd been together, I'd never once seen Lex without it. Her sexiness was as much a part of her as her big, beautiful brain, and I was wildly in love with both.

She cocked her head, dark curls spilling behind her shoulders, and fisted a hand on her hip. Unlike me, she was only wearing a black velvet mini dress over a white turtleneck and a short black peacoat open over the ensemble. I traced the line of her cocked hip, the length of her patterned-tight-clad legs, and wondered if it was too soon after our morning lovemaking to beg her to take me again.

"Get your mind out of the gutter and come help me with this, lazy bones," she scolded, but a little smile was wedged into the left side of her cheek.

"I was contemplating my next exhibition." I sniffed, still cupping my big mug of Earl Grey tea in both hands, raised to my mouth so the steam could warm my face. "If you must know."

"Sure," she agreed, but there was wickedness in the slow grin that claimed her face. "Are you finally planning on sharing the many, *many* nude photographs you've taken of me over the years? Because you have your sex face on right now, my love."

How could I be irritated with her, even playfully, when she called me her love?

It never failed to wow me that I'd won the deep and abiding love of someone so inspiring. It had been years, and I still found myself swooning over her beauty, shivering at a simple touch of her hand, in awe of every beautiful thought inside her head. She made me want to be better just by being herself while simultaneously showing me that I was perfect to her in every iteration of myself.

Love, they called it.

How simple a word for such a complex and stunning structure built between two hearts and souls.

"I don't want to disturb Shakespeare," I told her, stroking a hand down the soft fur of the King Charles Cavalier Spaniel we'd rescued the moment we landed foot in Cambridge.

A dog, Lex had said, *is an important part of our new British aesthetic.*

I loved that she went out of her way to live the kind of life that brought her pleasure, and Shakespeare had been such a welcome addition to our family that a year later when we bought our cottage, she declared a cottage couldn't be called such without a cat to curl up near the fire.

Virginia was inside doing just that.

Between the dog, the cat, and now Chrysaor, whom she'd just brought over to England, we had quite the menagerie.

Quite a family.

"Get your sweet buttocks over here, Luna," Lex warned. "The family will be here for dinner in an hour, and I have plans."

"Your mom and sisters are always late, and you know it."

"So you don't care if I don't have time to take you apart with my fingers, teeth, and tongue before they arrive?" she taunted with a raised brow.

I sighed dramatically but put my mug of tea on the railing and stepped off the porch to help her. Her smile was smug as I approached, so I ignored her, wrenching the rake out of her hands to finish off the remnants myself.

"Nice view," she leered, and when I turned my head, her gaze was fixed on my ass which was not at all visible through my many layers.

I snorted and her beautiful face broke open in a wide grin. When she reached for me, I dropped the rake immediately and stepped into her embrace.

"How'd I get so lucky?" she whispered against my lips, forehead tipped to mine.

I breathed in her earthy, floral scent and held it in my lungs as I kissed her lightly. "Luck had nothing to do with it. You worked for it."

"I wouldn't call it work," she argued, brushing her nose against mine, creating a warm cocoon between our bodies. "Not with you. I never knew what it was like to be happy before I decided to seduce you for my own nefarious gains."

I giggled, clutching at her open coat to haul her even tighter against me. "Neither did I."

"You lost a lot to be with me," she reminded me with a frown I smoothed out with a thumb. "Your mom. Most of your friends."

"The true ones stayed," I argued, which was true.

Pierce had actually flown in to visit us in the summer when he got a break from hockey. He'd managed to make his dreams come true, and he'd been signed to the Vancouver NHL team two years ago. Haley also kept in touch though she hadn't visited yet because she was busy working in New York for a not-for-profit where she'd met a lovely girl named Pauline.

"As for my mum..." I shrugged because even though it had been years, the dissolution of my love and hero worship of my mother still stung like lingering acid in my tissues. I wasn't sure I'd ever purge myself of the feeling. Agatha had told me once that there was no betrayal like that of a parent to a child because we were raised and biologically inclined to trust and rely on our parents. It made sense, even if it didn't make me feel better.

"I'd take you over her any day," I finished a little lamely. "Besides, you gave me your family, and they're the best."

They were.

Grace, Effie, and Juno had all followed us to England so of course, Agatha had followed. Some might call their relationships a little codependent, but I thought the kind of loyalty and love they shared was awe-inspiring. Grace lived in London and was scraping a living together as an actor. Effie and Juno both lived in Cambridge, the former as a journalist and the latter as a tech consultant. Agatha lived down the street from us and even though she was retired, she volunteered at the local library.

I loved them.

They were a family of choice instead of the one I'd been given, but that almost made them more special to me, because they made that choice every single day without failure. I wasn't a chore, or a puppet to be masterminded. I wasn't even just Lex's girlfriend.

I was me.

Luna Pallas, bookworm, jock, photographer, and perpetual optimist.

And they loved me.

"It's enough for you?" Lex asked, though her tone was bossy, almost a demand. Like she was daring me to tell her it wasn't.

I beamed at her, giving in to the impulse to brush a curly lock of dark hair from her face so I could cup her cheek. "It's everything to me."

She studied me with those stone-gray eyes, and I thought about how fierce they could be, how they'd turned men practically to stone with the threat of her violent vengeance. She'd given up her vigilante ways, even though she was a part of the Stay Safe program on campus here. Now, those eyes were filled with warmth and laughter more often than not. When she came home from work, red cheeked from the walk and giddy with talk of her research on feminism in Ancient Greek literature. When she woke up beside me in bed, our bodies curled into each other like halves of yin and yang. When she stared at me like this, right now, as if I was responsible for creating every good thing in her world and she couldn't quite believe she could hold me like this.

Finally, she nodded somewhat curtly and released me to step back, nodding at the lush pile of leaves.

"I did most of the work so it's really not fair, but I happen to love you unreasonably, so I will give you first go."

"Huh?"

A smile twitched her lips. "You know autumn is my favorite season and what happened at Acheron, before you, almost took that away from me. You gave it back. So I'm magnanimously allowing you to have the first jump in the leaf pile."

I laughed and the sound was bright and clear in the cold air. "You must really love me."

"Oh, yes," she agreed then crossed her arms. "Now, go before I change my mind."

I bit my lip to curb my smile and looked at the high stack of leaves, deciding on my best approach. Finally, I took a few shuffling steps back and then just flung myself at the pile.

It was a bit like falling in love.

The reckless rush of hurling your entire self into a relationship with only a tenuous hope you'd find a soft place to land.

And I did.

I sank into the fragrant, sweetly spiced leaves with a loud yipping yell of joy, closing my eyes as I was buried beneath them. I stayed there for a second, enjoying the autumnal womb, smiling because I had a lot to smile about.

I emerged with it stretched so wide between my cheeks, it ached, my mouth open to say something silly to my girlfriend.

Only, the words crashed to a halt on the back of my tongue because I stopped breathing.

And I stopped breathing because Lex Gorgon, the girl I'd first noticed standing like an unconquerable warrior across the quad at Acheron University, was on one knee before me.

With a ring in one hand lifted to me in offering.

My gaze flickered madly between the two gold snakes curling around a large diamond in their center and the solemn, striking face of my lover.

"Falling in love with you was like stumbling from a dark haunted house into sunlight for the first time. I felt more warmth and acceptance from you in the first hour we spent together in the library than I ever had from anyone else in my entire life. You scared me, because in my experience, everything good was merely pretty gift wrap around a ticking bomb. You can't know what it's been like to discover every single day since then that with every layer I unwrap from you, there is only more goodness to be found. How much that has changed me and how I view the world. You are not just the light in my darkness anymore, *lux mea*. You've driven out so much of the shadow and now, you're the light of my entire life. Of my soul. You accept every inch of me, even the dark deeds I've felt compelled to see done, and it feels like a miracle. It's not enough to call you my girlfriend anymore, I want more than anything to call you my *wife*."

She sucked in a deep breath, the only sign that she was anything other than composed. Still, I knew better because her eyes burned as they stared into mine and I felt every single word she spoke seared into my soul.

"Marry me, Lux," she said, not a question, not a demand.

An offering.

Something precious laid at the altar of a beloved and benevolent god.

We hadn't spoken about marriage. Not because it was something I dismissed, but because, truly, I was so incandescently happy already I didn't figure anything could make it any better.

Obviously, I was wrong.

Because looking at the face of the woman who had changed my life so much for the better and shown me who I could be if I was just brave enough to embrace it, I was overcome with awe.

Struck dumb with pure, unfiltered euphoria that lit up my veins like a drug.

"Lux?" she asked after a long moment where I could only gape at her, hand pressed to my pounding heart, eyes filling with tears.

"I'm so happy I can't speak," I tried to explain in an odd breathy gasp because I also couldn't breathe.

Her pink mouth twitched. "Yeah?"

I nodded vigorously.

Her smile spread, white teeth peeking between split lips. "Should I take that as a yes, then?"

Another nod, this one so hard I almost threw out my neck.

"Good," she said, relief and joy breaking open on her face as she stepped forward into the pile of leaves and gathered me into her arms.

My knees went soft the second she touched her mouth to mine, and when her tongue swept through my lips, I swooned fully. Lex laughed against me, holding me carefully as she lowered us to the leaves. Somehow, she found my left hand and slid the ring onto my finger without breaking our fierce embrace.

"I love you so much," I said, and I realized I was crying *hard*, tears streaking down my face into the leaves beneath my head.

Lex grinned down at me, thumbing the wet off my cheek. "I love you just the same."

I lifted the ring between us, admiring the intricately curled bodies of the two snakes, one totally gold and the other littered with small emeralds, the center diamond a perfect circle.

"Two snakes and a moon," she murmured to me, tracing the ring with a fingertip. "I designed it myself."

"It's absolutely perfect," I breathed, sucking in a deep breath to steady myself.

"Because it's us," she said simply.

Us.

I let myself have a moment to wonder at the nature of the revenge that had instigated our relationship. Lex had thought to use me to get back at the powers that be who had done her such wrong. How wonderful it felt now to know that this was the very best revenge.

Us.

Together and happy, still touched by the past but no longer tainted by it because our love had washed us clean and given us a new start.

"Us," I agreed. "I think it might be the best word in the entire English dictionary."

And even though it was cheesy, and Lex would usually tease me for my sappiness, she just brushed a thumb over my mouth and then claimed it with her own.

THANKS ETC.

There are so many things I could say about being a woman, but it would be too much to fill the simple page and a half I usually take for my acknowledgments. Women are complicated and perhaps therefore, easily and woefully misunderstood. Even by each other. Even by themselves. There is so much power in being female. No wonder so many spent so long trying to suppress and oppress us. The myth of Medusa has always fascinated me because the wrong that was done to her is irrefutable and taken by ancient poets and writers as justifiable fact. Medusa was a virginal priestess of the virgin goddess Athena who was taken against her will in the latter's temple. And instead of punishing the abuser, the great and mighty god, Poseidon, Medusa bore the consequences. She lost her great beauty to a monstrous form, unable to look upon anyone without turning them to stone. She was isolated and tortured for living her life, her fatal and unconscious flaw being so beautiful as to tempt a weak man into committing an atrocious sin.

For years, I harbored a deep, compelling need to give this woman a happily ever after. Who else in this story but her deserved one?

I hope you know this isn't a story written by a man hater. This is a story written by a woman who wishes more than most things that women would stop being seen for the vessel of their bodies. Stigmatized for their emotionality when our hormones move us like the moon her tides. Fetishized for our virginity when lovemaking should be a celebration and not a shameful death. Judged for being beautiful and judged for being ugly. Women are so much more than their looks and stereotypes. My wish is that Lex and Luna showcase that even a little bit.

Lex's journey was also a personal one. Like many women, I've been sexually assaulted. Even typing those words brings bile onto the back of my tongue, and the truth is, not all of that is directed at my attackers. I think that is the cruelest part of being a victim of sexual assault, that no matter how many times you tell yourself you didn't deserve it, you did nothing to incite it, a small part of you feels deep, enduring shame. One of the only ways to mitigate this feeling is, I believe now, to share it with each other. It took me over a year to tell anyone I was assaulted after it happened. Even now, I struggle to say the actual words *rape* and *assault*. I struggle to even allow myself to think of it or how it impacted me. But to struggle in silence is to struggle in vain and in sharing Lex's experiences with you, I've found healing within myself too. My heart goes out to all the women and men who have survived such trauma. Please know, even in your darkest moments, you are not ever alone.

If you or anyone else has been a victim of sexual assault, please seek out help through the National Sexual Assault Hotline (800.656.HOPE, online.rainn.org *y* rainn.org/es) or your local resources.

On another more positive note, Luna's journey resonated with me, too. I remember in high school a girl called me a "dyke" because I was predominately friends with men, played numerous sports, and was built with the muscled physique of a longtime athlete. It was the culture of the early 2000s when saying words like "dyke" and "gay" were insults even though they never should have been taken as such. I'm not sure if that's why it took me a while to find the words to describe myself as liking women. It's sad to think that a single comment could have made me afraid of something so beautiful as who I might love or my own sexuality, but it happens to all of us at some point in some way or another. The power of society's collective judgment on a single psyche can be grossly overwhelming. Now, like Luna by the end of this story, I am a happy bisexual woman at peace with my identity.

Now, to the people who make all this possible.

First, my darling Annette, whose support and care for me eclipses all the darkness in my life. You are a constant and a joy to me. I remain forever humbled and grateful to have you in my corner.

Sarah, for stoking my creative spirit and chatting with me about craft and beauty and art. You inspire me, warm me with your love, and awe me with your strength. You are my forever friend.

I want to thank my friend, Ella, who shares my love of the feminine mystic and chaotic bisexuality. Thank you for always being my sounding board and my ride-or-die friend. You are my Gorgon sister and I'll love you until the end.

Allaa, my love, without you I would be rudderless in stormy creative seas. Thank you for talking out my ideas and always being my hype girl.

Nina, my PR guru, do you have any idea how much I adore you? I'll love you forever and you shall never be rid of me.

Valentine, my girl, I loved you from the moment you first made me laugh with your wicked dry sense of humor. Thank you for being my friend and cheerleader.

Jenny, working with you is a dream. Thank you for polishing my very rough drafts and for always being so sweet and supportive.

To Sarah Plocher, who I am delighted to call my friend and fabulous proofreader. Thank you for bringing this manuscript to a high shine and for always being such a light.

Bex and Tacie, thank you for sensitivity reading Lex and Luna's love story for me! Your support and advice means the world to me.

Cat at TRC Designs, thank you for always making my covers and interiors so damn beautiful! You are such a joy and an inspirational young woman.

My Darlings, you buoy me the way the Man Eater Patrol buoys Lex. Thank you for always standing so staunchly behind me and for being so positive and excited about my words. I am grateful to have the best readers in the world every single day and the feeling of awe you inspire in me never fades.

My Street Team is compiled by some of the most creative, kind, and wonderful women in this industry and I'm so lucky to have their support. Thank you from the bottom of my heart for everything you do for me, my loves!

My M, for being the first and for loving me still and forever as a best friend.

To Fiona, Lauren, Madison, Armie, and Bridget, my bridesmaids, my ride-or-dies, my queens. The sisterhood I wrote about in this book is inspired by you. Thank you for supporting me, loving me, and encouraging me to be my best self.

My sister, Grace, who Lex's sister is named after. Thank you for believing in my dreams before I even had the courage to do so. You're the best sister a girl could ask for.

And to my other sister, Beth, who blazed a trail in the LGBTQIA+ community, who always stands up for what she believes in and never allows a bully to get the last word. You're a pillar of strength and confidence who always inspires me.

For my mother, who broke through the glass ceiling and achieved great success but always, *always* has time to mentor and uplift other women. Thank you for inspiring me to be the best, most formidable woman I could be and for loving me so deeply.

Last as always, but never ever least, for my husband, the love of my life, the man who accepts me for everything I am and everything I've been through. I have struggled my whole life with the desire to be seen through to my bones and with the fear of making myself so vulnerable as to achieve that. Thank you for being my safe place, my sword and my shield against the tragedies of the world.

ABOUT GIANA DARLING

Giana Darling is a *USA Today*, *Wall Street Journal*, Top 40 Best Selling Canadian romance writer who specializes in the taboo and angsty side of love and romance. She currently lives in beautiful British Columbia where she spends time riding on the back of her man's bike, baking pies, and reading snuggled up with her cat, Persephone, and Golden Retriever, Romeo.

Join my Reader's Group

Subscribe to my *Newsletter*
Follow me on *IG*
Like me on *Facebook*
Follow me on *Goodreads*
Follow me on *BookBub*
Follow me on *Pinterest*

OTHER BOOKS BY GIANA DARLING

Anti-Heroes in Love Duet

Elena Lombardi is an ice cold, broken-hearted criminal lawyer with a distaste for anything untoward, but when her sister begs her to represent New York City's most infamous mafioso on trial for murder, she can't refuse and soon, she finds herself unable to resist the dangerous charms of Dante Salvatore.

When Heroes Fall
When Villains Rise

The Evolution of Sin Trilogy

Giselle Moore is running away from her past in France for a new life in America, but before she moves to New York City, she takes a holiday on the beaches of Mexico and meets a sinful, enigmatic French businessman, Sinclair, who awakens submissive desires and changes her life forever.

The Affair
The Secret
The Consequence
The Evolution Of Sin Trilogy Boxset

The Fallen Men Series

The Fallen Men are a series of interconnected, standalone, erotic MC romances that each feature age gap love stories between dirty-talking, Alpha males and the strong, sassy women who win their hearts.

Lessons in Corruption
Welcome to the Dark Side
Good Gone Bad
After the Fall
Inked in Lies
Dead Man Walking
Caution to the Wind (The Fallen Men, #7) Coming Soon

A Fallen Men Companion Book of Poetry:
King of Iron Hearts

The Enslaved Duet

The Enslaved Duet is a dark romance duology about an eighteen-year old Italian fashion model, Cosima Lombardi, who is sold by her indebted father to a British Earl who's nefarious plans for her include more than just sexual slavery... Their epic tale spans across Italy, England, Scotland, and the USA across a five-year period that sees them endure murder, separation, and a web of infinite lies.

Enthralled (The Enslaved Duet #1)
Enamoured (The Enslaved Duet, #2)

The Elite Seven Series

Printed in the USA
CPSIA information can be obtained
at www.ICGtesting.com
LVHW051959271124
797803LV00003B/317

* 9 7 8 1 7 7 4 4 4 0 4 7 6 *